The LAST ENCHANTER

Book Two of *The Celestine Chronicles*

by

Laurisa White Reyes

Tanglewood • Terre Haute, IN

Published by Tanglewood Publishing, Inc., October 2013
Text © Laurisa White Reyes 2013

Cover art by Tristan Elwell & interior art by Kathleen Everts
Design by Amy Alick Perich

Tanglewood Publishing, Inc.
4400 Hulman Street
Terre Haute, IN 47803
www.tanglewoodbooks.com

Printed by Maple-Vail Press, York, PA, USA
10 9 8 7 6 5 4 3 2 1

ISBN-13 978-1-933718-93-4

Library of Congress Cataloging-in-Publication Data

Reyes, Laurisa White.
  The last enchanter / Laurisa White Reyes.
    pages cm. -- (The Celestine chronicles ; book 2)
    Summary: With the help of his old friends Clovis and Bryn, joined by new friend Lael, a feisty girl in search of her mother, Marcus uncovers a powerful secret that will change the course of his life forever.
    ISBN 978-1-933718-93-4 (hardback)
    [1. Magic--Fiction. 2. Fantasy.] I. Title.
  PZ7.R3303Las 2013
  [Fic]--dc23
                              2013022263

For my daughters
Carissa & Brennah

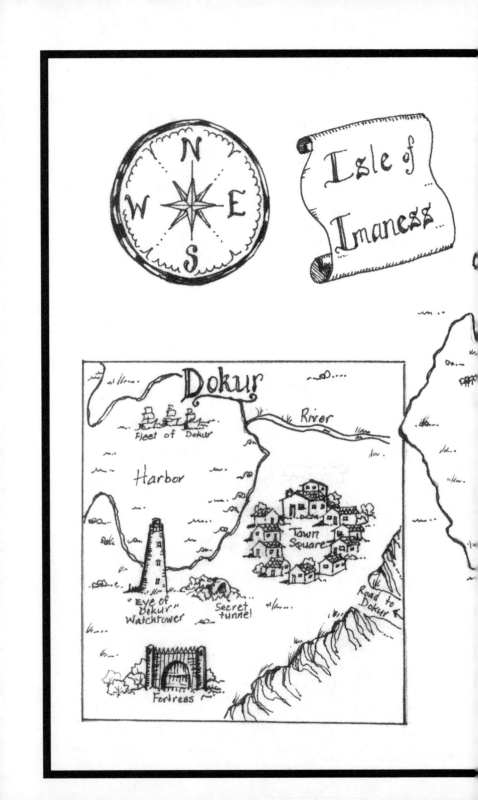

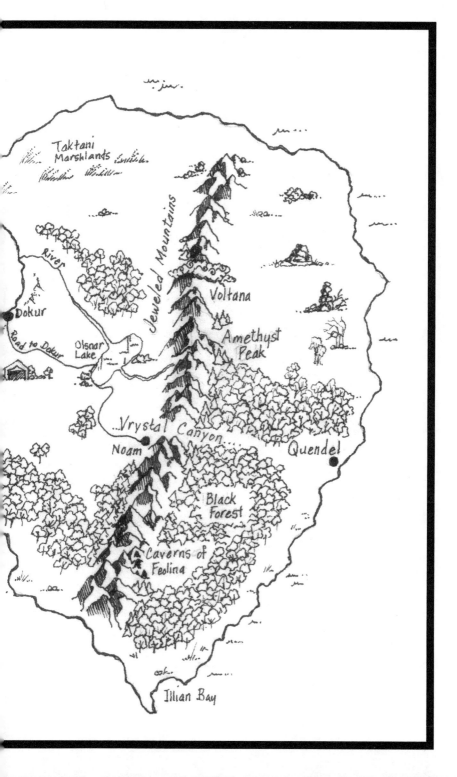

Prologue

Fredric, ruler of Dokur, stared out his window toward the sea. The sounds of the cutting and hammering of wood and of men shouting came to him on a crisp salty breeze. Below in the bay, Dokur's navy was busy rebuilding its ships. Eight months earlier, Fredric's own son had led their enemies to these very shores, and Dokur had nearly fallen by their swords. But soon these ships would set sail for the mainland and take revenge on the Hestorians.

Fredric heard the door open behind him. The gentle clinking of crystal against silver was the only introduction the visitor needed.

"Is it time already?" Fredric asked without turning. "I would like a little wine to soothe my nerves before bed."

Arnot filled a goblet and handed it to his king with a slight bow. Fredric downed the contents and returned the empty goblet.

"I fear I have grown too old for battle," said Fredric, crossing the room to his bed. "These eyes have witnessed too much bloodshed, too much suffering."

Fredric held out his arms while the attendant removed his royal robe and replaced it with a linen nightshirt. Once Fredric was dressed, Arnot went to the bed and pulled back the covers. "Your bed is prepared, Your Majesty."

Fredric rested his hands on the edge of the mattress. "My stomach," he said. "It bothers me so."

"Perhaps you should rest, Sire," replied Arnot.

Fredric rubbed his stomach and then raised his hand to his forehead, where beads of sweat had formed. "I am not well tonight," he continued, sighing. "But such is to be expected at my age."

Suddenly, Fredric clenched his teeth, and his hands balled into fists against the mattress. He groaned as his entire body began to shake. Fredric grabbed the quilt in both fists and pulled with such force, the fabric tore. A moment later he dropped to his knees, gasping for air.

"I am in pain," he cried. "Fetch my doctor!"

Arnot remained where he stood and stared at Fredric with cold eyes.

"Arnot," called Fredric, reaching for the attendant with both hands. "Please help me!"

A faint smile appeared on Arnot's lips—so faint Fredric wondered if his eyes were playing tricks on him. When the attendant finally crossed the room to the door, Fredric felt relieved that help would be found. He lay down on the floor, too weak now to lift himself into the bed.

"Tell my doctor to hurry," he whispered. "Tell him I am very ill."

Arnot looked back at Fredric. The smile on his lips was now unmistakable, and there was a look of pleasure in his face.

"You are not ill," he said coolly. "You have been poisoned."

Then Arnot slipped through the door, shutting it quietly and securely behind him.

AN
UNWELCOME
JOURNEY

One

The air was unusually cold when Marcus stepped out of his cottage near the village of Quendel. He cupped his hands around his mouth to warm them, and wisps of white escaped through his fingers. At the well, he lowered his bucket, listening for the crunch of wood breaking through the thin sheet of ice below.

After filling the animal trough with water, Marcus dropped the bucket into the well once more and left it on the hearth inside the cottage. Back outside, he untied Agnes's tether and led her toward the fields to graze. Agnes, his master's goat, bleated in protest. Marcus tugged at her lead.

"C'mon, you lazy animal, don't make me drag you," he said. "I've got better things to do than babysit a scrawny old maid like you. You aren't fit to be a goat, have I told you that lately?"

They trudged across the field until they reached a patch of grass. The morning frost was just beginning to thaw on the small, green shoots, but Agnes was impatient. She snatched the first crispy bunch between her teeth and yanked it clear out of the ground, roots and all.

"Take it easy there, girl," said Marcus, letting go of Agnes's lead. "Leave some for the other goats, why don't you?"

It had been eight months since Marcus had returned from his quest. He and five other boys from the village had gone in search of the Rock of Ivanore, a medallion made of Celestine crystal that had once belonged to Lady Ivanore, daughter of Fredric, ruler of Dokur. Years ago she broke the seal into two pieces and gave one to her husband Jayson (whom she also called her *rock*), when her father exiled him. The other half was divided into two smaller pieces, one for each of their two sons, Marcus and Kelvin.

Marcus considered the discovery that he was of royal blood, something he had thought a lot about since his return. Sometimes he could hardly believe it was true. Now Kelvin was in Dokur learning the ways of court with Fredric, and Jayson was on the far side of the Isle of Imaness in the marshlands of Taktani preparing the Agoran people to return to their homelands, a promise Fredric had made as a reward for their bravery during the battle with the Hestorian invaders.

"And here I am with you," said Marcus, tossing a

dandelion to Agnes. "So much for having royal blood. I'm nothing more than the king of goats."

Marcus reached for another dandelion, when something stung his neck.

"Ow!" he said, rubbing the spot with his hand.

A second later, a small pebble pelted him in the back of the head. Marcus spun around to see someone running across the field, an empty sling in hand. Marcus took out after the culprit.

"Come back here!" he shouted. "Come back, you coward!"

Marcus soon caught up. He grabbed anything he could reach—belt, hand, hair, leg—and both of their bodies toppled to the ground. Marcus had his attacker pinned in an instant.

"Thought you could get away with it, eh?" said Marcus, his chest heaving for breath.

The girl struggled to break free, but to no avail. She was Marcus's age, fourteen, and just as tall. She wore a simple tunic and trousers, and her long, yellow hair was kept in a tight braid.

"You're a pest, Lael," Marcus said. "You should be home playing with dolls."

"I prefer weapons to dolls," snapped Lael.

"And what does your papa say to that?" asked Marcus, a wry grin on his face.

Lael frowned, her face turning red. "My father is a farmer," she said. "What does he know of weapons?"

"More than you, most likely," Marcus said, laughing.

"You'll hurt yourself with that thing."

"I could have hurt you, Marcus Frye, if I'd wanted to."

Marcus snatched the sling from Lael.

Her arms now free, she jumped up, furious. "Give that back!"

"How does this work again?" teased Marcus. "You put a stone here . . ."

He picked up a rock from the ground and placed it in the small leather hammock. Then he began to spin the four long, leather straps in a circle over his head.

"And you swing it around like this . . ."

"Marcus, don't!" shouted Lael.

Marcus released two of the straps, but instead of sending the rock flying, it snapped back, hitting him square in the forehead. He dropped to the ground as still as the stone that had struck him.

Two

Marcus!" shouted Lael. "Are you all right?"

Marcus blinked. For a moment, he wasn't sure where he was, but as he gazed up into the face that stared down at him, he realized he was lying on the ground.

"Let me help you up," offered Lael, holding out her hand.

Ignoring her, Marcus struggled to his feet. He felt a little dizzy and lightheaded. "I'm fine," he said gruffly. He touched the tender spot on his forehead and found a swollen lump there.

"Are you sure you're all right?" asked Lael.

Marcus took up Agnes's lead. "I'm going home," he said. He didn't get far, however, before he felt a twinge of

7

guilt. Lael had only been teasing him, after all. He had been the stupid one, using a weapon on which he was untrained. And then when she tried to help him, he'd been rude to her.

Marcus stopped. He could see a plume of smoke rising from the chimney of his cottage, which meant Zyll was awake and preparing breakfast. If Marcus hurried, he might reach home while the food was still hot.

He glanced over his shoulder at Lael walking slowly toward the village. By the slump in her shoulder, he knew he had hurt her feelings. He would have to go back and apologize.

He called to her. "Lael, hold on!"

At hearing her name, Lael turned around.

Marcus patted Agnes's rump. "Go on home, girl," he told her. The goat obeyed and scampered off in the direction of the cottage, while Marcus started back across the field.

The pain struck without warning, an invisible fist thrust into his chest. As he fell, he saw Lael running toward him. A moment later he was on the ground, no longer aware of anything beyond his own suffering. His body shook, his fingers clutching at the soft soil. He wanted to scream, but no sound escaped through his clenched teeth.

At the very moment that Marcus was sure he would die, a strange warmth filled his body. It rose up from the earth and rained down from the sky. His muscles relaxed, and his arms fell limp beside him. He opened his eyes and saw a woman with golden hair and skin as bright as the sun.

He knew this woman. He had seen her before in his dreams and thought she was an angel, but now he knew her true identity. She was Ivanore, his mother.

Ivanore held out her hand toward Marcus as though she wished to grasp his hand in hers. Her lips moved, but Marcus heard no sound. Then, with despair in her eyes, Ivanore's image began to fade. Marcus wanted to reach for her, to feel his mother's touch for the first time, but his arms were like lead, lying useless beside him on the ground.

Ivanore vanished, leaving a dark void behind. The blackness swirled above Marcus, threatening to pull him in. Again he clutched at the soil, but the force was too strong. He felt his body lifting from the earth. Marcus opened his jaw and screamed.

Three

"There now, you are in good hands."

A familiar voice broke through the blackness. Marcus slowly opened his eyes. He lay on his own cot, a damp rag across his forehead and a blanket pulled up to his chin. He tried to sit up, but a stabbing pain forced him back to his pillow. Master Zyll leaned over him, examining him through a pair of silver-rimmed spectacles.

"Better now?" he asked, removing the rag and dipping it into a bowl of water on the floor beside him. He wrung out the rag and replaced it on Marcus's forehead. Marcus felt its soothing coolness against his skin.

"The pain hit so suddenly," he said, "I couldn't scream."

"Oh, you screamed all right," remarked Zyll with a

chuckle. "Half the village heard you and came running. And as you can see," he added, "some of them are still here."

Marcus looked toward the doorway and saw two boys standing there. Both were about his age, though one was short and rather plump, while the other was a good head taller and very thin.

"Clovis, Tristan," said Marcus. "It's good to see you."

"You, too," replied Clovis, the plump one. "We didn't know who had screamed until we reached the field."

Tristan reached over his shoulder for a scratch. "Thought it was a girl," he said, chuckling.

Clovis jabbed Tristan in the side with his elbow. "Well, naturally, we would think that, wouldn't we—when we saw Lael," he said. "That is, until she told us you were hurt."

"Lael?" asked Marcus.

"That's right," said Tristan. "She led us to you. The three of us carried you home."

Marcus glanced around the room. "Where is she?"

"She left once she saw you were safe," explained Zyll. "She seemed upset, though. Said something about a sling?"

Marcus touched his forehead. The lump was still there. He groaned.

"I was fooling around with her sling and hit myself on the head with it," said Marcus. "She probably feels responsible."

Clovis fidgeted with the crossbow. He had surprised himself and everyone else with his skill during the battle with the Hestorians. Now he carried it with him wherever he went. "We had better get back, Tristan," he said. "My father will be wondering where I am."

Tristan nodded. "And I was supposed to be at work an hour ago."

"That's right," replied Marcus, cracking a smile. "You two have responsibilities now. Clovis Dungham, the bow maker and Tristan Tether the cow slayer. So how are things at the tanner's?"

"Fine, just fine," answered Tristan.

"Can't you tell by the smell?" added Clovis.

Tristan glared at Clovis and then sniffed at his sleeve.

"Don't make me laugh," Marcus said. "It hurts!"

Marcus said goodbye to his friends, though he longed to go with them. As they turned to leave, Marcus heard Tristan ask, "Smell's not that bad, is it?"

Four

Once Tristan and Clovis had gone, Marcus carefully rolled onto his side and adjusted the pillow beneath his neck. Even that small amount of effort caused him pain, and he moaned.

Zyll stroked the white stubble on his chin. "The pain still persists?"

Marcus nodded. "The stab wound I got from Arik healed months ago. But just when I'm feeling strong again, the pain comes back."

"Your wound has healed," said Zyll. He rose from the stool at Marcus's bedside and reached for Xerxes, his walking stick carved with an eagle's head. Crossing the cottage to the hearth where a pot of broth was warming, he lifted the ladle to his lips and tasted it.

Marcus adjusted himself on his cot again, trying not to worsen the pain. "I haven't healed," he told Zyll. "I hurt more now than I did when that traitor stuck a dagger in my back."

As Zyll leaned on his walking stick, its wooden face moved. Eyelids flickered open, and Xerxes yawned.

"Well, well," said Zyll. "It's about time you awoke. Had you intended to sleep *all* day?"

Xerxes yawned again, a faint squawk escaping from his beak. "Sleep?" he said groggily. "How can anyone sleep with so much racket? All you humans do is talk, talk, talk, talk, talk!"

When Xerxes caught sight of Marcus on the cot, he ground his beak furiously. "And you complain *I* sleep too much! Up! Up, lazy boy! The day's half gone!"

"Now, now, Xerxes," said Zyll. "The boy's not well. He's had another attack."

Xerxes gasped, though Marcus sensed a hint of mockery in it. "Another attack? How convenient."

Zyll leaned Xerxes against the hearth and laughed lightly. "If you will excuse us a moment, my old companion," he said. "Marcus and I were just discussing the situation and would like to continue our conversation."

Xerxes rolled his eyes and clicked his beak impatiently.

Zyll lifted a fist to his mouth and cleared his throat. "In private," he added.

Xerxes closed his eyes, and just before he returned to his still form he said, "I'll expect no more complaints about *my* sleeping in after this."

Zyll carried a bowl of broth to Marcus who accepted it gratefully. The steaming liquid satisfied his hunger and took the edge off his pain.

"I saw her again," he said, setting the empty bowl aside. "I saw Ivanore."

"Oh?" replied Zyll.

"The vision was clearer than ever before. She looked so real, and she was trying to speak to me."

Zyll held out his hand. "A little more?" he asked.

"Yes, please." Marcus handed him the bowl, and Zyll returned to the hearth and filled it again. He filled another for himself. "I wish I knew more about my mother," Marcus continued. "I know she died when I was born, but sometimes, like when I have those visions, I feel her close to me. Silly, isn't it?"

The enchanter paused, staring at the bricks of the hearth. Marcus recognized that look. It meant Zyll's thoughts had gone someplace else for a moment. Then Zyll blinked and finished filling Marcus's bowl.

"No, of course not," answered Zyll, setting the ladle aside. "It is only natural for a boy to wish to know his mother." He turned to Marcus. "How are you feeling now?"

"A little better," Marcus confessed, "though I still hurt a lot."

"Earlier you were speaking of the wound in your back," said Zyll. "Is that the source of your pain?"

Marcus considered his question. "Come to think of it," he said, "the pain is mostly in my chest, as though my bones were being crushed."

Zyll set one bowl of broth on the table before returning to the cot. He handed Marcus his bowl, his expression serious. The steam rose into Marcus's face.

"Think back to that day in Dokur," he said. "Your brother Kelvin was mortally wounded from a fall. Using magic, you revived him by exchanging your life force for his."

Outside the cottage, the wind beat against the thatched roof. It reminded Marcus of that terrible day months earlier—the loud flapping of dragons' wings, waves crashing against the shore, and the screams of people dying. These were memories he had tried—yet failed— to forget.

"I don't understand," said Marcus.

"Magic comes with a price," said Zyll. "Greater magic demands greater sacrifice. Look at me. I limp when I walk, and my eyes grow dim. Magic has taken its toll on me one spell at a time. Do you ever feel spent after using magic?"

Marcus remembered his quest and the lessons in magic he had received. Each spell had left him breathless and tired, but the feeling had soon passed.

Zyll continued, "Most acts of magic result in moments of exhaustion, small aches and pains. To manipulate organic substances, whether plant or animal, requires greater effort and exacts a higher toll. The most difficult feat is healing human flesh. Most magicians will not attempt it. And even more, to call someone back from death itself . . ." Zyll shook his head. "You are the first I know of to survive it."

"How can that be?" Marcus asked. "I'm only an apprentice."

"How you survived, I do not know," answered Zyll, "but you have been left with a reminder of your sacrifice. Your body carries within it the shadow of Kelvin's wound and death. You will feel its effects forever after."

Zyll eased himself into a chair at the table. "Let us finish our supper," he said, lifting the bowl between his hands.

Marcus watched as Zyll brought the bowl to his lips and drank, but he was no longer hungry. The old man smiled at Marcus as if to comfort him, but Marcus did not feel comforted. Instead, he felt afraid. Deathly afraid.

Five

The Sotherby cottage looked gloomy in the fading daylight. Its roof sagged in spots, and the walls showed signs of age and neglect. In contrast, a brightly colored flower garden grew at its doorstep. Each day when Lael returned from the marketplace, she would spend a few moments picking out weeds, loosening the soil, and watering her cherished plants.

Today after plucking off a few dying blossoms, Lael sat on the porch step and gazed out across the now barren fields that stretched out in front of her home. The harvest this year had been the best yet, and there was talk that next season would be even better. But she didn't care about next season, or even next month or next week. She wasn't even sure if she cared about tomorrow.

From inside the house came the sound of glass shattering.

Lael sighed. "Another empty bottle," she said, rising to her feet. As she did so, the step beneath her creaked.

"Lael?" called her father's gruff voice. "Is that you?"

A moment later, a scruffy-looking man filled the doorway, the air around him smelling like liquor. He stepped out onto the porch, swaying unsteadily.

"Well?" he asked, holding out his hand.

Lael held up a small, linen sack and shook it. The bright sound of clinking coins brought a smile to her father's lips.

"How much?" he asked.

Lael opened the sack and emptied the coins into his palm. As he counted them, his smile disappeared.

"Only seventeen? I expected twenty at least."

"We waited too long," said Lael. "You know the price drops at the end of the season. Still, it's more than last time."

Sotherby grunted and squeezed the coins in his fist. "Thieves! Always trying to cheat a man. And you," he continued, turning his angry gaze on his daughter, "if it weren't for your idle ways, we could have taken the harvest to town a week ago and gotten double!"

She should have seen it coming, but when her father's fist came down across her left ear, she was taken by surprise. The blow was sudden but far from serious. His drunkenness left him weak, and his aim was bad. Still, Lael cried out.

Her father raised his hand to strike again. "If I didn't know you better," he said, "I'd swear you've been stealing from me. Why else would the likes of Farnall Dungham be richer than me when I have nearly twice the land he does?"

He stared down at his daughter, who held her hands up to ward off the next blow, but it never came.

"Nah," he said, tottering past Lael down the steps. "You wouldn't have the nerve to steal from your own father, not when you know what would happen if you did. I'm going to town." He waved his fist full of coins. "I need to fetch a new bottle."

Lael watched her father walk down the road toward town. He would not return until morning, when his belly was full of ale and his money was gone.

Lael blinked back tears and hurried inside the cottage. She went to her bed and reached into her tunic. There, concealed beneath her clothes, was a woolen scarf made by her mother years before that Lael kept tied around her body. She untied it now and carefully laid it across her bed. She ran her fingers beneath one of the folds until she found the treasure hidden there: three silver coins, the remainder of the price of this season's harvest. She rubbed the warm coins against her cheek.

Setting them on the floor beside her, Lael loosened the threads in one corner of her mattress and pulled out a small, wooden box she kept hidden in the straw. She opened the lid. Inside were twenty more coins to which Lael added the three.

Lael closed the lid, returning the box to its hiding place. Then she picked up the scarf and held it to her face. The fragrance that had once been so strong was only a faint memory now, but if she tried hard, Lael could still smell the sweet scent of lilacs, her mother's favorite flower.

"Nine years," she whispered to herself, forcing back tears. "Nine years since you've been gone. But I finally have enough to bring you home."

Six

In the cottage at the edge of the grazing fields, Zyll gave a quiet command. A small flame bloomed on a candlestick, lighting the room and the table on which sat a copper bowl filled with water. Peering into the bowl, Zyll hoped to see some of the latest news of the island. He wondered how his son, Jayson, was coping in the marshlands. He wondered, too, if his grandson, Kelvin, was happy in Dokur. What he saw, however, was far from comforting.

When the image finally faded, Zyll rested his hands on the edge of the table while his tears fell into the bowl.

"Master?" a voice behind him whispered. "Grandfather?"

Zyll turned. "Marcus, why are you out of bed?" he asked, drying his eyes with his calloused fingers.

Marcus stood beside him dressed in his nightshirt, trembling slightly in the cool, night air. "I couldn't sleep," he said, stepping closer. He saw the bowl on the table and the dampness on Zyll's face. "What is it?" he asked. "What did you see?"

Zyll sat down at the table, motioning for Marcus to do the same. Soon they were seated across from each other, the candlelight casting dancing shadows on their faces.

"I'm afraid I must leave," said Zyll.

"Leave?" asked Marcus. "But why?"

"Something terrible has happened, and I must go to make things right—if I still can." Zyll paused before continuing, his voice barely a whisper. "I did not want to tell you this," he said, "but you will hear of it eventually, anyway. In my vision, I saw Fredric, your *other* grandfather, in great agony."

"Is he sick?" asked Marcus.

Zyll shook his head. "It was over quickly," he said. "Fredric has died."

Marcus slumped back into his chair. He had known his maternal grandfather only a short time, but still the news took him by surprise. A new realization struck Marcus. "If Fredric is dead," he said, "that means Kelvin is the new ruler of Dokur Province."

"Yes," replied Zyll. "I will go and offer my services to your brother. Perhaps this old man may still be useful in some way."

"Do you really have to?" asked Marcus. "I mean, it's such a long journey."

"I wish there were some alternative, my boy, but there is none."

"But I don't understand. Kelvin has an entire court at his beck and call. I know he's your grandson, but so am I, and I want you to stay here with me."

Zyll's gaze turned to the flame in the fireplace. He did not answer for some time, and Marcus began to wonder if he ever would. Finally, Zyll looked back at Marcus, his expression resolute.

"What I am about to tell you, Marcus, is known only to me. It is important that it remains so until I have evidence."

"Evidence of what?"

Zyll lowered his voice. "Fredric did not die of natural means," he said somberly. "He was murdered."

Seven

"urdered?" said Marcus in disbelief. The shock made the pain in his body flare up briefly. He breathed deeply for a moment until the discomfort subsided. "Are you sure?"

"Sadly, I am," answered Zyll.

"But how? Who? Was it the Hestorians? If they've sent a spy—"

Zyll reached across the table and patted Marcus's hand reassuringly. "There's no need to cast blame on the Hestorians. I am fairly certain they are not responsible."

"But they are our enemy."

Zyll pressed his hand, warm and dry, against Marcus's hand. "My boy, do not confuse the people of Hestoria with those who govern them. You know full well that in his younger days, Fredric was responsible for many unjust deeds. Did his actions make us all evil?"

Marcus shook his head. "Of course not."

"Good," said Zyll with a nod. He then rose from the table with some difficulty.

"Maybe what you saw hasn't happened yet," suggested Marcus. "Maybe something can still be done."

"The past is always certain," Zyll said. "It cannot be changed."

Hanging from a hook in the wall was a worn leather satchel, the same satchel Marcus had so reluctantly taken with him on his quest for the Rock of Ivanore. Zyll removed it now, filling it with a set of clean clothes, a rolled blanket, a small pot, some dried fruit, and a wedge of cheese. "Fredric is dead," he continued, "and I fear that the man responsible intends to do the same to your brother."

"Then we should leave right away," said Marcus.

"Not 'we,' dear boy," said Zyll, lifting the satchel to his shoulder. "You are not well. Perhaps once things are settled in Dokur, I will send for you."

Zyll pulled on his cloak and cap. Then, taking up his walking stick, he strode out the front door into the darkness.

Marcus got up from the table and went after him. "Wait!" he called. "You can't leave me behind. I want to go with you."

In the east, the first glimmer of sunlight made its appearance. Marcus clutched his chest, trying to hide his pain, but Zyll would not be fooled.

"Rest, my boy. Regain your strength," said Zyll.

"Tend to Agnes for me until I return. She needs company as much as I do."

Zyll turned and started off across the field. Marcus pounded his fist against the cottage door. He wanted to run after Zyll and demand that he be allowed to come along. He was strong enough, after all. The pain was not half as bad as it had been yesterday. Then he thought of Fredric and Kelvin. Knowing that Kelvin might be in danger and that he would not be there to help his brother made Marcus angry. But then if the pain came again, Marcus would only delay Zyll's journey and further endanger his brother.

Marcus went back inside the cottage. He hurried to the bookshelf and took down a wooden chest. Setting it on the table, he opened the lid. There were items of all shapes and sizes inside, nearly filling it to the rim. The Celestine ring Fredric had given him lay on top, but he pushed it aside. He did not have time to sort through everything now. He took the item he wanted in his fist and slammed the lid shut.

"Grandfather!" Ignoring the pain, Marcus ran as fast as his weakened legs could carry him. Zyll had just reached the opposite side of the field and had paused at the border of the forest where a thick wall of trees greeted him. He turned now to watch Marcus with mild amusement.

"Grandfather!" repeated Marcus, nearly collapsing into Zyll's arms.

"I told you before, boy, you cannot come to Dokur," Zyll said. His voice was stern, but his eyes revealed a tenderness that Marcus had recently come to know well.

Marcus shook his head. "I know," he said, "but please take this with you."

He held out his hand. Across his palm lay a small, metal object. Zyll took it, narrowing his eyes to examine it more closely.

"It's just a key," continued Marcus, "just an ordinary key. You gave it to me once, remember? Said it would unlock my destiny."

Zyll nodded, and a slight smile formed on his lips. "And so it did," he said. "So it did."

The old man placed the key in his satchel and wrapped his arm around Marcus, pulling him close. He held him there for a long time. When he finally let go, there were tears in his eyes.

"I will treasure it always," he said. Then Zyll passed through the trees into the forest, leaving Marcus standing alone, shivering in the cold.

Eight

Two days after Zyll left, Marcus arose from his cot and stretched his arms over his head. The pain that had nearly crippled him before was now nothing more than a dull ache. Maybe by tomorrow he would feel well enough to go to town.

Marcus made his way to the fireplace, where Zyll had left a pot of soup warming over enchanted coals. Marcus dipped the ladle into the broth and emptied it into a bowl. Then he carried it to the table.

He took several spoonfuls before he noticed what was in front of him. Zyll's divining bowl was dented from years of wear. It sat just where Zyll had left it before his hasty departure.

Marcus looked into the dark water. Zyll had seen Fredric's death. He had sensed danger, betrayal. Marcus desperately wanted to see it, too. And why shouldn't he? He wasn't half bad at magic now.

In his mind, he formed an image of Dokur. He remembered the crowded streets, the jutting cliffs above the shore, the grand yet menacing Fortress. The vibrant colors filtering through the stained-glass window in the king's council chambers and the scarlet robes Fredric wore were as vivid now to Marcus as they had been when he had first seen them eight months earlier.

He focused on his memory of Fredric's face. Could he really be dead? And was it true that his brother, Kelvin, was in danger? Marcus peered into the water and tried to summon up the past. Suddenly it felt like someone had taken hold of one of his ribs and snapped it in two. He doubled over, clutching at his chest. He took slow, measured breaths until the pain began to subside.

What Zyll told me was true then, he thought. Magic is to blame for the attacks I've been having.

In a sudden burst of anger, Marcus swung his arm across the table, knocking the divining bowl to the floor. The bowl landed with a sharp ping, and the water spread across the wooden floor, leaving a dark, widening circle in its wake.

"Then I won't do magic," he said through clenched teeth. "Not ever again!"

Marcus stood up and snatched the rag still draped over the edge of his cot. He knelt at the edge of the spill and placed his hands in the water. He wondered at the stillness of it. Its surface was as smooth as a mirror, so smooth Marcus could see his reflection in it.

Within moments, Marcus realized the sounds were gone. The crackle of the fire, the soup boiling, the window shutter creaking in the wind—all had gone silent.

And then he realized everything was gone. The world around him had vanished—the table, the fireplace, the cottage—everything. All that remained was himself and the puddle of murky water.

Marcus stared at his face in the water. As he did so, the reflection changed. It was not *his* face he saw now, but an older face bearing the marks of years of hard work and of magic. Zyll stared right back as though he could see Marcus through the water. The image widened, and Zyll's entire body came into view. Zyll lay on his side on a patch of brown earth. The front of his robe was covered in blood flowing into the soil beneath him. As Marcus watched in horror, Zyll's eyes flickered for a moment and then closed. His body lay as still as the earth.

As the water turned dark again, Marcus desperately waited for some other image to appear. He wanted to see Zyll stand up and walk, to hear him laugh and tell Marcus to do his chores. But no image came, only the pale, frantic reflection of Marcus's own face.

Nine

Marcus did not notice the world returning, nor the sound of the knock at the door. He may not have heard or seen anything at all had someone not grabbed him by the back of his tunic and pulled him to his feet.

"What are you doing?" asked the boy standing in front of him. It was Tristan. "Are you hurt?"

Marcus looked around. The cottage was back to normal. "What happened?" he asked. He realized Clovis was there, too, and had pulled out a chair for him. Clovis held Marcus's arm, helping him into it, though the pain Marcus had felt minutes earlier had nearly gone.

"We should ask you that question," said Clovis. "We knocked and knocked. When you didn't answer, we thought maybe you'd had another attack."

37

"I'm fine," said Marcus, "but I have to go."

"Go where?" asked Tristan.

"Dokur."

Marcus looked around the room. He wouldn't need much, just enough food and water to last a few days. He could refill his water skin at Lake Olsnar. He would also need a weapon. On his quest he had had Xerxes, who doubled as a sword, but Zyll had taken the walking stick with him this time. Marcus had no sword of his own, so he would settle for the long knife Zyll used to cut squash from the garden. It was a good ten inches in length with a sturdy handle. Luckily, Zyll kept it sharp. It would have to do.

"Marcus, you're acting very strange," said Clovis. "What's going on?"

"You wouldn't understand," said Marcus.

"Try us." Tristan crossed his arms and waited.

Marcus wanted to hurry, but he knew his friends wouldn't let him go without some kind of explanation.

"Two nights ago Zyll left for Dokur," he began. "He saw something in his divining bowl that made him believe Kelvin might be in danger. Today, just now, I saw something, too. I saw Zyll."

Marcus stopped. The image he had seen passed through his mind again. It was almost more than he could bear.

"I saw Zyll dying."

Tristan huffed in disbelief. "Zyll can't die."

"Yes, he can," said Marcus. "I have to get to him as soon as possible."

Marcus got up from the table. He fetched Zyll's knife and tied it to his waist with a long strip of cloth. Then he took a blanket from his bed, placed some figs, cheese, biscuits, and dried meat on it along with some coins, and tied the corners together. After taking one last look around the room, he picked up his bundle and headed for the door.

"Are you sure?" Clovis asked. "Sure about Zyll, I mean. Maybe he's just sick, or maybe it hasn't happened at all."

"It's happened," answered Marcus, "or is happening. Zyll uses magic to see things in the past and present. The images in his divining bowl have never been wrong. Not once."

"Then I'm coming with you," said Clovis.

"No," said Marcus, "you've got responsibilities here."

"That's right," said Tristan. "It's busy season at the tanner's. I can't just up and leave. And Clovis's father's got more bow orders than one person can handle."

"I wouldn't let you come," said Marcus. "Besides, I need someone to look after Agnes while I'm gone."

"Tristan will take care of the goat, won't you, Tristan?" said Clovis.

Tristan shrugged. "Yeah, sure I will."

"And he'll tell my father where I've gone. As long as I'm back before the first snowfall in a couple of weeks, he won't mind."

Clovis held tight to his bow, his wide, brown eyes gazing expectantly at Marcus. Clovis had proven a loyal friend during their quest, though the journey was at times demanding for the slightly overweight boy. But he had grown taller since then and had slimmed out a bit. Maybe Clovis would be up to the task after all. And besides, Marcus reasoned, the crossbow would come in handy for hunting.

"All right, then," said Marcus. "Grab some extra bread and cheese from the cupboard and anything else you need, and let's go."

Clovis eagerly gathered up some supplies and followed Marcus out the door, grinning from ear to ear. When they'd gotten halfway across the field, Marcus glanced back at the cottage where he had lived with Zyll his entire life. He wondered whether he would reach Zyll in time or arrive in Dokur only to learn that he was too late to save his grandfather. He shuddered to think about that. He decided it was best to put Zyll out of his mind and to focus on the journey ahead.

He looked back once more. A sick feeling filled him, one he could not ignore, no matter how hard he'd try. It was a feeling that he would not be returning—at least not anytime soon.

Ten

wilight.

For humans, this was the time of day when light blended into darkness, creating a muddled picture of the world, but Jayson was not human—at least not entirely.

Jayson had been born of a forbidden union between human and Agoran. Like his Agoran mother, Jayson's eyesight, hearing, and sense of smell were far more acute than his human cousins'. What he gained from his father was a strong skeletal system and powerful human muscles.

He used these attributes now as he prowled the marshlands of Taktani, the northern part of the island where the Agorans had lived for most of Jayson's life. Creeping through the underbrush, he pursued the scent that had attracted him hours earlier. He could have ended the hunt in minutes, satisfying himself with a warm meal, but he delighted in the hunt itself, savored the act of tracking and trapping his prey. In truth, he doubted he would even make the kill. There was no need. There was food to spare in the village, but still, something in him felt driven to this occasional pleasure.

He pressed on as daylight continued to fade, his cat-like vision unhampered by the dimness. Several yards ahead, a warboar grunted and pawed at the ground, preparing its nest for the night. Jayson, hunched and ready, extended his claws. His muscles twitched anxiously, but still he waited.

There would be a midnight feast, he decided at last. He would resist the urge to eat the kill himself and instead carry it back to the village where the elders would prepare it. A bonfire would be lit, and everyone would gather to celebrate the return of his people to their homelands in the forests of Imaness.

Jayson smiled. Yes, this was reason to celebrate. The village he had called home as a child would welcome his hunt. It would be his gift to them, his offering of goodwill.

The warboar was resting now, unaware of Jayson lurking behind the willows. Jayson's attack would catch it by surprise, rendering it helpless before it could consider the possibility of escape.

Jayson flexed his muscles and pressed his heels into the soft earth. He would need instant speed. His claws glistened in the moist, night air. They would make quick work of the warboar's thick hide. Steady now, thought Jayson, pacing the warboar's breathing with his own. Steady . . .

In the distance, a voice called out. The warboar shifted in its sleep. The voice called again, strained, worried. Jayson knew that voice well, and immediately the thought of the hunt left him. He turned and sprinted off toward the village. The warboar would live another day.

Eleven

The hours passed too slowly, and Marcus wished more than anything that he could travel faster, but if he pushed himself too hard, the pain might come back. He would be useless to Zyll then. Better slow than not at all.

Clovis didn't seem to mind. He passed the time by describing every detail of every hunting trip he'd been on in the past few months, none of which interested Marcus, but listening to Clovis did keep Marcus's mind off Zyll for a while.

As daylight faded, Marcus started to feel anxious. The last time he had spent the night among these trees, he had nearly become a giant snake's meal. He was sure there were other creatures lurking in the shadows, and he did not want to meet any of them.

Marcus walked faster. He couldn't shake the feeling that he was being stalked.

"You must be feeling better," said Clovis.

"What?" asked Marcus.

"You're walking faster than before."

"I just want to get out of the forest."

Marcus wasn't afraid of the dark, at least not anymore. He had overcome that fear months ago in the shadows of Dokur's watchtower when he fought Arik, the man who betrayed Dokur to the Hestorians. However, Marcus still didn't like the darkness. Darkness had a way of settling into his bones, like a winter chill or a sickness. At home, he always managed to have his chores done before nightfall. By the time the sun said its last goodbyes and tucked itself behind the mountains, Marcus had long before put Agnes in her pen, drawn water for the next morning, and shut the cottage door tightly behind him.

Before Dokur, before he had conquered his fear, he understood why he was afraid. Everything made sense. But now, as the sky grew dark above the forest of trees, the uneasiness he felt made no sense at all.

It's nothing, he told himself, but with each step the light grew dimmer and his courage grew weaker.

"We'll stop here," he said, tossing his bundle to the ground.

Clovis walked another few paces and then tossed his knapsack beside Marcus's. "I guess here's as good a place as any," he said through a yawn. "Should I get some wood?"

It would have been easy to make fire. The enchant-ment that had once seemed so impossible now came almost without thinking, but Marcus hesitated. He thought of the pain it would bring on, and what Zyll had told him: Magic is power, but power comes with a price.

Luckily, Clovis had come prepared. His flint and wool made quick work of the kindling, and they soon had a warm fire. After Marcus and Clovis ate some food from their packs, they spread out their blankets and lay down for the night.

Just as Marcus had convinced himself that it was safe to fall asleep, something in the darkness caught his atten-tion. It wasn't anything he could see. It was more of a feeling that someone—or something—was there.

Marcus shook Clovis by the shoulder. Clovis, who had already fallen asleep, groaned as he sat up. When he saw the knife in Marcus's hand, he reached for his quiver, drawing out two arrows. Marcus placed a finger to his lips, motioning for silence.

"What is it?" Clovis mouthed.

Marcus leaned close and whispered in his ear. "We're not alone."

Twelve

By the time Jayson reached the edge of the village, darkness had fallen, and the wide, grass huts stood guard in the moonlight. He slowed his pace a little and listened. Once more, the voice called for him by name. He went toward it and found Nathar waiting for him.

"I came as quickly as I could," said Jayson. "What is it?"

Nathar was one of the pureblood Agorans Jayson freed from the Celestine mines. He was tall and proud, though the web of scars on his back showed what he had endured there. Jayson recalled the anger that had burned in Nathar's eyes upon their first meeting. That anger served Nathar well in the battle with the Hestorians. Nathar had been Jayson's closest friend ever since.

"The elders have called for you," Nathar said.

"The elders? But why?"

Nathar pressed his eyelids shut. "I can't believe this. Not really," he whispered more to himself than aloud.

"What has happened?" Jayson asked.

"A messenger just arrived from Dokur. It's Fredric . . ." The Agoran's voice broke off, but he quickly regained control of himself. "He is dead."

The words struck Jayson to his core. It was true that he had never liked Fredric. Rather, he had more than ample cause to hate him, but hate him he did not. Despite Fredric's past crimes, the king had been one of the few links Jayson had to Ivanore.

Jayson clenched his jaw, his heart filling with sorrow, not for himself but for his sons who had lost their grandfather. Jayson wished he could be with them to comfort them.

"You said the elders want to talk to me?" Jayson asked.

Nathar nodded again. "They plan to send you to Dokur."

"Of course," replied Jayson, "but I am still needed here. We are to return to our lands soon. There is still much to do to prepare."

"As it stands, there may be no return."

"What are you saying, Nathar?"

"This is what I dread telling you, my friend. Fredric's order to return the Agorans to our homelands has been revoked."

"Revoked?" cried Jayson with growing fury. "But he swore an oath, signed a binding agreement! What right does anyone have to change that? Who is responsible?"

Nathar bowed his head, reluctant to continue. Jayson took a deep breath to calm himself. "Tell me," he said, "by whose authority has this happened? I must know so that I may plead our case before him."

Nathar's shoulder began to tremble. "I saw the name on the document for only a moment, but there is no doubt," he said. "It was Kelvin Archer, your son and heir to the throne of Dokur."

Thirteen

"Did you hear that?" asked Marcus, crouching low behind the fire. Beside him, Clovis knelt in the dirt, readying his bow. Marcus noticed the tip of Clovis's arrow trembling slightly.

From the edge of the firelight came a slight stirring of leaves. Marcus crept toward a large stone. As he approached, he was sure the sound of his heart beating was as loud as thunder. Summoning his courage, he leapt behind the stone, hoping to surprise whatever was hiding there. From the corner of his eye, Marcus saw Clovis trying to hold his bow steady. Sounds cut through the silence—scuffling, grunting, someone crying out in pain.

A moment later, Marcus had it by the hair and dragged it, kicking and squirming, into the light. Marcus pulled back its hair and looked at the face, red and out of breath.

"You!" Marcus shouted, letting go. "You've been following us all along!"

Clovis lowered his arrow. A smile crept onto his face, and he covered his mouth with his hand to keep from chuckling.

Lael angrily brushed the dust from her tunic.

"Why?" Marcus demanded.

"Why do you think?" Lael scowled at him. "I want to come with you to Dokur."

A laugh burst from Clovis's mouth, but he quickly swallowed it. Marcus clenched his teeth. He had been afraid, and for what? To be humiliated by Lael once again. All he wanted was to be rid of her once and for all.

"You can't come," said Marcus. He scooped up a handful of kindling and pitched it into the fire.

"Who are you to tell me where I can and cannot go?" answered Lael. "I've as much right as you to travel these woods."

"Lael, look at you!" said Marcus, waving his hand up and down the length of her. "You're not ready for this sort of journey."

"Not ready? I'm more ready than you were when you went on your quest. You know as well as I that I'm just as strong as you and better with any weapon. In fact," she added, "from what I hear, you two could use someone like me along for protection."

The kindling ignited, the flames rising higher. Marcus felt the heat on his face. Or was the heat coming from inside him?

"Go home, Lael. Your papa is calling."

From the look in her eyes, Marcus saw how deeply his words had stung her. Why did he always say the wrong thing?

Stepping closer to the fire, Lael held out a small, leather pouch in her fist. She shook it. The coins inside jingled like tiny bells.

"I'll pay you," she said. "Be my guide, and I'll make it worth your while."

"Are those *silver* coins?" Clovis asked, swallowing hard.

Lael emptied the bag into her palm. The firelight reflected off the shiny coins.

"That's at least a year's pay!" said Clovis.

"More," replied Lael. She held up a single coin and returned the rest to her pouch. "And I will gladly share it all if you will take me with you."

"I don't mind," said Clovis, reaching for the coin.

Marcus grabbed his hand. "We don't want your money, Lael."

"We don't?" asked Clovis. "No, right. Of course. We don't want your money, Lael."

"Where did you get all that, anyway? Did you steal it?" asked Marcus.

Lael ignored his question with a defiant glare. "Will you take me or not?"

Marcus stared at Lael over the tip of the flame. Behind her, the Black Forest seemed vast and endless. Marcus noticed, too, that Lael's eyes were almost as dark as the forest.

"All right," Marcus replied finally. "You can go to Dokur."

Lael's shoulders relaxed.

Marcus couldn't help but grin. "But," he continued, turning from the fire, "you'll be traveling there alone."

"Marcus Frye!" shouted Lael. "You're a tyrant! That's what you are!" She pulled back her arm and chucked her coin at him. It hit him on the shoulder and fell soundlessly to the earth.

Marcus bent over and plucked it up. "Thanks!"

"That's mine!"

"You just threw it at me, so I believe the coin now belongs to me."

"Give it back, Marcus!"

"No."

Lael paced between the stone and the fire. She reminded Marcus of Agnes in her pen.

Finally, Lael stopped and faced Marcus. A mischievous grin spread across her face, her nose tilting to the air. "Fine," she said, "keep the coin, but I am going to Dokur. And what's more, I'm going to camp right here tonight— with you."

"Here?" asked Clovis, casting a wary glance at Marcus.

"Yes, here. So if you two don't mind," she added, unrolling her blanket and smoothing it out on the ground beside the fire.

A stunned Clovis politely moved his blanket over several inches. Lael lay down on hers. "Good night, boys."

"Good night, Lael," said Clovis, a second before Marcus stuck an elbow into his ribs.

Once they were all settled, Marcus held up Lael's coin and studied first one side and then the other. As much as he felt justified in keeping it, he tossed it onto Lael's blanket instead.

Lael looked at the shiny disk for a moment before closing her fingers around it. She looked up only briefly, her expression still hard. Then Lael rolled away from Marcus onto her side, choosing to face the darkness rather than him.

Fourteen

The next morning, Marcus was already tying up his belongings when Clovis awoke with a yawn.

"Why does it have to be so cold?" Clovis asked, pulling his cloak tightly around him. He got to his feet and stretched. "Where's Lael?"

"She wasn't here when I woke up," answered Marcus. He handed Clovis a biscuit from his pack.

"Oh," said Clovis, disappointed.

"Don't tell me you wanted her to come with us." Marcus was still angry at her from the night before and was glad she had gone.

"What if something happens to her?" Clovis said. "What if she gets hurt?"

"Lael get hurt?" said Marcus, finishing his biscuit and starting another.

"She might meet a wild animal."

"Then it's the animal I'll worry about," Marcus scoffed. "She probably had a rough night and decided to head for home. That's what I'd do if I were her."

"But you're not me," said Lael, stepping through the trees. She held up a dead rabbit by its legs, a triumphant grin on her face. "Breakfast!"

It was good of Lael to share her morning's catch, considering the way Marcus had treated her the night before. After they cooked and ate their meal, he mumbled his thanks. Then he put out the fire and started off toward the edge of the Black Forest. Lael tagged along, keeping far enough behind the boys to not be bothersome. A few hours later, they emerged from the forest and found themselves at the foot of a rock mountain split by a tall, narrow opening.

"Vrystal Canyon," Marcus announced before drinking from his water skin.

Clovis paused beside Marcus and let his gaze travel up to the cliffs above. "Do you think we'll meet any more of them in there?" he asked nervously.

Lael marched past them into the canyon, but Marcus grabbed her by the shoulder.

"Let go of me," she said, but the serious look in Marcus's eyes silenced her.

"Last time I was here I was attacked by a groc," he told her.

"That's right," added Clovis, "shape-shifters. Monsters that parade around in human form waiting for the perfect moment to strike."

Lael pulled her arm free. "I know what a groc is. I heard you talk about him in the village. Name was Bread, wasn't it?"

"Bryn," said Marcus. "His name was Bryn."

"Bryn ended up saving you from King Fredric's soldiers, didn't he? Well," added Lael, "if all grocs are as noble as Bryn, then we haven't anything to worry about, have we?"

As Lael disappeared into the mouth of the canyon, Clovis and Marcus gave each other a worried glance. Marcus drew his knife, and Clovis readied an arrow. Only then did they follow.

Fifteen

The canyon was even colder and darker than Marcus remembered. The air rushing through the winding passages moaned as if the mountain were in pain. Marcus brushed his hand against the smooth, stone walls coated with a thick layer of damp moss. He had once believed the canyon was the remains of a dried-up river or the scar left behind from an ancient earthquake. But Kelvin had said that behind these walls was an underground lake. Marcus wondered if there was some way into the rock itself so that he could find out.

Marcus kept Lael in his sights as best he could. It was obvious by the way she now marched ahead that she didn't think she needed protection, and maybe she was right. She was dead on with her sling and could down any prey with ease. However, as the pathway narrowed and twisted, Marcus doubted there would be space or time enough to use her weapon.

Nearly an hour passed without a problem, but Marcus's dread did not let up. Rather, each step made his heart beat faster. Several times Lael disappeared around a curve, and Marcus would hurry to catch up with her, but then he would lose sight of Clovis.

Lael had once again gone out of his sight while Marcus struggled to keep up. He finally found her leaning back against the canyon wall.

"Why did you stop?" asked Marcus, grateful for a moment to rest.

Lael closed her eyes and tried to slow her breathing. "Guess I've tried so hard to get away from you that I finally wore myself out."

"Get away from me?"

"You made it very clear last night that you don't want me along. So I figured I'd do my best to put some distance between us."

"This isn't the place to travel alone, Lael."

"I can take care of myself, apprentice."

"Really?" replied Marcus. "Then why did you offer to pay me to be your guide?"

"I just thought it would be nice to have some company."

"That's a high price to pay for company."

"Too high for yours, at least!"

"Listen, Lael, this isn't Quendel. You really don't have any idea—" Marcus stopped suddenly and cocked his ear.

"What was that?" asked Lael, but Marcus put his hand up, signaling silence.

After a few moments he spoke cautiously. "Clovis?"

Clovis had fallen behind again, but he should have caught up by now. There was a sharp, grating sound, like rock scraping against rock, and Marcus thought Clovis would appear at any moment. But when he didn't, Marcus felt the same fear he had felt that day he first met Bryn, the day Jayson had appeared out of nowhere and sent the groc running. If it hadn't been for Jayson, that day might have been Marcus's last.

The sound came again, closer this time, but now there was also a low hum—or mumbling. What was Clovis saying? wondered Marcus. As he tried to make it out, he realized that what he heard was not one voice, but many, like the soft murmuring of a hundred whispers.

He took Lael's arm and shoved her forward. "Run!" he hissed. "And no matter what, don't look back!"

Sixteen

ael didn't look back. Instead she ran, just as Marcus told her to. She didn't have to know why. The urgency in his voice was enough to convince her that whatever they were running from was dangerous at the least, deadly at most. Lael soon outpaced Marcus. Only seconds had passed, half seconds really, before she realized she was running alone. For a half second more, she wondered whether she should keep running or turn back for Marcus and Clovis. But half a second was all she had.

A horde of creatures unlike Lael had ever seen came up behind her. The creatures varied in form and size: Some were ferocious monsters with thick tails and razor-sharp claws. Others had arms and legs and faces that were almost human. Still others were something in between.

They not only chased Lael on level ground but also crawled behind and above her along the cavern walls like the spindly-legged spiders that nested in Lael's barn at home. Soon these creatures had passed her and started climbing down the walls directly in front of her. Lael had no choice now but to stop running. She was surrounded. The hideous creatures circled her in ever-shrinking rings. She held the leather straps of her sling in her hand, but the creatures were too close for her to use it. She searched desperately for anything she could use as a weapon. There was nothing.

"Stop!" a voice growled. The creatures eyed Lael hungrily as they parted to allow one of them through. Though not as tall as the others, this groc was still frightening. Its gray skin was covered in lizard-like scales, with claws as long and sharp as daggers. Its snout carried several rows of jagged teeth. Its breath smelled of rotten flesh.

"Wait," the creature said, grasping Lael's upper arm in its paw.

Another groc with the distorted face of a man but with a body more like some animal clung to the rock wall overhead. "Why wait?" it bellowed. "This meal easy for us all!"

"No!" shouted the first. "Hyer wants them! Eat we our catch, and leave nothing for him?"

"Hyer does not know!" said the second. A trail of saliva dripped from its mouth, landing on Lael's shoulder.

"Hyer knows all! The stone knows all!"

A murmur rose from the crowd of grocs, and Lael noticed that some even backed away from her. The first, however, tightened its grip on her arm.

"Who takes first bite?" it asked, lifting Lael off the ground. A sharp pain shot through her shoulder. She struggled to free herself, but the groc only held her higher. "Who eats," it continued, "and be forever banished?"

No reply came from the crowd. The groc with the human face growled and then crawled away. The first groc lowered Lael and motioned to another groc beside him, one with green scales and a long, broad tail. It held a stone in its hand, which it lifted above Lael's head. The last thing she remembered was the loud crack against the back of her skull as a sudden darkness descended.

Seventeen

arcus awoke in darkness. It was impossible to tell whether hours had passed, or days. He remembered running and being attacked by what could only be grocs. His head still throbbed from being hit from behind. He blinked now, waiting for his eyes to adjust to the weak light cast from a single, smoldering torch stuck in the ground nearby. Both Clovis and Lael lay unconscious beside him.

Marcus reached over and pushed Clovis's shoulder to wake him.

Clovis groaned, rubbing the back of his head. "What a dream I had," he started to say. Then he opened his eyes, blinked, and glanced around. "Or was it a nightmare?"

"Neither," said Marcus. "It was all real."

Lael awoke then and immediately scrambled to her feet, only to lose her balance and collapse onto Marcus's lap. She glanced up at him and then pushed him back.

"Hey!" Marcus said.

"Where are we?" Lael asked, ignoring him.

Clovis got to his knees. His bow was there beside him, his quiver of arrows still slung across his back. Marcus was relieved to find his knife nearby, too. The grocs, it seemed, had no fear of human weapons.

"Are we in a cave?" Clovis asked.

The three of them stood up, but Lael wobbled unsteadily. "I'm a little dizzy," she said. Clovis offered his arm, and she leaned against it gratefully.

Marcus walked forward a few steps into a shallow pool of water. The darkness of the cave made it difficult to see more than a few feet ahead. He bent over, picked up a small rock, and threw it as far as he could. A few seconds passed before a faint *kerplop* sounded in the distance. "Kelvin was right," he said. "We're standing at the edge of an underground lake."

"Actually," said Lael, "I think we're *in* the lake."

Sure enough, they were standing on a small mound of earth, no more than ten feet across, surrounded by water. No matter how far they threw their stones, each one landed in more water. They could see nothing but darkness all around them.

Without knowing how far the water extended or what might be lurking in it, none of them dared try to swim to safety. Instead they stood and waited.

Soon they heard the splashes of a boat paddling toward them. Marcus could just make out a small speck of light that grew larger and larger until he could see the outline of a boat and the tall, monstrous creature standing in its bow.

The creature wore a pack of some kind that partially hid its hunched back and elongated snout. Only its claws were visible. As it approached their little island, it said nothing but motioned for the three prisoners to step into the boat, which they did without a word. The groc turned the boat with a long oar, and they glided slowly away.

Marcus peered into the darkness. There was light ahead of them, several torches on a distant shoreline. As they drew nearer, he saw dozens of grocs awaiting them. The boat slid quietly onto the sandy shore. Their guide stepped out and helped Marcus and the others do the same. It walked forward, silently beckoning for them to follow.

Eighteen

hy are you here?"

The voice was gravelly and hoarse. At first Marcus could not tell who had spoken. He, Lael, and Clovis were surrounded by grocs of all shapes and sizes, but one groc, so thin the outline of his bones was visible through his sickly yellow skin, sat on a tall boulder rising from the sand. His face was hidden in shadow.

"Why are you here?" repeated the groc, whom Marcus assumed was the leader.

Marcus hoped Clovis or Lael would answer, but by the fear in their faces it was clear the honor fell to him. Their guide still stood beside them, saying nothing.

"We are on our way to Dokur," Marcus said, mustering as much courage as he could. "My brother is ruler there and needs our help."

"Fredric has no brother."

"Fredric was our grandfather. He's dead. My brother rules in his place."

"Fredric dead?" asked the groc leader. "How?"

"I don't know," answered Marcus, and he didn't, though if he had known, he wouldn't have revealed anything to this monster.

"And your brother now rules?"

"Yes."

"He is a wise ruler, a just ruler?"

"I suppose so. Why?"

"Because for many years grocs are captured, tortured, killed! Perhaps your brother changes that."

"Maybe grocs are killed because you eat humans."

The groc leader lifted his snout in the air and roared. The sound of it made Marcus shudder in fear.

"Perhaps we eat humans because we are killed!" said the groc.

Marcus wondered just how far he could go before he pushed his host too far. "If you want justice from the new king, then maybe you should show some justice yourself. Let me and my friends go, and I promise to talk to my brother about your, um . . . people."

"I see your face before," the groc said thoughtfully. "That is why I send for you."

"You sent for me?"

"You are the one in the stone."

Marcus was confused now. The groc was curious about him, but he knew grocs rarely took the time to chat with their prey before eating it.

"I don't know what you're talking about," said Marcus.

"You challenge me? The stone sees everything! The stone never lies!" The groc's voice rose to a frenzied pitch. "Do you know who I am?" he shouted, his teeth glinting through his drool. "I am Hyer, keeper of the stone's secrets!"

"I don't understand," said Marcus. "What stone?"

Hyer growled and thrashed his head from side to side. The other grocs growled back. Hyer held up his hands and spread his webbed fingers.

"Many seasons past she come to us. Alone. She has only her child. When I learn who she is, I want to make her suffer. Make her father suffer! But she is wiser than I. She swears oath that my kind will one day walk in daylight, drink from the rivers, not be tormented by other creatures of Imaness. To prove her word, she show me vision of future."

Hyer lowered his hands and fell into silence. He stared at Marcus with a strange longing, as though he were waiting, or hoping, for something to happen. After a few moments, Marcus began to feel uncomfortable and wondered how long he had before he and his friends would be eaten.

"You said you saw me before," said Marcus.

"I see you in the stone! The stone does not lie!" Hyer shook with rage.

Clovis, who had been quiet until now, leaned forward to whisper in Marcus's ear. "Maybe he's talking about Ivanore's Celestine seal."

Marcus thought about what Clovis said. When Marcus and Kelvin's mother, Ivanore, ran away from Fredric, she would have had to pass through Vrystal Canyon to reach Zyll in the village of Quendel. But she had broken her seal and given half to Jayson before she escaped. And even now, restored again, the seal was simply that—a royal seal. Marcus had never even seen his own reflection on its polished surface, let alone a vision of the future. But he did not doubt she had somehow convinced the grocs to believe her promise and free her.

"So," said Marcus, "you saw a vision of me in the stone. If so, then what are your plans for me?"

Hyer remained silent for a few moments, though he grew more agitated by the minute. "The stone," he shouted, "reveals that you are to go free!"

"Well, I'm glad to hear it," replied Marcus, relieved. "We'll need a guide to find our way out. Now, if you don't mind, we'll be going."

"Yes, you go free," repeated Hyer, pressing his webbed fingertips together. "But the others must stay."

Nineteen

I won't leave without my friends," Marcus said.

Hyer pulled his knees up to his bony chest and rested his jaw on them. "You are not glad to be released?"

"No!" said Marcus. "I demand you release all of us."

Hyer stared at Marcus from his perch on the boulder. The other grocs stood by, but Marcus sensed a growing uneasiness among them. Some of them paced restlessly, while others let out low, growling sounds. Still others glared hungrily at Marcus and his friends as if they were imagining what they would taste like.

"Well?" said Marcus.

Hyer straightened his scaly legs and raised himself to his full height, which was much taller than Marcus had thought. This brought Hyer out of the shadows so that Marcus could see him fully.

"They want to eat you," Hyer said, his voice laced with delight. "They will not long resist before they give in to their hunger."

Marcus realized then that Hyer might very well decide not to free him, vision or no vision. He was running out of time.

Their groc guide, who still stood beside Marcus, leaned close so that his snout nearly touched Marcus's ear. "Get in the boat," he whispered.

There was something about the voice Marcus recognized. The shape of the beast's face, the look in his eyes seemed familiar. He looked at the groc more carefully.

"Bryn?" whispered Marcus. "Is that you?"

The guide suddenly stepped between Marcus and Hyer's throne. "The stone does not lie!" the guide shouted to the crowd of anxious grocs. "The stone reveals this boy and his friends should go free."

"*All* of them free?" growled a groc who stood nearby. "Hyer says only the one in the stone goes. We can have the others!"

An angry grumble rose from the crowd. Hyer raised his hands for silence. "You will have what I promise!"

"I will take the boy back to the human world," Bryn said. He bowed several times, each time taking a step backward, forcing Marcus, Clovis, and Lael closer toward the boat.

When the boat was at their backs, Bryn hissed, "Get in the boat! Hurry!"

The grocs roared in confusion.

"What's going on?" asked Lael.

"You heard him!" said Marcus. "Get in the boat."

Clovis climbed in without hesitation. Then he offered his hand to Lael.

"But why?" said Lael. "You don't expect me to trust some overgrown lizard."

"Lael—"

"How do we know it hasn't planned its own personal feast?"

"Lael!" said Marcus. "Get in the boat—now!"

Lael glanced over Marcus's shoulder at the grocs who were growing more and more restless. Then she climbed into the boat. Marcus and Bryn scrambled in after her.

From his perch, Hyer shouted a command to stop the escaping prisoners, but the crowd of complaining grocs drowned out his voice. Bryn rowed the boat several yards out from shore. Hyer roared louder, "Follow them!"

Several of the grocs jumped into the water and started swimming after them. Others disappeared into a nearby cave and then returned, dragging two more boats behind them. Soon these boats, filled with shouting grocs, were steadily gaining on them.

"We need to go faster!" said Marcus.

Lael stood up in the back of the boat. Loading her sling with some small rocks she'd snatched up on the shore, she swung the weapon over her head and let the stones fly. They hit several of the pursuing grocs, resulting in some painful yelps. One even lost his balance and fell into the water.

Bryn rowed the boat into the darkness of the cavern. Soon it was so dark, they could not see each other let alone the boats chasing them, and Marcus wondered where they could possibly be headed. They continued on for several minutes, and then suddenly the bow of the boat rammed into something solid. The impact threw everyone forward and nearly out of the boat.

"What happened?" asked Lael, rubbing her sore knee, which had smashed against the boat's wooden bottom.

"The cave's outer wall," answered Bryn.

"Is this the way out?" said Clovis.

"The only way out is the tunnel we brought you through before," replied Bryn. "But I don't think you want to go back there now."

"You mean it's a dead end? We're trapped?" Lael's voice rose in a panic.

"Marcus will save us," said Bryn.

"What?" asked Marcus, suddenly alert. "What can I do?"

"You have magic."

"No, I don't."

"But I've seen it," insisted Bryn. "You command fire and water and earth! You can get us out of here."

"No! I won't do magic. I can't!"

"You must, Marcus, or we will all die."

Marcus heard the two groc boats cut through the water only yards behind them. He knew grocs had much keener eyesight than humans and suspected they could see him clearly. He did not want to use magic. He worried it would cause him pain, and he didn't want to feel magic's effects on him again. But at the moment, not using magic was even more frightening.

Marcus leaned forward over the hull of the boat and pressed his palms against the cavern's wall.

The shouts of the grocs grew closer as Marcus tried to decide what to do. Suddenly, the boat jerked back. One of the grocs had grabbed it! Bryn swung his paddle through the air. The thump of it hitting something was followed by a splash.

"Hurry!" shouted Bryn.

Marcus didn't wait a moment longer. He formed the word *open* in his mind.

At first, nothing changed. Then the stone beneath his hands gave a little. Marcus clutched his fingers, grabbing handfuls of mud. The cave walls were absorbing water like a sponge.

"Bryn? I think we should back up a little—"

Before Marcus could say anything more, the entire cave wall crumbled outward. One moment there was blackness and a solid wall, the next there was brilliant daylight and open air. The gaping hole in the side of the canyon was at least twenty feet above the ground, and the sudden rush of water that cascaded out of it filled the canyon with a deafening roar. Marcus, Lael, Clovis, and Bryn had barely enough time to hunker down low in their boat before they slipped over the crest of the newly born waterfall.

Twenty

Marcus, Lael, and Clovis screamed until they thought their lungs would burst. Then, after a brief yet terrifying drop, the boat landed with a heavy thud on the churning water below, now rushing like a mighty river through the snaking canyon. As narrow as the canyon was, their boat struck its walls again and again so hard Marcus was sure it would be dashed to pieces. Miraculously the boat held together—for now.

Marcus glanced up and saw blue sky ahead.

"Hold on!" he shouted and then ducked his head as far down into the boat as he could. The boat shot out of the canyon like an arrow and arched through the sky, taking flight before landing once again in the now-slowing river below.

Marcus cautiously peered over the boat's edge as it traveled lazily through the town of Noam at the base of the Jeweled Mountains, past its gawking citizens, and down what once had been a road. Eventually the boat ran aground near some trees.

They lay in the boat not speaking for a long time. Marcus's chest burned, and he felt completely drained of energy. He kept his eyes closed and tried to focus on the rhythm of his own breathing. After several minutes, he heard the others stirring around him.

Clovis was the first to sit up. He gripped the side of the boat and lifted his trembling body over it. Then he dropped onto the wet, muddy earth on the other side. He raised himself to his knees and finally, slowly, to his feet.

Lael moaned. "Are we dead?" she asked, shading her eyes. Clovis reached down and took her hand, pulling her to a sitting position.

"*We're* not dead," he said, "but I'm not so sure about him."

Lael shook Marcus by the shoulders. "Come on, Marcus," she said, her voice breaking into laughter. "Believe it or not, we're all in one piece."

Marcus rolled onto his side and used his hands to brace himself as he stood. He winced from the pain in his chest, which thankfully was beginning to fade.

"Are you all right?" asked Clovis.

"I'm a little weak." In truth, Marcus hurt more than he cared to admit.

"Here," said Clovis, "lean on me."

Marcus draped an arm around Clovis's shoulder and gingerly stepped out of the boat. He took a few shallow breaths, steadying himself, and then glanced around for Bryn. He found a boy with disheveled, black hair squatting in the field nearby, studying a butterfly perched on a mustard blossom. The boy stretched out a finger and managed to touch its delicate wings before it took flight.

"Who's that?" asked Lael.

"That's Bryn," replied Marcus. He strolled over to the little boy and tousled his hair. "Thanks for getting us out of there."

The boy looked up with amber-colored eyes and grinned happily. "You got us out of there," he said, picking the blossom and holding it beneath his nose. "I just got us *there*."

Lael gaped at them both. "You don't mean he's that . . . I mean, that little boy is that . . . that . . . thing?"

"Groc," said Clovis. "I told you, grocs are shapeshifters that take human form."

"Yes, but he's a . . . a child!"

Bryn stood up and walked over to where Lael straddled the boat with one foot out and one foot still in. She shrunk back as he approached. When Bryn held out his small, yellow flower to her, she cast uneasy glances toward Marcus and Clovis.

"Go ahead," said Marcus.

Forcing a smile, she accepted the flower. "Thank you," she said, "but—"

"But?" asked Marcus.

"His clothes," she said, indicating the shabby trousers and tunic he wore.

Bryn's face lit up as he raised the pack he had been wearing earlier. "I carry everything I need in here," he said proudly.

"I think we're near Lake Olsnar, about halfway to Dokur," said Marcus, pointing in the direction of the trees. "There's a road not far from here that leads through the forest to the lake. We can fill our water skins there and rest for the night."

The four of them soon found the road and spent a good part of the afternoon traveling north on it. The last time Marcus had traveled through these woods, he had been on his way home from Dokur after the battle with the Hestorians eight months earlier. But he had been on horse-back, and the journey had taken far less time. Before that, he, Clovis, and Bryn had arrived at the lake and visited with a band of cyclopes. It was the cyclopes who fought against the Hestorians and finally tipped the scale in Dokur's favor. There would be no cyclopes now, however. Winter was coming, and cyclopes were nomadic, traveling from one place to another as food and weather permitted. Last Marcus heard, they were spotted in the foothills near the hot springs of Amethyst Peak in the northeastern part of the island. They would not return to Lake Olsnar until spring.

Marcus and the others reached the lake shortly before sundown. After filling their water skins, Marcus suggested they gather some tree branches and construct a shelter for the night.

"Bryn, why don't you handle the hunting? I'm sure we all could use a good meal."

Bryn dashed off happily into a dense patch of underbrush. Marcus knelt in the dirt and began clearing the area of rocks and leaves.

"Clovis," he said, "can you and Lael fetch that fallen branch over there? It'd be a perfect brace for the other branches."

But Clovis did not respond.

"Clovis, did you hear me?" Marcus asked again.

"There's something over there," Clovis whispered. Marcus followed his gaze to a grove of trees not far from where they stood. They waited. A few moments passed. Then they heard movement and a low grunting sound. The brush just beyond the nearest trees rustled.

"Please don't let it be a warboar," said Clovis.

"Maybe it's a deer," suggested Lael.

Marcus crouched low and drew his knife. "Clovis," he said, "I think you should get your bow ready."

Twenty-one

Marcus inched forward with Lael close behind him, her sling raised. The brush rustled again, and there was more grunting, louder this time. Then suddenly—

"By the gods!"

Marcus looked back and met Lael's astonished glance.

"Drat these brambles!" said the voice.

Clovis crept up to them. "A talking deer?" he asked.

One final, violent shudder of the brush was followed by the sound of fabric tearing. A man emerged, examining the ragged hole at the hem of his robe. "Of all the trials the gods could send, they send me bushes with thorns! Can't a man relieve himself without getting ensnared? How am I to mend this?"

Marcus lowered his knife. "Grandfather?"

Zyll glanced up and, at the sight of Marcus and his companions, immediately forgot about his robe. "Marcus, my boy!" he said, approaching with arms extended. Marcus ran to his grandfather and threw his arms around him. "Well, well," said Zyll, peering at him over the rim of his spectacles. "Seems you've recovered nicely. But I must scold you for following me. I told you not to—"

"You're alive!" shouted Marcus. His eyes burned with tears. "You're really alive!"

"Well, yes. Last I checked. What is it, boy? Had you hoped I'd be otherwise?"

"No, Grandfather, of course not. It's just that—"

"Out with it. You obviously expected to find me in some other condition than I am in at present."

Marcus wanted to tell his grandfather everything— about the vision in the water and his reasons for leaving Quendel—but Marcus was so happy to see Zyll, he didn't want to spoil it. Obviously there had been some mistake. Marcus was no enchanter. He was just a boy apprentice. His vision had been wrong, and he was relieved to know it.

"I'm just glad you're safe," said Marcus. "I was worried about you and didn't want you to go on this journey alone."

"I'm not surprised you caught up to me, as old and as slow as I am. And I see you've brought company."

"You remember Clovis and Lael?"

"Yes, Clovis the bow maker. And Lael, did you say? Lael, that troublesome girl from the village?"

"I tried to make her go back, but she refused," said Marcus. "I had no choice but to let her come along."

"I see," said Zyll.

Lael's face went red, but Zyll's smile set her at ease. "Such a pleasure to see you again, my dear."

Lael and Clovis excused themselves to finish gathering the necessary wood.

"And Bryn is with us, too," continued Marcus. "Oh, you've never met Bryn. He's the groc I told you I met before."

"How did you run into him?"

"It's a long story, actually."

"And I'd love to hear it, but it appears as though you are setting up camp. May I be of assistance?"

Another voice sounded from the thicket, accompanied by a frustrated squawk.

"Leave me behind, will you?" cried Xerxes. "If I wasn't made of wood I'd—"

Zyll reached a hand into the thicket and pulled out Xerxes. "There now, old friend. I had no intention of leaving you behind again."

"Again?" asked Marcus.

"Seems I was a little absentminded the first night in the forest," replied Zyll, rolling his eyes.

"A little absentminded?" said Xerxes, ruffling his feathers indignantly. "I laid there for an hour before you returned for me."

"I was bathing in the stream."

"And then there was last night in Noam."

"It was merely a joke, Xerxes."

"He threatened to use me in a game of stick ball!"

"I should have endowed you with a sense of humor when I made you. Marcus, how did you endure so many days with him as a companion?"

"It wasn't easy," replied Marcus, laughing.

Xerxes clicked his beak angrily. "Well, now that I know my company isn't wanted—"

"Now Xerxes, really," said Zyll, trying not to laugh. "You are far too sensitive. Come now, we are only having a bit of fun at your expense."

"At my expense is right. No, I shall endure no more of it. And don't expect me to come hopping the next time you need a thorn plucked from your backside!"

And with that, Xerxes went still, returning to his inanimate form.

"I think you hurt his feelings," said Marcus.

"It wouldn't be the first time. Don't worry, my boy. He may have an ill temper, but he's the only true friend I've ever had. He'll forgive me . . . eventually. In the meantime, we must get our rest. We still have a day's more travel before we reach Dokur where your brother, Kelvin, awaits us."

Twenty-two

he heat from the fire was more than the small flame could possibly produce on its own. Marcus suspected Zyll had cast a spell so that it could warm everyone present despite the chill in the air. In time Clovis, Lael, and even Bryn nodded off to sleep, huddled peacefully beneath their blankets. Marcus thought Zyll must have had something to do with that, as well. Soon only Zyll and Marcus were awake, watching each other over the flame.

Looking at Zyll now, Marcus could still see the vision clearly in his mind. The sight of his grandfather lying in a pool of his own blood made his stomach churn.

"You seem troubled," said Zyll, stirring the embers at the edge of the fire with the point of his walking stick. "Are you going to tell me about it, or do I have to slip you a vial of noorweed serum to loosen your tongue?"

Marcus smiled at Zyll's good-humored threat. "It's hard to explain," he began. "When you left, I tried to use your divining bowl."

"And what happened?"

"Nothing at first. But then later I saw . . ." Marcus stopped. He turned away from Zyll, ashamed to let him see the tears that formed now against his will. "I saw you."

He looked back at Zyll and saw in him the man who had raised him, loved him, taught him everything he knew. Zyll had been more than a grandfather to him. He had been his mentor and friend. He could not imagine his life without Zyll in it.

Marcus stood up and took several steps away from the fire. He couldn't sit still. "It was a mistake," he said. "It had to be."

"What did you see?" asked Zyll.

"Enchanters see the past," continued Marcus, the words tumbling out of him, "but you're here, right in front of me. So it had to be a mistake."

"Marcus, tell me what you saw."

Marcus could hardly continue. The tears came freely now, and he choked them back. Zyll stood and walked over to Marcus, placing his aging hand on the boy's shoulder.

Marcus felt the gentle weight of Zyll's hand, but he could not meet his eyes. "I saw you, Grandfather," he whispered, "and you were dead."

Zyll nodded thoughtfully. "Enchanters do only see the past."

Marcus sighed with relief. "I knew it," he said, almost laughing. "I knew it was a mistake—"

"But you are not an enchanter."

"What?"

"You're not an enchanter," repeated Zyll, "at least not merely an enchanter. From the time you were a small boy, I knew there was something special about you. You see, enchanters are nothing more than magicians. We cast spells, manipulate objects. Once there were many of us, but now I believe I am the last of my kind."

Marcus sat down again beside the fire, but the chill he felt was not from the night air.

"Do you know what a seer is?" asked Zyll.

Marcus shook his head.

Zyll continued. "A seer sees the future, translates languages, can look into people's very souls."

Marcus recalled his visit to the Noamish library during his quest, searching for information about Ivanore. It was there he learned that Ivanore was Lord Fredric's daughter—a princess—and that she had disappeared fourteen years earlier. Marcus had not yet learned that Ivanore was his mother. When he first arrived at the library, he saw an inscription above the door in the ancient tongue. Though he had only a basic knowledge of the language, Marcus translated it easily, as if the words themselves changed before his eyes.

"How does someone become a seer?" asked Marcus.

"Oh, seeing cannot be learned or taught," replied Zyll. "A seer is born a seer."

Marcus realized Zyll was staring at him. No, not at him, but into him as if there were something inside of him to be marveled at or admired. Marcus didn't like being looked at that way. There was nothing special about him, about the boy who spent his mornings in the company of goats, his afternoons cleaning out the fireplace back home. He preferred it that way, preferred to be like everyone else—though somehow he knew Zyll was right. He had never been like everyone else.

"But I'm just an enchanter's apprentice," he said, as if saying the words would make them true.

"No, my boy," said Zyll, "you are more. Much, much more."

A GUARDED SECRET

Twenty-three

he rest of their trek to Dokur was uneventful. Marcus didn't mind their slow pace now that he knew Zyll was all right. When their journey brought them within a mile of the Celestine mine, Clovis reminded Marcus that he had never been there and asked if they could see it.

"It's just a big hole in the ground," said Marcus. "It's been abandoned since the Agoran slaves were freed."

But Bryn and Lael both wanted to have a look, too, so off they went. When they arrived, however, the mine was all but abandoned. Four log buildings had been constructed near the rim of the pit, and the area around the mine was dotted with dozens of fires. There were soldiers everywhere, some by the fires, some grooming their horses, and others keeping watch. Three drew their swords the moment Zyll, Marcus, and the others came into view.

"State your business!" shouted the largest of the three. They all wore red tunics with embroidered yellow crosses, the symbol of Fredric's army.

Zyll did not hesitate but stepped forward with his hands up in a show of peace.

"The grandson of Lord Fredric is in our company, Captain," he said calmly. "We are accompanying him to Dokur where his brother, the young King Kelvin, awaits his arrival."

The captain kept his sword raised, a cautious expression on his face. "The king is dead," he said.

"Yes, we know," replied Zyll. "We just thought we'd take a little detour and visit the mine. We expected it to be abandoned."

"It is," said the captain, "except for thieves intent on getting their hands on whatever Celestine they can manage to steal. Our duty is to protect it until a more permanent solution is worked out."

Behind the guards, Marcus could just make out the rim of the pit where he had first seen Agorans being whipped. Though he knew the captain spoke the truth, he wished he could see for himself that they had all gone.

He felt a tug on his pant leg. Bryn gazed up at him, fear in his childlike eyes. The last time they met Fredric's guards, Bryn had been taken captive. No wonder he was afraid now.

"We should get going, Grandfather," said Marcus. He took Bryn by the hand and started away from the soldier's camp.

"Wait," said the captain. Marcus froze. He felt Bryn's hand stiffen in his. He heard the scrape of metal as the captain sheathed his sword. "You should not be traveling alone," he said. "You never know what trouble you'll run into. Even Dokur isn't safe anymore. Just two days ago the royal navy's flagship was burnt to ashes by rebels."

"Rebels, you say?" said Zyll.

"Yes," the captain continued. "Let me send an armed escort with you to Dokur. One of my men was just about to leave to deliver our weekly report to the king at the Fortress. He could accompany you."

Marcus heard Xerxes squawk in surprise. Bryn's grip on his hand tightened, yet he dared not say anything to Zyll. What would happen if the guard discovered that Bryn was a groc?

Zyll scratched thoughtfully at his whiskers. "Your offer is a generous one," he said, "but Dokur is less than a day's walk from here. I'm sure we'll be fine."

The captain waved off his two companions. One strode over to the men with the horses and said something to them that Marcus could not hear. The other mounted his horse and took off at a gallop toward Dokur, leaving a cloud of dust in his wake.

"We'll be on our way then," said Zyll. "Good day, Captain."

Zyll said nothing to Marcus as he led them back

toward the road. Clovis and Lael were silent, too, but the captain called after them.

"My rider will let the Fortress know where you are and when you are expected to arrive. That way," he said, "if you never show up, they'll know something's happened to you."

Twenty-four

Despite the captain's warning, they arrived in Dokur early the following morning. The town had changed since Marcus saw it last. He remembered all too well how it had looked after the invasion by the Hestorians: its blackened buildings, charred by flaming dragons' breath, and the heap of bodies in the center of town. As he entered the city now, however, Marcus noted that many of the buildings had been repaired. Instead of the horrors of death and battle, the streets of Dokur were lined with row upon row of colorful silken tents. Tables laden with scarves, blankets, jewelry, pottery, weapons, and all kinds of food crowded every inch of space. Merchants haggled with customers. Drums, pipes, and dulcimers filled the air with music. Some people actually danced in the street.

Xerxes did not hide his disapproval. "After all this city has suffered," he said to Zyll, "you'd think they'd show a little more self-control."

"Now, now, Xerxes," replied Zyll. "These people have mourned long enough. This is their annual harvest celebration. I imagine after all the hard work of rebuilding their city and caring for the families of those who died in battle, the Dokurians deserve a little merriment, don't you?"

In contrast to all the celebration, however, were the soldiers standing guard throughout the square. Bryn stayed close to Marcus as they followed Zyll through the crowd. When they reached the immense stone fountain at the center of the city, they drank from it and splashed water on their faces. Once refreshed, Marcus sat down at the edge of the fountain. The smell of freshly baked bread made his stomach rumble.

Zyll raised an eyebrow. "Those meat pies over there look delicious," he said, placing a coin in Marcus's hand. "Why don't you buy a few to hold you until supper? In the meantime, I'll find a courier and send word to the Fortress of our arrival."

"Don't tell me you plan to leave these children alone?" squawked Xerxes. "They're certain to get into trouble."

"Calm yourself, Xerxes. They will be fine. And besides," Zyll added with a wink, "whatever trouble they get themselves into, I will not hold you accountable."

"Well, then I suppose it would be all right to leave them," Xerxes said in a serious tone, "for a short time."

Zyll laughed again and waved over his shoulder as he

and Xerxes disappeared into the crowd. Marcus thought he heard Xerxes say, "Oh, I feel an ill wind blowing." Of course, Xerxes' comment was lost on Marcus, who had already turned his attention to the display of pies. He bought four and gave one each to Bryn, Lael, and Clovis. They ate them slowly, savoring each bite of seasoned pork and gravy. When Marcus had finished, he turned his attention to the other nearby tents and the many people swarming around them. He wondered how much longer Zyll would take. The couriers were usually quick in delivering their messages, and news that he and Zyll were in Dokur would surely have reached the Fortress by now.

When several more minutes passed without Zyll's return, Marcus walked over to one of the tents to look at some wooden carvings of birds. He picked one up, rubbed its polished surface, and put it back down again. As he walked back to the fountain, he noticed a glint of light coming from another tent at the opposite end of the square.

"Look over there," he said, pointing.

Clovis stopped eating long enough to glance up. "Where?"

"There, where the ornaments are hanging by the bunch."

"I see it," said Clovis with little interest.

"I've always wanted a dragon amulet. Do you think they'll have one?"

"I guess so. These merchants sell just about everything. Why don't you go see?"

"Nah," replied Marcus, shaking his head. "Zyll said he wouldn't be long. We'd better stay put until he returns."

"I'll go," said Lael as she finished off her last bite of pie. She had already crossed half the square before Marcus caught up to her.

"Lael, let's do this later. Zyll might not see where we've gone."

"Clovis," called Lael over her shoulder, "if Zyll comes back, tell him where we've gone, all right?"

Clovis mumbled something, his mouth again full of food.

"Now come on," said Lael. "Let's see if we can't find you the biggest dragon amulet in Dokur."

Twenty-five

The tent was much larger up close than it had appeared from the fountain, as tall as the neighboring building, with thick, red fabric supported by heavy, wooden posts. From the crossbeam above hung hundreds of amulets made from gold, silver, and many gemstones of all colors. Some of the stones were round, smooth, and clear, and others were cut into diamond shapes. Tiny rainbows danced like stars inside the tent.

Some amulets were shaped like demons or fairies. Each one hung from a sturdy leather cord. Marcus let the tips of his fingers brush against the bottoms of the amulets. The sound of the gems colliding against each other was like the tinkling of glass.

He had worn something similar only once in his life, when he wore his brother's Celestine shard around his neck. Later, he and Kelvin learned that it was one of three pieces of their mother's royal seal, the Rock of Ivanore. A second piece belonged to their father, Jayson, while the third piece belonged to Marcus. Using the magic he had learned from Zyll, Marcus had reunited the three pieces into one. The restored medallion was given to Kelvin, the rightful heir to the throne—and to Ivanore's seal.

"Did you say you want a dragon amulet?" asked Lael from the opposite end of the tent.

Marcus looked at the item in her palm. A silver figurine with wings folded neatly against its body gazed back at him. Every detail was perfect—every feather in its wings, every strand of fur, the proud pose of its head, and the gentle yet powerful curve of its beak.

"That's not a dragon," said Marcus, "it's a gryphon."

"Oh, my mistake," said Lael. She turned to replace it on the empty hook, but just then a woman approached. She was dressed in a blue hooded robe with gold coins sewn onto the sleeves. Her hair, the color of rich soil, lay in soft curls upon her shoulders. She was much older than Marcus and quite beautiful.

"Do you like the gryphon?" she asked.

"Actually, I'm looking for a dragon," explained Marcus, "but I don't see any here."

The woman narrowed her eyes, studying Marcus's face. "Not for you," she said. "The dragon is a symbol of demons. They serve the evil ones. No, not for you."

The woman leaned close to Marcus and pointed at the amulet in Lael's hand. Then she reached beneath her collar and pulled out a pendant of jade. On it, carved in relief, was a gryphon.

"The gryphon," she continued, "is the guardian of the gods. It stands watch over the sacred treasure and protects the divine oracle. It is an honor to wear its likeness."

"All right," said Marcus. "I kind of like it. How much?"

"For you only two coins—and your blessing."

Marcus started to laugh but then stopped when he saw the serious expression on the woman's face. He looked at Lael, who returned his glance with a shrug. Then Lael placed the leather strap around his neck.

There was something about this gryphon Marcus liked. He had planned to buy a dragon to remind him of the one he had fought during the Hestorian invasion, but he felt satisfied that he had found something more suitable.

The merchant woman held out her hand for payment. Marcus dug in his pouch for the coins, while Lael wandered toward the neighboring tent.

As Marcus placed the coins in the woman's hands, a loud crack sounded. Marcus glanced up just in time to see Lael rushing toward him. She rammed into him and knocked him to the ground, forcing the breath right out of him. At the same time, more cracks sounded. People shouted. Marcus looked over Lael's shoulder and saw the tent's huge wooden frame collapse in a heap. The massive central pole lay on the ground—right where Marcus had been standing just moments before.

Twenty-six

Marcus lay on his back on the rough stone that paved the streets of Dokur. His right elbow and shoulder ached from the sudden blow. But he was not thinking about the pain. He was thinking about the fact that Lael had landed on top of him, her face only inches from his.

"I'm sorry," she stammered, scrambling to her feet.

Marcus wasn't sure whether to smile or scowl. "It seems landing on me has become a habit," he said, choosing a smile. Lael's expression told him he had chosen wrong. He was about to roll over onto his not-so-sore left side, when a shadow fell over him. Marcus closed his eyes and groaned, waiting for the lecture that was sure to follow.

"I told you he'd get into trouble," said Xerxes, "but do you ever listen to me?"

"I can explain," started Marcus as Zyll held out a hand to help him up. The merchant woman who had sold him the gryphon amulet bent over the mass of broken wood and torn silk. She already had dozens of pendants strung up and down both arms and was searching the wreckage for more. Marcus was relieved she had not been hurt.

Zyll picked up a tangle of leather cords and held them out to her. "Here you are," he said with a smile. The woman reached for the amulets but stopped short. Her eyes grew wide as she took them from him.

"The tent just suddenly collapsed," Lael was explaining. "It wasn't Marcus's fault."

"Zyll, are you listening to this?" Xerxes snapped.

Zyll looked away from the merchant woman. "Hmm? What was that, my friend?"

"Are you all right?" Marcus asked his grandfather.

The space between Zyll's eyes creased. He glanced back toward the tent, but the merchant woman had gone.

"Nothing," said Zyll. "I thought I recognized her, that's all. Just my aging memory playing tricks, I suppose. Now, what were you saying?"

By then Clovis had reached them, out of breath from running. "I heard the commotion, but I didn't realize how close—by the gods, Marcus, you're bleeding!"

Marcus touched the damp spot on his cheek and found a small scratch there, but the injury wasn't as bad as it could have been.

Clovis took Marcus's arm as though he were helping an invalid.

"I'm fine, Clovis," insisted Marcus.

"You look pale. Maybe you should lie down."

"Really, Clovis," said Marcus a little too sharply. It was just that he hated that sort of attention, and other than feeling a little bruised here and there, he was quite capable of walking on his own. "I'm okay," he added. "We should be getting to the Fortress to see Kelvin."

Lael shook her head. "I'm not coming."

"What?" asked Clovis. "Why not?"

"I didn't come here for Kelvin, remember? I have my own business in Dokur."

"That's fine," said Marcus. He agreed with Lael. He hadn't wanted her coming with him in the first place, and he certainly did not want her tagging along on his visit to his brother. "If you need a place to stay, there's a tavern across the square. The girl who works there, Kaië, is a friend of mine."

"I'm staying, too," said Bryn. "You know what happened the last time I went to the Fortress."

"What happened?" asked Lael.

"He was arrested and sentenced to death," said Clovis. "He only escaped because of Marcus."

"And Kaië," added Marcus.

Bryn smiled. "I can stay here with Lael."

Lael's eyes widened with concern, but she said nothing. Marcus wondered if leaving them alone together was a good idea. While he was certain Bryn could take care of himself, he wasn't quite so sure about Lael. She'd never been away from the village of Quendel before, especially in a city like Dokur. She might run into trouble.

Marcus pulled Clovis aside. "Clovis, I have a favor to ask."

"Anything."

"I know you came all this way to help me," said Marcus. He hoped what he was about to ask would not hurt his friend's feelings, but Clovis interrupted him.

"Marcus, do you really think we should leave Lael alone? I mean, I know she's handy with her sling, but maybe I should stay here—to keep an eye on her—and maybe Bryn, too."

Marcus patted Clovis's shoulder, relieved that he didn't have to make the suggestion himself. "I think you're right," he said. "In any case, Zyll and I will be back tomorrow after we've had a chance to meet with Kelvin."

A smile crept onto Clovis's face. Then he led Lael and Bryn toward the tavern.

Marcus watched them for a moment and turned to go his own way. "Are you coming, Grandfather?" he asked.

Zyll, who had been looking over the wreckage, nodded. "Yes, of course," he said. Noticing the scratch on Marcus's face, Zyll reached up to touch it, when something else caught his attention. He gazed curiously at the silver figure at Marcus's throat. Then his demeanor abruptly changed. "Yes," he repeated with a smile, "I think your brother will be quite surprised to see us."

Allowing Marcus to lead the way, Zyll held back a moment. He looked at the collapsed tent once more.

"Trouble seems to follow that boy," said Xerxes,

clicking his beak disapprovingly. "I've warned you before, he cannot be left alone."

"I believe you might be right, old friend," replied Zyll. "Perhaps I will take your advice and keep a closer eye on him."

Xerxes squawked in surprise. "Since when do you ever take my advice?"

"Since I discovered that this tent's main support rope was deliberately cut."

Twenty-seven

The Seafarer Tavern was one of the few buildings in Dokur that had survived the invasion of the Hestorians several months earlier. Despite the swath of charred wood across its front, it still reeled in visitors and locals alike. Lael, Clovis, and Bryn hoped for a hot meal and place to sleep. What they found was a dining room full of men singing loudly and off key. The three stood in the doorway, staring at the spectacle. Bryn cowered behind Lael's legs like the child he was. Only when the singing finally stopped did someone notice them.

"Look, Mother," said a ragged-looking man wearing a leather apron. "We have more customers. Come, come," he continued, approaching them unsteadily, "here's a table for you."

119

Mother, a round woman with few teeth and a patch of scraggly, red hair atop her head, came out of the kitchen carrying a platter of steaming baked potatoes.

"All right then, Mr. Peagry, enough with the ale! You've had your entertainment. Now why don't you see what the *real* customers will be having tonight?"

Mr. Peagry, the tavern owner, led the young visitors to a small table near the kitchen and invited them to sit down. "Will you be needing a booster for the little one?" He plopped his dirty hand onto Bryn's head and gave it a friendly rub. Bryn curled his lips back and growled, but the owner was too drunk to notice. "What'll it be?" he said.

"A bowl of chowder," replied Lael. "And the same for the boy."

"I'll have some stew," said Clovis.

Mr. Peagry nodded. "You heard that, Mother? Two chowders and a stew!"

"I heard 'em!" shouted Mother as she passed them on the way back to the kitchen. "And tell that good-for-nothin' Kaië she'll be docked a day's wages for comin' in late!"

"Don't worry, luv, she's not talkin' about you," Peagry said to Lael.

"Excuse me," said Clovis, choosing an apple from a bowl of fruit on the table. "Your wife mentioned a girl named Kaië. Is she here?"

Peagry's lips parted in a grin, revealing a set of discolored, crooked teeth. "You know the little mouse then, do you?" he said. "No, she ain't here—yet. Never know when she'll show up. She's gone half the time up at that castle hanging around with the royalty!"

Mother had just stepped through the door again, setting the bowls out on the table. "Mind your mouth, Mr. Peagry," she said, then added proudly, "Some folks say she's got a mind to marry that young king of ours."

"Marry Kelvin?" said Lael, stifling a giggle.

"Not right away, of course, but in two or three years when he's old enough. Imagine that! A servant girl marrying a king!"

"I think she's gone and wheedled her way into high society, that's what I think," added Peagry. "Well, let her have her gold and her fancy clothes. She can rot up there for all we care! Isn't that right, Mother?"

"Keep your thoughts to yourself! Your gossip's gonna get us into trouble."

With that, Mr. and Mrs. Peagry disappeared together into the kitchen, leaving their young visitors alone to enjoy their supper.

Bryn eyed Clovis's apple and licked his lips. He tried to snatch the sweet jewel from Clovis's grasp, but Lael had his fingers clutched in her fist before he could succeed.

"Mind your manners," she said, giving the boy a warning glance. Bryn lowered his eyes and placed both hands beneath the table away from view.

"Don't tell Marcus about Kaië, okay?" said Clovis. "He might not take it well."

"Why not?" asked Lael.

Clovis ran his fingers around the rim of his mug. Suddenly, Lael burst into laughter. "Don't tell me he cares for her!"

"What does it matter?" said Clovis defensively. "From what the innkeeper said, she's marrying Kelvin."

Lael took a bite of her meal. "I guess some girls might find Kelvin attractive," she said, "but then I'd think anyone with brains would want more than good looks in a man."

"So, you think Kelvin's good looking?" asked Clovis.

Lael shrugged. "I guess. But I'd want someone better."

"Better than a king?"

"A woman who marries for money will never find true happiness."

"So she should marry someone poor and plain?"

"That's not what I meant and you know it," said Lael.

"Maybe instead of Kelvin," Clovis went on, "Kaië should marry someone from humbler circumstances, like me. Or like Marcus."

"That's not funny, Clovis."

"Now that would be something, wouldn't it?" Clovis laughed. "I can see it now. A double wedding! Kelvin and Kaië, and you? You'll marry Marcus."

"Stop it—"

"Better yet, *you'll* marry Kelvin and become queen!"

"I said stop it!" Lael slapped her hand on the table so hard, the utensils jumped.

"What?" said Clovis. "I was only joking."

"I won't marry anyone!"

"Then what's all the fuss about?"

"I don't know!" answered Lael. "You brought it up, talking about that girl marrying Kelvin."

"I didn't bring it up. The tavern keeper did!"

They both turned toward the sound of someone biting into a crisp apple. Bryn, his cheeks full, held the confiscated fruit in his hand and a delighted look on his face. Lael glared at him while trying to conceal an amused grin.

"I was hungry," he said, taking another unrepentant bite.

Twenty-eight

Marcus and Zyll stood before the towering doors of the throne room in the heart of the Fortress. This was the very spot where Bryn had faced Fredric's guards while Marcus and Kaië escaped. Marcus wasn't so sure how he felt about being here again.

"I hate leaving Clovis and the others behind," Marcus told Zyll. "Do you think it was the right thing to do?"

Zyll brushed a spot of dust off Xerxes' beak. "Bryn told you himself he did not want to come, and I can't say I blame him after what he endured here. And Lael has her own matters to take care of."

"Then I'm glad Clovis offered to stay with them," added Marcus. "That makes me feel a little better."

Xerxes narrowed his eyes and huffed like an annoyed

child. "So it should," he replied. "I'm sure they'll be better off as far from you as possible."

"Xerxes . . ." chided Zyll.

The doors swung open on their mighty hinges, and a guard beckoned Zyll and Marcus to enter. At the far end of the room, three steps led to a throne on a raised platform. Marcus remembered it well from the day Fredric awarded him and his friends their Celestine rings. It felt strange not to see Fredric there now. Marcus sensed things had changed here—and not necessarily for the better.

The throne sat empty, but a frail-looking man with a sculpted gray beard approached them.

"Welcome," said Chancellor Prost, extending a stiff hand to Zyll, who shook it briefly. "When my attendant announced your arrival, I almost thought him mad. Zyll, thought I, traveling such a distance? Surely it isn't possible, but here you are before me."

Prost's tone was mocking. Marcus stole a quick glance at his master to see if he was offended, but Zyll just nodded his head respectfully.

"Chancellor," Zyll said, tipping the top of his walking stick toward Marcus, "my grandson, Marcus Frye."

"Ah yes, we've met. You're here to visit your brother, no doubt. Unfortunately, the king is busy this morning. A boy of his position has many responsibilities."

Prost's voice made the hairs on the back of Marcus's neck bristle. It must have had the same effect on Xerxes, because Marcus noticed his wooden feathers puff up ever so slightly. Zyll stroked Xerxes' head and neck.

"We are not here for a visit, Chancellor," said Zyll. "We have come to offer our services to His Majesty."

"Services?" asked Prost, one eyebrow rising to a pointed arch. "What sort of services?"

"Anything my brother needs, sir," said Marcus.

Marcus knew that he should show respect to this man, but he could not help but add the slightest edge to the word "sir." Zyll shot him a warning glance.

"I am sure His Majesty will appreciate your kind offer," said Prost, "but he has no need of any more servants at this time. Perhaps if you return tomorrow . . ."

Prost was about to dismiss them, but the sound of a door opening at the back of the room made him stop. Marcus recognized that door. Beyond it was the king's personal chambers and the secret tunnel that led outside. Marcus and Kaië had escaped through the throne room and that very door after freeing Bryn from the Fortress dungeon.

The door opened, and an attendant dressed in a glittering silver tunic stood at attention. A moment later, Kelvin walked in.

Twenty-nine

The boy king looked much like he had when he and Marcus had gone on their quest together eight months earlier. Though Marcus had grown a few inches since then, so had Kelvin, who was still a little taller than his younger brother. However, Marcus sensed Kelvin had changed in ways other people might not notice: the apprehension in those eyes and uncertainty in his step.

Kelvin stopped when he saw who was in the room, a look of disbelief crossing his face. Zyll bowed. Marcus did the same.

"Your Majesty," said Zyll.

After a moment's hesitation, Kelvin hurried over to them and embraced Zyll. "Grandfather!" he said through a wide smile. Then he turned to Marcus and hugged him, too. "Marcus! I had no idea you were coming. Why didn't anyone tell me?" he asked, directing his question to Prost.

"They only just arrived, Sire."

"I'm so glad you've come!" said Kelvin.

Marcus looked Kelvin over and nodded. "Royalty suits you, brother," he said.

"I know, it seems strange, doesn't it?" answered Kelvin, laughing. "Me—a king. Why, just a few months ago I was working alongside my adoptive father in the fields of Quendel, and today—well, here I am. Although I would give anything for Fredric to still be here. You must have heard about his passing."

"We left for Dokur the moment the news reached us," said Zyll. "We are so sorry for your loss but extend to you our humble congratulations."

"There's no need to be so formal with me, Grandfather."

"Of course. We were just explaining to your advisor that Marcus and I have come to offer our services in your court."

"What a wonderful idea! Chancellor Prost?"

Prost watched the reunion with a scowl on his face. He stepped forward now, his bony fingers laced together at his waist, like a skeletal sash about his crimson robe.

"Sire," said the chancellor.

"Find something for them to do, won't you, Prost? I want them close to me. We'll have dinner together tonight."

"I assume you'll be staying with us?" Prost asked of Zyll.

"If His Majesty pleases," said Zyll.

"Of course!" said Kelvin. "Chancellor Prost, do you think—"

"Then I will show you to your rooms immediately," answered Prost.

Marcus hesitated. "I was hoping we could spend some time with you, Kelvin. We came a long way to see you."

Kelvin smiled. "Yes, that would be—"

Again Prost interrupted. "The king will certainly make time for you later, but he has an urgent matter to attend to just now. You'll have to excuse him."

Kelvin's smile vanished. "Yes," he said, disappointed, "of course. I'd almost forgotten."

Zyll and Marcus nodded their respects to Kelvin before they followed Prost out of the throne room. Marcus noted that Zyll seemed strangely quiet despite having just been reunited with the grandson he had not seen in many months.

Ahead of them, Prost led the way down a narrow corridor. "So what did you have in mind?" he asked, directing his comment to Zyll. "Vizier, perhaps? Or jester? I'm sure you could entertain His Majesty with palm readings and prophesy. And the younger brother would make a fine captain of the guard. Hmm?"

Marcus bristled, but he felt angrier that Zyll did not respond in kind to Prost's rudeness.

"Ah, here we are," said Prost, stopping beside a pair of ornately carved wooden doors. "Your room, Marcus, is here. Zyll's is just across the hall. A servant will be in shortly to tend to your needs. I'll send someone to fetch you for dinner. Oh," he added, "I believe I have just the job for both of you. I'll have you instructed first thing in the morning."

With that, Prost turned and strode briskly down the hall and back to the throne room without giving Zyll or Marcus a second glance.

Thirty

"Alone, finally!" squawked Xerxes, stretching his beak wide. "That Chancellor Prost is such an unpleasant creature."

Marcus opened the door to his room and entered, followed by Zyll with Xerxes.

"I could not agree with you more, my old friend," said Zyll, "but we must remember our manners while in his company."

Xerxes rolled his wooden eyes in disgust.

"So remind me why we're here?" asked Marcus, dropping his pack on an upholstered velvet chair near the door. "Oh, that's right: to protect Kelvin from meeting the same fate as Fredric. Only it seems he's already got Prost for that job."

Zyll strode across the room, his steps muffled by thick, plush carpeting. The bed where Marcus would be sleeping was made of carved mahogany with red silk drapes and a matching down comforter. Zyll leaned against it and let his hand sink into the billowy thing. "I sense sarcasm in your voice," he said.

"And why shouldn't I be sarcastic when my brother could spare no more than a minute for us?" said Marcus.

"You're disappointed."

"I thought he'd be happier to see us."

"He seemed happy enough."

"But you heard Prost. 'The king has an urgent matter to attend to just now,'" said Marcus, imitating the old man. "And don't you think it was odd that Kelvin didn't know we were coming after that captain at the mine sent word that we were?"

"Yes," agreed Zyll, "odd indeed."

Marcus turned to the window overlooking a grove of trees. From the open pane he could hear the sounds of construction hidden from view by a wide, stone parapet. Marcus leaned out the window, straining to catch a glimpse of the navy's new ships. He could just make out a few sails.

"Perhaps we could arrange a tour of the Fortress." Zyll's voice was cheerful.

Marcus would have preferred that the old enchanter felt as resentful as he did—or at least a little annoyed.

"I doubt Kelvin will have the time," he said. "Too busy with his royal duties, you know."

"Now, Marcus, jealousy is unattractive and not at all suitable to you."

"Me? Jealous of Kelvin? I don't think so."

A sound came from Xerxes that Marcus could swear was a chuckle.

"Well, if you were jealous," said Xerxes, "no one could blame you. He is not quite a year older than you, yet it was he whom Fredric invited to court and he who has inherited the throne."

Marcus was about to offer a snide comeback when Zyll spoke up. "Kelvin bears a heavy burden for one so young. I would not envy him if I were you."

Marcus stood back from the window and glanced at Zyll, who was unpacking Marcus's belongings into a cedar chest.

"I suppose you're right," he said. "I shouldn't be jealous of Kelvin. He may have an entire kingdom, but thanks to you I've got everything I ever wanted."

Zyll glanced up for only a moment before turning back to the chest, but in that moment Marcus saw a smile beneath the old man's whiskers.

"My room is across the hall," said Zyll, folding Marcus's blanket and laying it inside the chest with the other items. He then went to the door. "I am a bit stiff after that long journey and am in need of a good night's sleep. If you need anything at all, just shout. Xerxes will be sure to hear you," he added with a sly wink.

Once alone, Marcus sat down on the bed, bouncing a little. Then he lay down and rubbed his palms across the smooth silk. The cot in his small cottage in Quendel was all he'd ever known and was comfortable enough for him, but now, cradled in luxury, he could hardly recall a single night he'd spent there.

Marcus closed his eyes and imagined himself drifting on a cloud across a clear, blue sky. It was as if the air itself held him aloft. It was the most pleasurable sensation he had ever felt. But then his thoughts turned to Kelvin, who surely had a bed like this one, maybe even bigger, and would never have to sleep on a cot again, or hunt for his own food, or sweep out the chimney, or slop the pigs. He tried to picture Kelvin dressed in his royal robes taking Agnes the goat for her morning walk across the pasture, mud and stickers clinging to his hem. Marcus stifled a laugh at the image, and as he drifted off to sleep, a smile remained on his lips.

Thirty-one

Dokur awoke with merchants' wagons rolling into town behind sluggish oxen. They came from all over the Isle of Imaness. Dokur, the island's only port city, was the hub of trade, where price of even the smallest piece of the precious Celestine crystal was high. At one time, the stones had become almost common, but since Fredric had shut down the mine and freed the Agoran slaves, the well of Celestine had dried up—and the demand for it had grown.

Lael stood outside the Seafarer Tavern and watched as the colorful tents of the marketplace were raised. By the time the sun had come into full view over the horizon, Dokur was wide-awake.

Lael stepped forward and was instantly swept into the crowd. She set her jaw and wore a serious expression. She had no intention of being taken for granted here. She meant business and hoped to get that point across to everyone she might meet.

She didn't have any specific destination in mind as she walked the narrow paths between the tents. Her goal was to find her mother, not that she expected the task to be as easy as stumbling on her by accident here (though perhaps she did entertain a childish wish that very thing might happen). No, she would first need to find out who had taken her and where his path might have led.

Lael paused beside a produce vendor selling vegetables from wide, shallow wooden boxes. It was possible that her mother was no longer on Imaness at all, but Lael had to start somewhere, and Dokur was as good a place as any.

"Pardon me," said Lael to the man behind the display. He was counting out radishes for a woman with a baby in her arms.

"Tomatoes are in back," the man barked, "so the children can't bruise them."

Pouring the handful of little, red roots into the woman's basket, he accepted her coin and nodded a quick thanks before turning to Lael.

"I'm not here for tomatoes," said Lael.

"No?" asked the man.

"I am looking for a woman. A slave."

The man snickered, and his long, pointy nose and pinched cheeks reminded Lael of the rats that often raided her fields back home. "You are awfully young to be a master of slaves," he said. "What do you need one for, anyway? To be your nursemaid and tuck you into bed at night?"

His nose twitched when he talked, and Lael imagined a stone striking him between the eyes, a direct hit from her sling. No more difficult than hitting those rats.

Lael moved on, carefully observing each face that passed by as if one of them might reveal some hidden truth that would lead her to her mother. Maybe, too, she hoped she might recognize the man who had taken her those many years ago when Lael was a small girl—the man who came through Quendel looking for workers willing to sell their lives in exchange for enough gold to pay their debts.

Lael's memory of that day was rough at best. She was a girl of five years, still much in need of her mother's care. That afternoon her parents argued over supper. What the argument was about Lael didn't know, but it had ended when her father stormed out of their house. Lael's mother had held her and kissed her for a long, long time. Then, with tears streaming down her face (How many wasted hours had Lael spent trying to remember that face!), her mother placed ten gold coins on their table and walked out their front door. Lael had run to the back window and seen her mother join a man on the road behind their house. They walked away together. Her mother never looked back.

Lael had tried for years to understand why her mother left. The only explanation she had came later from her father: The man was a slave merchant from Dokur, and Lael's mother had sold herself to pay the mortgage on their farm. That was all Lael would ever know about that day and about the man who took her mother away from her. Now, standing among hundreds of nameless faces, she realized any one of them could have been that merchant, and she would never be able to recognize him.

"Are you lost, child?"

The voice was familiar, and Lael glanced up. The merchant woman whose tent had collapsed the day before stood in front of her, dozens of amulets dangling from her arm. The gems were dazzling in the sunlight, and their beauty set Lael at ease.

"I'm searching for someone, actually," Lael replied. "I'm trying to locate a slave collector."

"Ah," said the woman, nodding. "There is someone who might be able to help you. Brommel is an old friend of mine. He knows much about those things."

"Brommel? Could you tell me where to find him?"

"He isn't here," the woman said. Lael felt disappointed, but the woman continued. "You'll find him in the shadows."

"The shadows? What do you mean?"

The woman gently grasped Lael's arm and turned her. "There, in the darkness," she said, pointing toward the older, battle-scarred part of the city.

"But how will I know him?"

The woman smiled, her expression surprisingly tender. Lael couldn't help but smile back.

"How will you know Brommel?" the woman said with a gentle laugh. "Trust me. You can't *not* know him."

The woman turned away and was quickly swallowed up in the mass of people. Lael rubbed her arm where the woman had held her. The spot was warm. Finding someone in the shadows, in the darkness. How absurd! But as she let her eyes wander through the crowd, Lael saw something that made her pause.

Across the town square, Lael noticed a narrow strip between two rows of buildings. The roofs were too close together for the sunlight to penetrate. It must be the darkness, the shadows the woman spoke of.

Lael started forward through the crowd, intent on reaching that dark place as soon as possible. She did not notice the stranger following close behind her.

Thirty-two

arcus was up before dawn, his stomach grumbling too much to sleep anymore. The night before, he and Zyll had been ushered into a great hall with a long dining table laid with gold utensils and crystal plates. The linens were fine silk, and gold candlesticks adorned each end of the table. At first, Marcus was impressed by all the finery, but when they were told they would be dining alone, Marcus lost his appetite. He had hoped to spend the evening with Kelvin, but apparently the new king was still too busy.

There was a loud rap at his door. "Sir, I have been sent to bring you and your grandfather to the kitchen," said the voice from the other side.

Marcus dressed quickly and stepped into the hall where Zyll and the attendant were already waiting. The rumbling in Marcus's stomach was loud enough to be heard. Then he realized he could hear Zyll's stomach as well.

"Breakfast," said Marcus, rubbing his hands together. "I could eat a whole rack of bacon and a dozen eggs all by myself."

Xerxes clicked his beak. "Gluttony becomes no man," he said. Though no one but Marcus and Zyll could hear Xerxes, the walking stick's remark was still irritating. Marcus chose to ignore him.

The royal kitchen was larger than Marcus could ever have imagined. His entire cottage in Quendel could fit easily inside. A large man with a plump, pink face met them at the door.

"Ah, you have arrived just in time for breakfast," said the man whose chins jiggled as he spoke. "Come with me."

"Finally," Marcus whispered to Zyll. "I'm starving."

"Can you think of nothing but your stomach?" chided Xerxes.

Zyll leaned close to Xerxes and whispered, "I think this would be a good time for you to sleep."

"And if I choose not to?" asked Xerxes.

"Then I will take you back to our room and leave you there for the remainder of the day."

After that, Xerxes remained silent.

The man led Marcus and Zyll to a wide, iron stove on which sat a kettle of simmering liquid.

"You, Zip," he said, indicating Zyll, "shall prepare his

majesty's morning tea. And you, Martin," he added, pointing a sausage-like finger at Marcus, "will bake the biscuits."

Marcus scowled, but the chef ignored him.

"I, Val, the island's most talented chef, will make a most delectable cream gravy for His Majesty's meal."

Marcus stared at the man, his mouth agape. "You mean we're here to *make* breakfast?"

Val the chef opened a nearby drawer and tossed two cotton aprons to Marcus and Zyll.

"Chancellor Prost told me last night I would have two new assistants. I expect you here each morning an hour before His Majesty's breakfast and again an hour before dinner. You will have each afternoon off as I prepare His Majesty's lunch myself. If you are late or fail to obey my orders, you will be imprisoned. Have I made myself clear?"

Marcus and Zyll exchanged glances.

"Very clear," said Zyll.

"Couldn't be more clear," said Marcus.

"Now," continued Val, "I must collect the ingredients for the gravy. I will return shortly."

Val whirled on his heels and trotted off toward the pantry. After finding a safe place for Xerxes in the corner, Zyll pulled the apron over his head and tied it in back. On the counter beside Marcus sat a lump of dough on a floured board. Marcus poked it with the tip of his finger, leaving a dent in its side.

"'I will offer my services to your brother.' Is this what you had in mind when you said that?" Marcus asked angrily.

"We are here in the Fortress and are near Kelvin," replied Zyll, taking a ladle from a rack and dipping it into the kettle. "That was our plan."

"Our plan was to protect him from whoever murdered Fredric. So explain to me how answering to Val is going to help us do that."

Zyll lifted the ladle to his lips and took a sip of the tea. Then he took a canister from a nearby shelf and sprinkled some of its contents into the kettle.

"Patience, my boy. Patience," he said, adding one last dash from the canister before replacing it on the shelf. Then he gave a sly smile and winked at Marcus. Marcus rolled his eyes and groaned as he yanked his apron over his head. He pulled back his elbow as far as he could and rolled his fingers into a tight fist. Then, using every ounce of strength he could muster, he plowed his fist into the lump of dough.

Thirty-three

ael slipped into the narrow path between the two rows of buildings. It reminded her of the narrowest passages of Vrystal Canyon, except here the sunlight did not penetrate at all. She held out her arms and touched both walls. The wood was spongy with moisture.

She crept down the path, careful to avoid the puddles of muddy water. She hadn't gone far before she heard someone walking behind her. She wondered if whoever was following her might be Brommel, the man she was looking for, but she was too afraid to turn around and look. Instead she walked a little faster. She saw light up ahead and hoped it was the way out. She kept her eyes focused on it, but then all of a sudden the path was thrown into darkness. Something, or someone, had stepped into it, blocking out the light.

Lael stopped. Fear clutched at her. She could neither move forward nor turn back. The person who had been following her grabbed her from behind. She tried to scream, but a hand clamped over her mouth. Without thinking, she bit it. The sour taste of sweat and dirt filled her mouth.

Her attacker loosened his hold just enough for Lael to break free. She pushed past him and started to run back toward town. He grabbed her ankle, and she slammed face-first into the mud. Her attacker grabbed her other foot and flipped her over onto her back. He slapped her, his calloused skin tearing into her skin. Lael screamed. The attacker leaned in close enough for her to see the sneer on his face. And then his expression changed. He raised his eyes, widening in alarm, to stare at something behind Lael.

A large, dark shape loomed up from the shadows. It gripped the attacker by the throat and lifted him off the ground. Then it sent the attacker hurtling through the air. The man landed several yards away then scuttled off like a frightened rat.

Lael turned to face her rescuer, whose shape was already shrinking. In moments there stood only a little boy before her, shivering in the dark.

"Bryn, what are you doing out here?" asked Lael, unsure whether to thank or to scold him.

"You needed help," replied Bryn. "So I helped."

"You know the law against grocs. You've been seen. You could be in danger."

Lael realized Bryn was not alone. Behind him stood Clovis with his bow poised, an arrow drawn, ready to fire.

"Your face is bleeding," Clovis said.

"Clovis!" Lael shouted, ignoring his comment. "How could you let Bryn do this?"

"Me?" answered Clovis. "What about you? Sneaking off like that without telling us!"

"You were following me?" Lael asked.

"I promised Marcus I'd keep an eye on you." Clovis replaced his arrow in his quiver and adjusted his bow across his shoulder. "It's a good thing we did follow you, too," he added. "You could have been killed! What were you doing in here, anyway?"

Lael nodded and brushed the mud off her sleeves. "I was looking for someone."

Clovis was about to say something more when Bryn reached up and wrapped his small fingers around Lael's hand.

"Are you all right, Lael?" he asked.

"I'm fine," she said. Then she lifted her other hand to her face, raw and bleeding. She flinched from the pain. She looked at Bryn and the worried expression on his face. "Let's get back," she added, smiling down at Bryn to ease his concern. "You wouldn't want to miss breakfast, would you?"

As they headed back toward the Seafarer Tavern, Lael stole a quick glance behind her. There, standing at the edge of the shadows, was a large man with strange mark-ings on half of his deep brown face. He was not the man who attacked her, she was certain of that. Could he be Brommel? She watched him for a moment and then shiv-ered as she realized he was watching her, too.

Thirty-four

Only a handful of customers were seated in the Seafarer Tavern when Marcus and Zyll walked in later that afternoon. The aroma of sizzling ham and freshly baked bread made Marcus's mouth water. Finding a table near the window, Zyll brushed off a stool with his sleeve and sat down. He leaned Xerxes against the table beside him.

"Too bad you don't have a sense of smell," he said, tickling Xerxes beneath his wooden chin. "The food here smells heavenly."

Xerxes squawked in annoyance and rolled his beady black eyes. "I think your sense of smell has been damaged by the cooking at the Fortress," he retorted. "Enough of that stuff would leave anyone *sense*less."

Marcus spied Clovis and Lael coming down the stairs from the landing above. Bryn held Lael's hand. Marcus waved at them. Clovis waved back. When they reached their table, Clovis greeted Marcus with a slap on the shoulder.

"So you've returned from the mighty Fortress," said Lael, taking a seat beside Zyll. "What's the news from court? Have they been tossing rose petals in your path? Hand-feeding you with a golden spoon?"

"Not quite," answered Marcus. He had been with Lael for only a few seconds, and already he felt irritated. "We've been working in the kitchen."

Clovis's confused look prompted Zyll to speak. "'Tis true, I'm afraid. We are lowly kitchen servants."

"How is Kelvin?" asked Clovis, sitting down at the table. Lael pulled up a stool next to her and helped Bryn onto it.

"He is well," answered Zyll. "He makes a fine ruler, indeed."

"Did he ask about me?" asked Bryn.

"I didn't tell him you're here in Dokur," said Marcus. "The laws about grocs haven't changed, I'm afraid. You'll be safe as long as you stay with Lael and Clovis."

Bryn looked disappointed, but nodded.

"Other than that," continued Marcus, "we really haven't spent much time with Kelvin. Every time we've tried, his advisor says he's busy. I could almost swear Prost doesn't want us anywhere near—"

Marcus stopped abruptly. He peered closely at Lael from across the table. "What happened to your face?"

Lael self-consciously raised her hand to her wounded cheek. "I'm all right," she told him. "It's nothing."

"Nothing?" said Clovis with a huff. "A man attacked her, that's what happened."

"I'm fine," Lael insisted.

The door to the kitchen swung open, and a young woman appeared wearing a crisp, white apron over a pale blue dress, which matched her eyes perfectly. But it was her hair, dark and glossy as a raven's wings, that first caught Marcus's attention. He smiled when he saw her. Noticing his grin, Lael turned to see who had caught his attention.

The girl set the tray down on a table and passed out the mugs to the customers sitting there. Then she turned back toward the kitchen. "I'll be right with you," she called out to the table near the window, shooting them a quick glance as she turned. She paused, and her expression changed from disbelief to delight.

"Marcus?" she cried, coming to the table. "Is it really you?"

Marcus stood up and met her halfway. They wrapped their arms around each other and stood like that for a few moments. When they finally parted, their hands remained clasped.

"I promised I'd come back," said Marcus. Still holding the girl by the hand, he led her to where Zyll and the others waited and introduced them. "This is my grandfather, Zyll, and this is Lael, a girl from my village."

Zyll took Kaië's hand briefly, but Lael stiffened in her chair.

"This is Kaië," Marcus continued, oblivious to Lael's reaction. "Kaië, you remember Clovis and Bryn."

"Bryn? But I thought—" She knelt beside the boy and touched his face. "It's so good to see you, Bryn. I never got the chance to thank you for fighting off those soldiers so Marcus and I could escape. I always hoped you were all right."

Bryn gave Kaië a hug. "It's good to see you, too," he told her.

Kaië said her hellos to Clovis and Zyll.

Marcus turned to Lael. "Kaië is the girl I told you about," he explained, "the one who helped us during the invasion."

"Right," Lael snipped, "the one the tavern keeper said is—"

Her voice cut off abruptly as Clovis kicked her beneath the table. Lael cast an angry look in his direction.

"Oh?" asked Kaië. "And what did that old fool say about me?"

"Nothing," said Clovis hastily, but Lael ignored him.

"Only that you are marrying Kelvin," she said, "though why on earth you'd want to do that only the gods know."

"What?" Marcus wasn't sure he heard Lael correctly, and if he had . . .

Kaië's smile failed to mask her embarrassment. To ease the sudden tension in the room, Marcus pulled an extra chair up to the table. "Why don't you join us, Kaië?" he asked.

"I'd really love to, but I've got to serve lunch," said Kaië, pointing her thumb at the other customers. "I'll bring you each a plate hot off the stove and a round of cider on the house."

Kaië gave Marcus a quick hug and then disappeared into the kitchen. Marcus turned on Lael, ready to scold her for being so rude. But she was suddenly in a serious conversation with Bryn about the proper way to fold a napkin.

Thirty-five

What is the matter with you, Lael?" Marcus said sharply. "Why did you say that about Kaië?"

Lael turned to Marcus with a bored looked on her face, which made him even angrier.

"Why not say it?" she said.

"Because," interjected Clovis, "it's not true. It can't be."

"Kaië didn't deny it, did she?" asked Lael. "Besides, why should either of you care? She's too old for you." She said this directly to Marcus.

"What?" said Marcus, his face growing hot. "Did you think Kaië —? And me? That's ridiculous!"

But he could feel the heat in his face and knew it was as crimson as Prost's robes. Lael turned back to Bryn, and the two of them went on talking about table manners.

Marcus wanted to get up and march out of the tavern and right back home to Quendel, where he belonged. Why had he agreed to let Lael come along? But he hadn't, he reminded himself. She had followed him here. No wonder he had never liked her. She was a pest.

"Now, my boy," Zyll soothed, "no need to get upset at the poor girl."

"I'm not upset," snapped Marcus, annoyed.

"Of course not."

Zyll clasped his hands together on the table in front of him. Kaië had emerged from the kitchen again and was setting plates of food on a nearby table.

"You failed to tell me everything about Kaië," said Zyll, just loud enough for Marcus to hear. "She is quite a beauty."

Marcus watched Kaië move from table to table. She was graceful, like an angel, and she spoke so easily with the customers, as if she had known them all a lifetime. Kaië approached their table and set down platters of roasted vegetables and bowls of piping hot stew.

"Master Peagry is sending me to the bakers for some fresh rolls. Would you like to come along, Marcus?"

"Absolutely!" said Marcus, promptly forgetting about his hungry belly and the food in front of him. Then, remembering the present company, he turned to Zyll. "Do you mind, Grandfather?"

Zyll wiped his mouth with his napkin and laid it on the table. "Not at all, my boy. Actually, Xerxes and I have an appointment of our own, don't we, Xerxes? So why don't

I meet you back at the Fortress this evening? Hmmm? You two go on then."

"Great," said Kaië. "I'll grab my cloak, and we'll go."

Kaië gathered up a pile of soiled plates and headed back into the kitchen. As Marcus watched her cross the room, he was annoyed to discover that Lael was directly in his line of sight. Lael, with her blonde braid draped across her shoulder and her dark eyes flashing as she laughed at one of Clovis's jokes. But Marcus was so focused on Kaië, he failed to notice that Lael's eyes were fixed on him.

Zyll, his eyebrows raised, said in a voice only Xerxes could hear, "Yes, quite a beauty. Sometimes beauty lies right before our very eyes, and yet we see it not."

Thirty-six

Marcus waited near the well behind the Seafarer Tavern while Kaië finished up her work inside. The air was getting cold, and Marcus hoped he wouldn't have to wait too long.

The back door opened and Kaië stepped through, wiping her hands on her apron. "Sorry about that," she said, crossing the space between them in strong yet graceful steps. "Master Peagry's demands never end."

She took both of Marcus's hands in hers. Then she leaned forward and quickly kissed his cheek. "Shall we go then?" she asked.

They walked hand in hand around the side of the tavern toward a clump of older buildings. When they reached the first, they turned down a wide, cobblestone road lined with shops.

"I'm surprised you still work for him," said Marcus.

"How else would I pay for my keep?" answered Kaië. "But I don't want to talk about me. Tell me how you've been. It's been too long since I've seen you."

Marcus told her as much as he could recall from the time he had left Dokur after the Hestorians were defeated until now. He described his painful attacks, his strange visions, and his narrow escape with Bryn from the grocs' lair. All the while, Kaië listened intently, often stopping him to ask questions. When he had come to the end he paused, noticing for the first time the warmth of Kaië's hand in his.

"I wanted to come back here," he said, "just like I promised I would. You're happy I came, aren't you?"

"Of course I'm happy," said Kaië, laughing lightly. "Why wouldn't I be? We shared a great adventure, you and I, fighting the Hestorians and freeing Bryn from the Fortress prison. We're bound forever. Here we are."

They stopped in front of a shop with a wooden sign cut and painted to look like a loaf of bread. Several older women with baskets on their arms waited inside. Kaië walked right past them to the counter.

"Hello, Master Jacob!" she called. "I'm here for the rolls. Are they ready yet?"

A thin man, not much taller than Marcus, popped his head out from behind a brick oven. He had a tuft of black whiskers on the bottom of his chin, and Marcus could not be sure whether it was an intentional style or the baker had missed a spot shaving.

"Afternoon, Mouse," he said happily. "Aye, they are ready, indeed. I'll have them out to you in a wink." And his head disappeared once again.

"Here," said Kaië, pointing Marcus to a small table in the corner of the shop, "let's sit down."

They took the only two chairs in the place, and Marcus was glad to be alone with her. She was just as he remembered and no less beautiful than he had imagined her in his dreams. He had thought of her and of her parting words to him every day since he left Dokur. *I'll think of you often*, she had said.

"Why do you stare at me like that, Marcus?"

Marcus looked away. He hadn't realized he was staring. He decided it was best to change the subject. "Is it true?" he asked, sounding casual.

"Is what true?"

"That you and Kelvin are to be married."

Kaië's laughter took Marcus by surprise. "Do you believe the ramblings of every drunken tavern keeper?" she asked. "No, Marcus, it's not true. I deliver Jacob's pastries to the court, and the Peagrys think of any contact with the king as a golden opportunity. Besides, as much as I like your brother and would certainly love being queen, he is too young for me, I'm afraid."

"Here you are, Mouse," said the baker, who appeared so suddenly beside them that his presence startled Marcus.

"Thank you, Jacob," said Kaië, taking the linen bag stuffed with rolls. They left the bakery and started back toward the tavern. The air was growing colder by the moment.

"He's older than I am," said Marcus.

"Hmmm?"

"Kelvin," repeated Marcus. "He's a year older."

"And still four years my junior," answered Kaië.

"What's wrong with that? In time, that will seem like nothing."

When they returned to the tavern, Kaië took Marcus by the hand and led him back to the well. It was made of many large, round stones with a wooden support above it.

"I didn't mean to upset you, Marcus. I hope I haven't offended you." She pressed her hand on top of his. "You know I'd never hurt you."

Her face was mere inches from his. If he leaned forward just a little, he could kiss her. He wanted to—more than anything. He wondered if she felt the same.

"I couldn't marry your brother even if he wanted me," she continued. "I'll marry one day, but no man has as yet captured my heart."

Then it struck him. She did not feel the way he did. Why hadn't he seen it before? Marcus slipped his hand from beneath Kaië's. He leaned against the well, both his hands clasped tightly together.

Kaië studied him for a moment. And then her eyes widened in embarrassment. "Oh, Marcus, I'm so sorry! I didn't realize—" She touched his shoulder but then pulled back her hand. "I didn't mean to mislead you," she said. "I do care for you, just . . . not like that."

"Nonsense," Marcus interrupted. How could he admit that he had thought he loved her and was disappointed she didn't love him back? "I care about you, too, Kaië," he answered, smiling weakly. "You've been like a sister to me."

"Yes, your sister," replied Kaië, her expression relieved. "When you grew so quiet, I thought—"

"Don't misunderstand me," said Marcus. "I feel sorry for Kelvin's loss. I think you would have made a wonderful queen."

They both gazed down into the well. The darkness seemed endless, as if it could swallow everything around it. Marcus wished it would swallow him. Even when Kaië kissed him again and said goodbye before going back inside the tavern, Marcus wished he had never come to Dokur, not now, not ever. Despite the fact that he had successfully fulfilled his quest, fought dragons, saved the life of his brother, and faced many other challenges most men never would in a lifetime, he was far too aware that to Kaië, and perhaps to everyone he knew, he was still just a boy.

Thirty-seven

Marcus stood alone on the cliffs of Dokur until the sun had set. The night air was cold and salty. In the distance, the sea roiled in deep shades of undulating green and blue. He watched as a lone gull soared along the coast, then pivoted and flew out to sea. It was peaceful here with the constant lullaby of the breaking waves. If Marcus hadn't seen the cobblestones stained red and the buildings burning in the moonless black of night, he would not have believed there had ever been a battle here. The Dokurians had almost completely erased every trace of the Hestorian invasion since then.

If only I could erase the war from my memory, thought Marcus, and my body. He placed a hand over his chest where even now, a dull ache reminded him of what had happened here. There had been no hesitation on his part, no second thoughts where Kelvin's life was concerned. Marcus knew the risk before he laid his hands on Kelvin and had fully expected to die in his place. What he had not counted on was that he would live and bear the burden of Kelvin's wound the rest of his life.

After Zyll explained this to him, Marcus had made a vow never to use magic again. He'd only made an exception to get them out of the grocs' cave, but that was the end of it. He did not want to end up old before his time, crippled and in pain. Most people lived perfectly happy lives without magic, and so would he. The aching in his chest would be his reminder to honor that vow.

It was getting late. He and Zyll would be expected back at the Fortress soon, but first he wanted to see the bay from the cliffs, the way he had when he'd visited Dokur before. Marcus walked toward the outlying parts of the city. Some of the buildings here had not been repaired yet. Their black scars were still visible around windows and doors and on the edges of rooftops.

He was about to continue on when a movement in the shadows caught his attention. He stepped behind the wall of the nearest building and glanced into the alley. A single lantern hung beside a door, the sign above it lit by the flickering glow. It read DRAGON'S HEAD INN. This place held more bad memories for Marcus. He had seen a man die here and had fought and killed a Mardok (a man-like beast from Hestoria) to rescue his friends.

The door to the inn opened, and two figures stepped

out into the lantern's light. The first was a man as tall as the door through which he had just passed, his shoulders nearly as broad. His skin was darker than most islanders, which meant he must be from the mainland, from Hestoria. A large tattoo extended down the left side of his face and neck, disappearing beneath his collar.

The second man was unmistakable. His shoulders were slightly stooped, and he leaned on a waist-high walking stick. Zyll held out a small, leather sack. The tattooed man took it, weighing it in his palm. Then Zyll turned away from the light and started walking down the alley toward Marcus.

Marcus ducked behind the building and waited until Zyll emerged from the shadows of the alleyway. He watched until Zyll went inside the Seafarer. Marcus realized then that he had been holding his breath. He let it out and gasped for another. The sea no longer interested him. Instead, his mind was filled with questions.

Thirty-eight

Marcus leaned over the large basin, scouring a metal pot with burned gravy stuck on the bottom. Zyll stood beside him, holding a towel in his hand. Five days had passed since they arrived in Dokur, yet most of their time had been spent in the kitchen. Marcus was beginning to wonder why they had come at all.

"And why am I doing the dishes again?" asked Marcus. He rinsed the pot in a tub of clean water and handed it to Zyll.

"Because hard work develops character," squawked Xerxes from his spot in the corner.

Marcus scowled at the walking stick. He was beginning to resent his unwelcome comments. He secretly hoped Zyll would follow through with his threat and leave

171

Xerxes alone in his room while they worked.

Zyll wiped the pot dry and set it down on the counter beside him while Marcus attacked another pot.

"So I guess that means," replied Marcus, "that I am the only one of us who needs to develop character."

Zyll shook out his towel and draped it over his arm. "My boy, at my age I have all the character I could possibly need."

Marcus shoved the pot into the water, splashing dirty suds onto his apron. He could not help feeling angry that Zyll had kept secrets from him. Zyll had met with the tattooed man and given him money. Marcus had come close several times to asking Zyll outright what he was up to, but he couldn't bring himself to do it. But now, standing here in the kitchen, he had decided to speak. He was just building up his courage when a guard appeared at the kitchen door and handed Marcus a note on stiff paper. Marcus read it quickly.

"What is it?" asked Zyll.

Marcus snatched Zyll's towel, dried his hands with it, and draped it back over Zyll's arm. "Looks like you'll be doing the dishes today," he said and then added with a grin, "It's Kelvin. I've been summoned."

*   *   *

The Great Room was larger than any enclosed space Marcus had ever seen, even larger than Quendel's entire town center. On the far end, against the outside wall, flames burned in a huge fireplace. Marcus tried to imagine how much wood it took each day to keep that fire stoked. He could feel its heat from the door.

In the center of the room stood a green-velvet settee and two matching chairs. All were edged in gold trim. The room was elegantly decorated in deep, rich hues of burgundy, blue, and gold. Natural light spilled into the room from half a dozen narrow windows that reached to the ceiling. The room was spacious, yet welcoming and comfortable.

Marcus heard the sound of hurried footsteps in the hall.

"I'm so sorry," Kelvin said as he entered. "It seems I am always in between meetings."

"Well, it's got to be better than working the fields in Quendel," remarked Marcus with a casual laugh.

"True, though there are times I think I'd prefer that sort of work to this. No one ever told me that ruling a kingdom would be so complicated."

They took their seats facing the fireplace.

"I'm glad you and Zyll came," said Kelvin.

"We should have come sooner," answered Marcus.

"Why did you come?" Kelvin asked, a curious look on his face. "Why now?"

Marcus looked at his brother. He seemed older somehow, as if he had aged years in the past few months. He realized that what he saw was the burden of responsibility, and he wondered not for the first time if Kelvin was really ready to be king.

"We were worried about you," said Marcus.

"Worried about me? Why?"

"When we heard about what happened to Fredric . . . well, we thought . . ."

Marcus paused to study Kelvin's expression. He thought of the moment he and Zyll first arrived in Dokur. Kelvin had been surprised to see them, but he had not acted as if anything was unusual and had said nothing about *how* Fredric died. Even now, Kelvin did not seem afraid or concerned about anything.

And then it dawned on Marcus. Kelvin didn't know! Zyll had seen Fredric's murder in his divining bowl, but that didn't mean Kelvin or anyone else understood what had really happened.

They must all assume Fredric died of natural causes, Marcus realized. Kelvin has no idea he's in danger.

"We wanted to come to help you, Kelvin," said Marcus finally. "We're family. We should be together in times like this."

Kelvin absentmindedly fingered the Celestine medallion strung on a leather cord around his neck.

"Is that Mother's seal?" asked Marcus.

Kelvin glanced down at it. "I always keep it with me," he said. "It reminds me of home."

Marcus had first seen Ivanore's seal, or a fragment of it, during their quest. Later, once the seal was restored, Marcus had held it on several occasions, but both he and Zyll had agreed that Kelvin was its rightful owner. Marcus had not seen it since Kelvin left for Dokur more than six months earlier.

Marcus was about to ask if he could hold it again, just for a moment, when they were interrupted by the arrival of Kelvin's young page. The boy dropped to one knee and, head bowed, held out a scroll.

"A courier brought this for you, Your Majesty. He's waiting for your reply."

Kelvin rose from the settee and took the scroll. As he read it to himself, the expression on his face grew taut with worry.

"He's here? In the courtyard?" Kelvin asked the boy.

"Shall I tell the courier to invite him in?"

Kelvin considered this a moment, then replied, "No. I need to meet with Chancellor Prost first. Tell him to return for dinner instead. I think that would be more appropriate."

"As you wish, Your Majesty," said the page.

The page left the room. Kelvin remained where he stood, still holding the scroll in his hand.

"Is everything all right?" asked Marcus.

"Yes," answered Kelvin a little too quickly. "Yes, why do you ask?"

"You seem upset."

"Do I? I suppose I am. You know, Marcus, I had intended eventually to take over for our grandfather, Fredric, but this has come far too suddenly. I am trying to be a good king, though."

"I'm sure you are."

"I've had to make some difficult choices, and there are those, even some who are quite close to me, who don't agree with what I've done, especially in regards to the Agorans."

In the fireplace, an ember popped. Kelvin still held the open scroll in his hand. This he tore in half, and then half again, tossing the pieces into the flames.

"Unfortunately, I have to cut our time together a little short," he told Marcus. "A matter of some urgency has come up, and I need to consult with my advisor. Can you find your way back?"

"Of course," said Marcus, hoping his face did not betray his disappointment. He stood and walked to the door. He glanced back at Kelvin and was surprised at how small his older brother appeared. Gone was the carefree confidence Marcus had once admired. Instead, Kelvin seemed fearful and troubled.

"Will you and Grandfather join me for dinner tonight?" asked Kelvin.

Marcus nodded, though he wondered why they had not been invited before now. Kelvin looked away then, his gaze focused on the fire. Marcus opened the door and let himself out.

Thirty-nine

he hall outside the great room was empty except for two guards farther down near the throne room. Marcus headed toward the staircase, which led to the lower floors. He paused at the top stair to look at a familiar door at the end of the hall. When he had last seen the entrance to the dungeon prison, it had been in splinters after he forced it open with magic. Kaië was with him then, as were Bryn and an Agoran named Eliha whom they had freed from the prison below. They had burst through that door and fought off armed guards in order to escape. Bryn had chosen to stay behind, willing to sacrifice himself for their freedom. Marcus again felt relieved Bryn had survived that day.

The door, which had since been replaced with one
made of iron, now stood unattended. As Marcus neared,
he saw that it was locked with a heavy bolt. He remembered the dark, damp stairway that led to the cells below.
Marcus tried the lock, but it was secure. Not that he
wanted to go back to that dungeon. He laughed at himself for even considering the idea. Surely Kelvin would not
keep anyone in such a place.

Marcus lay his palm against the metal door. Strange,
he thought, how warm it felt beneath his skin. He curled
his fingers and rapped lightly on it and then turned away.

A sound so faint he almost missed it reached him
through the door. Had he really heard something? Marcus
paused and listened. Nothing. His mind was playing tricks
on him. That was all. He lifted his foot to take another
step, but—there it was again!

Marcus pressed his ear against the door. He held his
breath and waited. He heard the sound once more, a low
rumbling followed by what could only be described as a
moan.

Someone was down there!

Marcus grabbed the bolt and tugged at it with all his
strength. The thought of anyone, even a criminal, locked
up in that horrible place made his stomach churn. How
could Kelvin have allowed it?

The lock, solidly fastened, might as well have been a
stone in his hand. The sound came again. Yes, thought
Marcus, someone was in there, moaning in misery. Marcus
pounded on the door with his fist.

"Hello down there!" he shouted. "Can you hear me?"

A sudden, deafening bellow rolled up from below like a thunderstorm. Marcus jumped back from the door, his heart thumping wildly. Then, without warning, something deep down below exploded with a fury unmatched by anything Marcus could describe with words, as if the entire Fortress had been shaken to its core and threatened to collapse around him. Marcus dropped to the floor and covered his head with his arms, but the Fortress did not collapse. The hall was quiet again. Marcus lifted his head to see if anyone had come running, but no one had.

Marcus stood up. Only then did he realize he was shaking. His legs felt weak. He reached out his hand and timidly approached the door again. He touched his palm to the door as he had before but immediately jerked it back from the pain. The door was so hot it had burned him.

Forty

So far dinner had been a grave affair, with little more than the tinkling of crystal and silver to offset the uneasy silence. Marcus had tried to start a conversation, but neither Kelvin nor Prost had paid him any attention. Zyll had left Xerxes in his room this evening (using Marcus's shoulder for support instead), so there wasn't even the walking stick's sarcasm for entertainment.

As the soup bowls were being cleared, a guard appeared at Kelvin's side and whispered something in his ear. Kelvin's already grim expression became even more serious.

"Would you prefer to have him wait in the throne room?" asked the guard.

Kelvin shook his head. "No. I've been expecting him. See him in."

The guard bowed stiffly and exited the room.

Prost leaned back in his chair, lacing his bony fingers together. His lips were pursed in a sour expression. Marcus couldn't help but wonder if his mouth was naturally formed that way.

"Not to worry, Sire," Prost said. "Remember, our motives are just."

"I'm not worried," replied Kelvin sharply.

A moment later the guard appeared again. "Jayson of the Agoran," he announced.

Marcus stood up the moment he saw him, nearly knocking his goblet to the floor. He flew to his father's arms. Jayson greeted him with a firm hug.

"What a surprise! I hadn't expected to see both sons today," Jayson said, his gray cat eyes sparkling with pleasure.

"Zyll and I got here a few days ago," explained Marcus, nodding toward his grandfather, who was savoring a bite of the braised boar the servants had just brought in. Zyll lifted his fork and waved a little hello.

"Hello, Father," said Jayson, and to Kelvin, "Your Majesty."

Prost carved off a small slice of meat with his knife. "Well, what a family reunion. Jayson, you did come to see your son, didn't you?" he said, slipping the bite of meat between his lips. "Or have you come on more pressing business?"

Jayson glared at Prost, not hiding the hatred in his eyes. He then looked at Kelvin, who had not yet spoken. Kelvin met his father's eyes only briefly, then dropped his gaze.

"No greeting for your father, Kelvin?" said Jayson, extending his hand. "Well then, how about a simple hello to a former travel mate, eh?"

"I know why you've come," said Kelvin, keeping his hands on the table.

"Do you?"

"You didn't come to visit your long lost son, so please don't insult me."

Jayson reached over the table and picked up a polished apple. He studied it a moment before biting into it, then chewed and swallowed. "All right," he said, "I'm here because of the rumor that my eldest son has abandoned his people."

"The Agorans are not my people."

Jayson's face remained calm. "Their blood—*my* blood—runs through your veins as much as your mother's human blood does," he said.

The servers came to whisk away the plates of the half-eaten main course and replace them with dessert. As one server removed Zyll's plate, Zyll struck out his fork and managed to skewer the remaining morsel of meat, which he then popped into his mouth.

The tension in the room was thick, and Marcus tried to think of some way to ease it a little. He tasted the pudding.

"This is really delicious, Kelvin. Is there nutmeg in it?"

Kelvin stared at Marcus with a blank expression. He blinked a few times before responding, taking the signal to change the subject.

"Yes, and cinnamon. I've been told the recipe has

been in the family for generations. I'm glad you like it."

"I do," replied Marcus. "You really should try it, Father."

"Yes," added Kelvin hesitantly, "please join us. Server, bring another dessert."

"By all means, Jayson, do have some pudding," added Prost coolly.

Marcus took another mouthful.

"I did not come for pudding," said Jayson, his voice becoming angrier. "I came to Dokur for one reason and one reason only: to make sure you honor Fredric's promise to the Agorans."

"What is he talking about, Kelvin?" asked Marcus, his spoon poised for another bite of pudding. "Have you broken your promise to the Agorans?"

Kelvin stood abruptly, his jaw and teeth clenched. "*I* made no promise!" he said.

"What about Fredric's oath to give them back their lands?" said Jayson. "What of Dokur's debt to them for spilling their blood in defense of this city?"

Kelvin stood still as stone, his face reddening under the questioning glares of everyone at the table. But it was Prost who answered.

"My dear Jayson. No one is keeping from the Agorans what they deserve. Kelvin is only doing what is best for Dokur and for the entire Isle of Imaness. We are preparing for war. As you well know, our navy was destroyed in the mainland's invasion earlier this year, and it has taken a great deal of time and money to rebuild it. We are in no position to just hand over half the kingdom."

"You stole that land from them."

"Not I, Jayson. You know full well that Fredric moved your people off their lands and enslaved them in response to *your* betrayal. So I suppose in some way you could say *you* are to blame for all this. Now, won't you sit down and have some pudding?"

Jayson hesitated, then stomped to the opposite end of the table and dropped down into a chair. A server promptly set down a bowl of yellow pudding in front of him, but he did not eat it. Instead, he glared down the long table at his Kelvin.

"I thought you'd make a wise ruler," said Jayson after an uncomfortable silence. "I believed you'd do great things. I never imagined that you would deprive anyone of what is rightfully theirs."

"I might change my mind," said Kelvin, "if the Agorans were an honorable people. So far it seems they are nothing more than a bunch of beggars and criminals and don't deserve to have any land other than the swamps my grandfather gave them when you were a child."

Jayson fumed. "How dare you say such things about my people!"

Kelvin threw his napkin onto the table. "Over the past few weeks, your "people" have done everything in their power to sabotage our preparations for war against the Hestorians. They somehow sneak into court and destroy my property. They write threats across the walls with the blood of my own guards. And shortly before you all arrived in Dokur, they succeeded in setting one of my royal navy ships on fire. It's gotten so that I go to bed at night fearing for my life!"

"How do you know the Agorans are to blame?" Jayson asked.

"Because a week ago one of my guards survived an attack. He saw the man's face, though he nearly died for the privilege."

"No decent Agoran would do such a thing!" Jayson rose to his feet.

Kelvin stood as well, pounding both fists against the table. "And I do not believe that Agorans are decent! So until your people stop their attacks, I will not fulfill Fredric's decree!"

Through the entire conversation, Zyll continued to eat his pudding. His bowl now empty, he pushed his chair back from the table and gave a loud, satisfied belch. The argument came to an abrupt end. Everyone gazed at Zyll, astonished.

"Pardon me," Zyll said with an embarrassed chuckle, but Marcus wasn't fooled. His grandfather had intentionally interrupted their dinner. If he wanted Jayson and Kelvin to stop fighting, thought Marcus with approval, his scheme couldn't have worked any better.

Forty-one

The mood in the dining hall immediately lightened, and Marcus noticed the slightest of smiles on everyone's lips. Zyll rose from the table and motioned for Marcus to give him his arm. "I've left Xerxes in my room. Would you be so kind as to help an old man to his bed?"

Marcus helped Zyll to the door. Zyll paused long enough to pat Jayson's shoulder. "Where are you staying, my boy?" he asked.

"In town at the Seafarer."

"Good. Good. I have business to attend to tomorrow afternoon. We shall visit you then. It warms my heart to see you." Then addressing the room, Zyll added, "Goodnight to you all."

"Goodnight, Father, Marcus," said Jayson.

Marcus gave Jayson a quick embrace. "We'll see you tomorrow," he said, addressing his father and Kelvin both.

Kelvin replied with an abrupt but gracious "Yes, good-night."

Marcus led Zyll down the hall. He was not entirely happy to have left the dining room just then. He wanted to hear more of the discussion between Kelvin and Jayson. As though sensing his thoughts Zyll said, "Some conversations are not meant to be overheard."

They walked slowly toward their rooms. Marcus noticed how frail Zyll's hand looked, pale and creased with age. He knew that Zyll's actual age was far younger than he looked, but years of conjuring magic spells had taken their toll and left Zyll ever more feeble. Marcus would never do anything to upset him, but he could not keep silent any longer.

"Grandfather," he asked, careful not to sound angry, "why haven't you told Kelvin how Fredric died?"

Zyll took a few moments before answering. "I'm not entirely sure," he said. "I suppose I've been waiting for the right time."

"The right time?" replied Marcus with surprise. "Don't you think he ought to know he's in danger? You heard about the attacks in the Fortress and on the ships. What if the Agoran rebels—"

"Fredric was not killed by an Agoran."

This revelation angered Marcus. His grandfather must have seen in his divining bowl who killed Fredric. Why keep it hidden?

"Another secret," said Marcus.

Zyll looked at his grandson, his eyebrows arched in an amused expression. "*Another* secret?" he asked.

"Yes," answered Marcus. "You collect secrets the way you collect all those trinkets in your chest back home. Like how you gave me the key, letting me believe it had some special power. Or never telling me about my father, or who my mother was."

If Marcus's comment surprised Zyll, he did not show it. Marcus went on, fueled by Zyll's silence.

"I know there are many things you haven't told me, things I ought to know. You think I'm too young or too vulnerable, but I'm not, Grandfather. And neither is Kelvin."

They reached their rooms and paused at Zyll's door. Zyll stood without speaking for a few moments, lost in thought.

"Perhaps you are right," he said at last. "You are no longer that little boy in need of protection. I do have much to tell you, but the hour is late, and I am weary."

Marcus felt a little guilty for losing his temper with his grandfather. In all his life, Zyll had never been angry with him. Marcus lowered his eyes, feeling ashamed.

"I just think we should tell Kelvin the truth about Fredric, that's all," he said.

Zyll nodded thoughtfully. "Do what you feel is best, my boy."

Hearing their voices through the door, Xerxes squawked angrily. "It's about time, old man! Leave me alone for hours with only this rude nightstand to talk to! What dreadful company!"

"I think Xerxes is a little upset," said Zyll, his eyebrows raised. "Perhaps he's afraid I might die and leave him without suitable companionship."

"Don't say such a thing!" said Marcus. The image of Zyll in the vision came flooding back.

"Well, I have to die sometime. And when I do, who will look after him?"

"You know I'd take Xerxes. Though I'm not so sure he'd want me to."

"Perhaps," replied Zyll, laughing. "You might like to know that Xerxes will not always be as he is now."

"You mean a critical, snobbish sliver of wood?"

"Precisely."

"Precisely what?" asked Marcus.

"Well," said Zyll, lowering his voice, "he will probably always be critical and snobbish, but on my death he'll be transformed from wood to flesh."

"Transformed?" Marcus repeated. "Is that possible?"

Zyll chuckled. "I don't know. It's never actually been done. I created Xerxes when I started growing old and needed both a friend and a support. But as the years went on I thought it would be cruel if he should die when I did. Wood and flesh are both living substances. It didn't seem too much a stretch to transform one into the other."

"But I thought manipulating organics is—you know—dangerous."

"Of course I couldn't manage it without doing myself

in," Zyll replied. "So the transformation will have to wait until I'm already dead, using whatever life force may still linger."

Marcus tried to imagine Xerxes as a real bird but couldn't conjure the picture in his mind.

Zyll laughed again and tousled Marcus's hair. "Never mind," he said. "It isn't anything to worry about now. Go to bed. We'll leave after breakfast. I'm sure your friends will be anxious to hear all your news." He turned the door handle to enter his room, but there was one more thing Marcus had to know.

"Wait, Grandfather," said Marcus, his courage almost leaving him. "A few nights ago, I saw you give something to a Hestorian, one with markings on his face."

Zyll's body stiffened. Marcus could see his knuckles turn white as he clutched the door handle. But Marcus continued.

"Who is he? What were you doing?"

Zyll's expression turned hard, though not angry. Marcus had never seen that look in Zyll's eyes before. It frightened him.

"That is one secret I pray to the gods you will never need to know," said Zyll. And with that, Zyll slipped into his room and closed the door behind him.

Forty-two

Marcus waited until he heard Zyll turn the lock in his door before heading back down the corridor. Zyll had told him to do what he thought was best, and that's exactly what he would do.

He passed several armed sentries, one at every door, as he made his way through the lower level of the Fortress. Kelvin was determined not to let the Agoran rebels get inside again. Maybe Marcus shouldn't worry about his brother. With all these guards around, Kelvin was far safer than Fredric must have been. Still, he deserved to know how their grandfather died. Secrets had nearly destroyed Marcus and Kelvin's relationship during their quest eight months ago. There would be no secrets between them ever again.

Marcus didn't want to go back to the dining room. Kelvin and Jayson were probably still arguing over dinner, and what Marcus had to say was private, anyway. He would go instead to Kelvin's council chambers and wait for him there.

Other than the sentries, the interior of the Fortress was quiet. Most of the servants had already retired to their rooms for the night. Marcus hurried across the vast entry hall toward the east alcove where the offices were located. He had made it halfway when he suddenly had the feeling that he was not alone. He turned and looked behind him, but there was no one besides the guard standing at the Fortress's main door. The light from several oil lamps left the corners of the room hidden in darkness. Someone could easily conceal himself in one.

This is silly, Marcus thought. I'm letting my mind play tricks on me. Still, he walked the rest of the way as fast as he could without actually running.

The door to Kelvin's council chambers stood just inside a narrow alcove. To Marcus's surprise, the sconces on the wall were not lit. The alcove was dark except for a weak glow from the lanterns in the great hall. He had expected to find a guard here, too, but the alcove was empty—or was it?

Near the door to Kelvin's chambers, Marcus saw a large, dark clump of something on the floor. He approached cautiously and touched it with his foot. An arm fell forward, hitting the floor with a dull thump. Marcus stepped back, his breath quickening. The dark clump was a sentry.

In the dim light, Marcus couldn't tell whether he was unconscious or dead.

Behind him, Marcus heard the sound of footsteps, which stopped abruptly.

"Hello?" Marcus called out, hoping it was one of the other guards. "There's a man here," he said. "I think he's hurt!"

When no one replied, Marcus realized once again his imagination was running away with him. But he did need to find help for the sentry. He was about to leave when he heard a new sound coming from inside the chamber: an unmistakable rattle as if something had fallen and rolled across the floor.

Marcus stepped over the guard's body and took hold of the door handle. Slowly he turned it, pushing open the door just an inch. Candlelight spilled through the narrow crack and into the alcove. Marcus saw now that the sentry's eyes were open, staring dully up at nothing. He was most certainly dead. And Marcus suspected that whoever was inside the room had done it.

Pushing the door open a little farther, Marcus stepped inside. Large tapestries hung from floor to ceiling against the walls. Three stories above, the stained-glass ceiling looked like a patchwork of black and gray. Charred remains of a log stood cold in the fireplace, though six candles burned in an ornate candelabrum beside Kelvin's desk. On the floor lay an ink bottle, dark liquid trailing from it like a tail. This must be what had made the noise. Marcus bent to pick it up. The glass bottle felt warm to the touch.

The air in the room was chill. So why would the bottle be so warm? Someone must have been holding it, Marcus thought, but who?

As he set the bottle back on the desk, he noticed movement from the corner of his eye. A tapestry fluttered ever so slightly. Marcus's heart raced. He reached for his knife but then remembered he had left it in his room, for he had thought he was just going to talk to Kelvin. What would he have needed it for? He reached for the tapestry with trembling fingers and jerked it aside, but the only thing behind it was a bare wall.

All of a sudden, something heavy hit him from behind. Sharp pain exploded across his shoulders, and Marcus's face smashed into the wall. He felt drops of hot blood trickle onto his lips. Licking them, he tasted copper, and he wondered whether the loud crack he'd heard had been his back breaking or something else. He turned and saw Kelvin's chair in pieces behind him on the floor. Someone had thrown it at him! He had only a second to think before something else came flying at him, but this time it was a man.

The man yelled. Marcus caught the glint of a blade in his hand just before it came down on him. Marcus twisted away just in time, the blade grating instead against the stone wall. But the man did not stop. He sliced his dagger wildly in every direction. Marcus jumped and slid his way across the room, doing his best to avoid the attacks. The man was slender, almost frail looking, yet was surprisingly fast and strong. He lunged at Marcus, not with the dagger, but with a set of bloodstained claws extended for the kill. It wasn't a man at all, Marcus realized. It was an Agoran.

Marcus grabbed the candelabrum. As he swung it in an arc, the candles flew off. Two went out as they hit the floor, but the other four still burned, casting long, unnatural shadows onto the tapestries. One lit the corner of a tapestry on fire, the flames soon licking the woven patterns like a hungry snake. The candelabrum hit the attacker with a force that would have knocked most men to their knees, but this one didn't even flinch. When the Agoran took hold of it, Marcus expected him to yank it out of his hands. Instead he thrust it forward, pushing Marcus off balance. Marcus fell onto his back, sending a fresh tremor of pain through him.

A second later, the attacker was on top of Marcus, holding the point of a blade to his throat. Damp tendrils of long, shaggy hair clung to his face. His pupils, narrow like a cat's, peered at Marcus, recognition slowly dawning. The Agoran and Marcus stared at each other, both remembering the day months earlier when they had first met.

Just then the door to the chamber flew open. A guard rushed in, his sword raised. Behind him came Kelvin and Jayson. The Agoran leapt off Marcus and crossed the room in half a breath's time. The guard ran after him, but the Agoran tore the burning tapestry free from the wall and flung it at him. The guard screamed in pain as fire engulfed his uniform. The tapestry dropped to the floor, the flames trapping the Agoran at the back of the room. Marcus managed to roll clear of it, though he felt his skin blistering with the heat and smelled the guard's scorched flesh.

Jayson ripped the burning fabric from the guard's body as Kelvin picked up his fallen sword. Kelvin slashed at the tapestry, trying to make a path through the fire. As he broke through, Marcus looked up to see what would happen next, but to his and everyone's surprise, the Agoran was gone.

Forty-three

What do you think you were doing?" shouted Kelvin, turning on Marcus. "There's a dead man in the hall, and my private chambers are in ruin!"

Marcus swallowed hard. He looked to Jayson for help, but he was busy tending to the injured guard.

"I came here looking for you. The guard was already dead when I got here."

"I could have guessed that much," said Kelvin. He lifted the blackened remains of the tapestry with the tip of his sword and flung it aside. Then he went to the back wall and brushed his hands over the paneling. "What I want to know is why you let that Agoran scum escape."

"What?" Marcus stood and faced Kelvin. His shoulder throbbed from where he'd been hit with the chair, but he did his best not to show it. "*I* barely escaped! If you hadn't come in when you did, he would have killed me."

Kelvin glared sharply at Marcus. "You know the trouble the rebels have caused. We've taken every precaution to stop them, and then you come face to face with one! But instead of calling for help, or better yet, capturing him yourself, you let him get away!"

"*Let* him get away?" Marcus was getting angrier by the moment. "How do you think I should have stopped him?"

Kelvin's rage was so obvious now, his teeth were clenched and his face pale. "Magic!" he shouted. "Or have you suddenly forgotten you're an enchanter's apprentice?"

Kelvin's words cut deeper into Marcus than any blade ever could. Magic. Yes, he could have used magic against the Agoran, and under the circumstances he should have used it, no matter how much pain it caused him. The realization that he had failed his brother, failed in the very purpose of his visit here, sickened him. What must Kelvin think of him now? Worse yet, what would Zyll think of him?

Across the room, Jayson finished wrapping a strip torn from his own tunic around the guard's burned arm. He helped the guard to the chamber door where two additional guards now waited. One was dragging away the dead sentry. The other took the injured guard's arm around his neck, bracing him as he walked.

"Take him to his room and call for the doctor," Jayson instructed. "Then send someone for the other man's family. They'll want to tend to him themselves."

Once the guards had gone, Jayson turned to his sons.

"So the rebel escaped," he said, kicking at the broken chair. "How?"

"He just vanished right before our eyes," Kelvin answered. "He must have used some hidden door in the wall."

Marcus suddenly felt as though his legs might buckle. He leaned against Kelvin's desk for support.

"What is it?" asked Jayson. "Are you hurt?"

The hidden door!

The pain in his shoulder, his bloodied face, even the ever-present ache in his chest was nothing compared to what he felt now. For a moment, he almost convinced himself that the reason he didn't use magic against the Agoran was because he was afraid, but that wasn't true— not completely.

He looked from Jayson to Kelvin and back again, shame burning inside of him.

"I didn't use magic," he said, "because I recognized the Agoran who's been attacking the Fortress. His name is Eliha," said Marcus. "He's probably been using that tunnel to get into the Fortress all along."

On the day the Hestorians invaded Dokur eight months ago, Kaië had led him through the tunnel into this very room. They had freed Bryn from the prison, freed Eliha as well, and then escaped the same way they had come in. Marcus was about to explain all this when Chancellor Prost appeared at the door.

"What's going on here?" he asked, taking in the damaged room at a glance. "I demand to know what's happened!"

"An Agoran rebel attacked Marcus," Kelvin explained. "We think he escaped through a secret door. Do you know anything about that?"

Prost gave an irritated *humph* before crossing the room and pressing his hand against the wood trim. A section of the wall swung open, revealing a dark hollow beyond.

"No one but those closest to Fredric ever knew about this," said Prost. "If an Agoran has been using it, then it's fair to say it isn't a secret anymore."

Jayson came up behind Prost and Kelvin and peered into the tunnel. "So," he said, rubbing at his chin, "which one of us is going to go catch him?"

Forty-four

The Dragon's Head Inn stood in a part of Dokur that still carried the scars of the invasion. Despite blackened roofs and patched-up walls, business was good, perhaps too good. Here was where the poor, the nonhumans, and the criminals gathered. Jayson knew it was the most likely place to find someone who did not wish to be found.

When Jayson entered the inn, his senses were repelled by the heavy odors of human sweat, spirits, and filth. No one even glanced up to take notice of the cloaked visitor, and Jayson took advantage of this fact to study each face in the crowded room.

At the tables, men haggled over pyramids of upturned shot glasses. Others stood by the fireplace gazing dreamily or unhappily into the flames. Still others sat hunched over the bar, their hands clenched around half-empty glasses of ale. Jayson searched for the one face here that would stand out from all the others.

He walked toward the bar and pulled back his hood. The clatter in the room fell silent as, one by one, all eyes turned to him.

"You, barkeeper," he said, leaning one elbow atop the bar, "tell me—any Agorans here tonight?"

The barkeeper, a young man with straight, dark hair down to his shoulders and eyes equally dark and wide, wiped a glass with a towel and set it on the bar in front of Jayson.

"I don't judge any man by his looks," he said, "only his wallet. What'll it be?"

Jayson plunked a coin onto the bar and waited while the keeper filled his glass. Seeing that he wasn't a threat, the men in the room went back to their haggling and drinking.

"I've heard rumors that someone's been causing problems at the Fortress," Jayson said, "and that the new king has a ransom out for the man responsible."

"Aye," said the keeper, "some of the servants come here on their days off and tell us the tales. Just before Fredric died, mysterious things started happening. Guards found with their throats slit, the treasury ransacked, messages scrawled in blood on the walls. Two of the navy's ships were burned and sunk."

"That can't all be the work of one man," said Jayson,

wiping the condensation from his glass with his thumb. "Can it?"

"Who's to say?" answered an older gentleman sitting beside Jayson. "You're not among the king's most loyal subjects here." The man burst out laughing and swayed so far to one side that Jayson thought he might fall off his barstool. But instead, the man dropped his head onto the bar and fell asleep.

At the far end of the bar, a figure dressed in a gray cloak stood up and turned toward the staircase at the back of the room. Jayson eyed him for a moment. Something about the smoothness of his movements made Jayson stand up, too.

"You there!" shouted Jayson. In response, the man bolted with such speed that it took Jayson by surprise. The man leapt over the railing onto the staircase and fled up to the second floor. As he reached the landing, his cloak fell away, revealing an Agoran face. Jayson was after him now, taking the stairs three steps at a time. He followed the Agoran down the hall to an open window. The Agoran climbed agilely onto the window frame, preparing to jump out. But Jayson grabbed him by the neck with both hands and flung him backward onto the floor.

"Are you Eliha?" demanded Jayson. "Are you the one who's been breaking into the Fortress?"

The Agoran spit in Jayson's face. Jayson yanked him off the floor and threw him across the hall. The Agoran hit the wall and slid to the floor where he sat, staring icily at Jayson.

Jayson drew his sword and pressed the tip of the blade into the Agoran's throat.

"Do you know who I am?" shouted Jayson.

"Everyone knows who you are, half-breed," said the Agoran. "You are a traitor to your people."

"There is a price on your head, and I've a mind to collect it!" said Jayson. "Your little games have cost our people their lands. Because of you, there may be civil war."

"Because of *me?*" said the Agoran, laughing a hollow laugh. "I don't see any scars on your back, Jayson. Where were you when your people were crushed under Fredric's whip? He drove our families to the swamps, forced our brothers and sons to wallow like pigs in his mine. He stole our dignity! And you say *I* have cost the Agorans their land?"

"Fredric gave you your freedom."

"He *gave* us nothing! This new king will never *give* us what we deserve. We have to take it! I fight for more than just a bit of land. My cause will win us back our pride!"

"No cause can justify murder, Eliha."

"You murdered us all when you married the princess, Lady Ivanore. You abandoned us that very day, Jayson. How can you justify that?"

Jayson had had enough. He punched Eliha square in the face. The Agoran went limp.

"Justify *that!*" said Jayson, rubbing his sore knuckles.

Forty-five

The kitchen was hot and steamy from the many vats of soups and sauces simmering over the red-hot iron stoves. Marcus carried two sacks of potatoes into the pantry and emptied them into the root bin. A cloud of dry, moldy dust coated his apron, and he flapped the empty sacks, trying to clear the air. His shoulder felt better today, but he couldn't hide the bruise on his face. He had to tell Zyll what had happened and, of course, had to endure two lectures: one from Zyll and one from Xerxes. He was glad when they were called to work, because it meant the issue could not be discussed further.

Marcus had to admit that working in the kitchen had grown on him. Maybe that was because he would get to see Kaië each morning when she delivered her pastries.

She arrived early that day and stayed for more than an hour, helping out where she could. Marcus was glad for the company, even if they were only friends.

Marcus closed the pantry and returned to the kitchen, passing Xerxes in the corner. The enchanted walking stick had been on his best behavior since being left in the room for dinner several nights before. At the counter, Zyll slid a pile of freshly chopped basil into a bowl. Beside him, Val, the head chef, explained the art of dicing vegetables.

"It's all in the way you grip the knife," Val said, holding a large butcher knife up for Zyll to see. "And you curve your knuckles over the carrot, like this." He demonstrated it by deftly slicing paper-thin circles from the carrot. Marcus thought it funny how Val's sparse mustache moved as he spoke, as if it were a live caterpillar wriggling around on his lip.

"That's right," Marcus said as he passed behind Val, "this old man has never cut carrots in his life."

From the grunt Val gave, Marcus could tell his comment was not appreciated.

"This is not some poor villager's stew," he said with a huff. "This is a very special recipe for the king himself. Everything must be perfect."

Marcus folded the potato sacks. There would be turnips delivered later, and he wanted the bags handy.

"I can just see it now," mocked Marcus, plucking a wooden stirring spoon from a crock on the counter. "Kelvin lifts a spoonful of soup to his lips and—'What's this?' he cries. 'This carrot slice is too thick! Death to the cook!'" Marcus tasted the invisible soup and then drew the spoon across his neck like a knife.

Val snatched the spoon away from him. "Laugh if you will," he said, "but there is a good reason why I am the chef and you are the storage clerk. Now you, Marco, prepare my tea while Zit and I finish the stew."

"Once again, I'm Marcus and he's Zyll," said Marcus, rolling his eyes. Val had proven bad at names.

Suddenly the door to the delivery area swung open, and there was Kelvin's young page gasping for breath as if he'd been running. "They have caught him!" he shouted.

"What? Who?" asked Val, his knife poised over a parsnip.

"The Agoran who burned the ship and killed the king's guards!"

"How do you know this?"

"The gatekeeper just told me," answered the page. "The guards are bringing the culprit before Chancellor Prost as we speak."

Marcus looked at Zyll, but Zyll had already removed his apron and was heading for the hall with Xerxes in hand. Marcus flung the empty potato sacks across Val's shoulder, following Zyll.

"Wait!" called Val. "Where are you two going? And who will serve His Majesty's tea?"

*   *   *

The door to the throne room stood open when Marcus and Zyll arrived. The throne was empty, but Prost stood beside it as usual and was speaking to someone else in the room.

"Kelvin has reconsidered his decision," Prost was saying. "He has decided to honor Fredric's decree."

"I see," said a voice Marcus recognized as Jayson's. "I'm certain the Agorans will be pleased to hear of it."

The attending guard announced Zyll and Marcus's arrival. Prost nodded, permitting them to enter. "Hello, Master Zyll, Marcus," said Prost. "How goes it in the kitchen?"

"Splendidly," answered Zyll, smiling. "I have learned that for the past fifty-seven years of my life, I have been defiling the very art of vegetable preparation. Ah, but we did not mean to intrude," he added, bowing respectfully. "Please, continue."

"Yes, of course," said Prost. "Jayson, Dokur owes you its thanks in locating the Agoran rebels. They are now in custody and will be tried and condemned for their crimes."

"*They?*" asked Jayson. "I only brought you one."

Prost nodded to the guard to open the chamber doors. Two more guards entered the room, leading two prisoners behind them in chains. One was Eliha the Agoran. He held his head high, though his face and back bore the signs of a serious beating. Beside him the second prisoner stumbled and would have fallen had the guard not yanked her back to her feet. Her hair, caked with dirt and mud, lay stiffly on her shoulders. As she passed by, Kaië's eyes met Marcus's, and the pleading look in them made his heart break.

"No!" he whispered, too stunned to say more.

Forty-six

Prost stepped closer to the two prisoners. "I believe you know each other," he said, addressing Jayson. "The girl's mother was Ivanore's lady-in-waiting. After her mother died, she lived with you and Ivanore—until you were exiled. Both she and Ivanore disappeared after that."

Kaië tried to speak, but the guard slapped her across the face. Marcus started forward, but a warning glance from Zyll stopped him.

"Well," continued Prost, "now we know where she's been all this time and what she's been up to."

Jayson was outraged. Marcus could feel the anger radiating from him.

"I brought you the Agoran," said Jayson. "Why would you arrest an innocent girl?"

"Because she is *not* innocent." Prost placed a bony finger beneath Eliha's chin, pressing it up. Eliha hissed at him through gritted teeth. "When we asked this rebel how he learned about the secret tunnel," continued Prost, "he gave us her name."

"Chancellor," said Jayson, pleading, "I've known this woman most of her life. She would never do such a thing!" He turned to Kaië. "Tell them you are innocent!"

Kaië's eyes filled with tears.

"Let her speak," Prost told the guards. "Go ahead, girl. Say what you've already told me."

Kaië swallowed. Her lip, swollen from being struck, had a thin line of blood on it. "During the invasion," she began, "I sneaked into the Fortress and freed the Agoran from prison. We escaped through the tunnel. It was I who showed the Agoran how to get into the Fortress unseen."

Marcus was stunned by what he heard. Kaië had purposely left him out of her story. It had been *his* idea to free the Agoran, not Kaië's. He would have explained it before if he'd had the chance.

Marcus tried to speak, "Father, I need to—" but Jayson cut him off before he could finish his sentence. Then Jayson gave him a look that told him to be silent or else they might all be endangered. Marcus reluctantly held his peace.

"Does Kelvin know about her arrest?" asked Jayson.

"I have full authority to act in Kelvin's name in these matters," replied Prost.

"I demand to speak to him."

"I cannot—"

"I *will* speak to my son NOW!"

Jayson's hand went for his sword, but the guards drew theirs first, stepping between Jayson and Prost. Prost gloated.

"I know how you must feel about her, Jayson," he said, "but their crimes are more serious than we first believed. We have reason to suspect they are responsible for Fredric's death and have been plotting against Kelvin, as well."

Kaië jerked forward, her chains pulling taut. "That's a lie!"

"You can't be serious!" said Jayson.

Prost's gaze grew icy. "I assure you I am deadly serious, Jayson," he said. "We found traces of poison on the rim of Fredric's wine glass, which, thankfully, we had preserved. It is clear the Agoran is guilty of murder, and since the girl was working with him, so is she."

Prost motioned to the guards. "Take them now," he said. "They will remain in custody until their trial."

The guards led the two prisoners away. The enormous doors shut heavily behind them. Prost turned to leave as well, but Jayson stopped him.

"You said before that Kelvin will honor Fredric's decree. Do I have your word on that?"

"You will have your lands—after our war with Hestoria is over."

"What do you mean, *after* the war?"

"As I said before, we need the resources on that land to provide for our soldiers and to rebuild our ships. The war won't last long, I assure you, and then the land is yours."

"But that is not what Fredric promised."

"It is all *we* can promise."

"The Agorans will want a war, too."

"Is that a threat?" Prost glared at Jayson. Then one corner of his mouth turned up in a smirk. "You really ought to control your son, Zyll," Prost said. "He's liable to get hurt."

With that, Prost motioned to the remaining guard to open the door to Kelvin's private chambers. He left Marcus, Zyll, and Jayson alone in the throne room.

The three of them stood in silence for several moments, not knowing what to do next. Finally, it was Jayson who spoke. He turned on his father. "Why didn't you do something?"

"What should I have done?" asked Zyll, leaning calmly on Xerxes.

"You're the enchanter!" said Jayson. "You could have freed her!"

"And bring the entire royal guard upon us? I'm a magician, not a miracle worker."

Until now, Marcus had stood rigid as a statue, but now his entire frame began to tremble. "This is all my fault," he said, his voice barely audible. "It was me Kaië led into the Fortress the day the Hestorians attacked. We rescued the Agoran. Now he's used his freedom to put us all in danger. And even worse, he betrayed Kaië! If it weren't for me, Kaië would be safe."

"I can't let her stay in prison," said Jayson, pacing back and forth, from one end of the room to the other like a wild cat trapped in a cage.

"We could break her out," suggested Marcus. "I did it once before."

"And barely survived the attempt, so you've said," remarked Zyll. "No, we must prepare an argument in her defense and do our best to clear her name at her trial."

Jayson stopped suddenly. His eyes were filled with both rage and sadness. "I don't care what it takes," he said, "I will save her. I swear it."

Forty-seven

Marcus did not sleep that night. How could he, knowing that Kaië was shivering in a cold, damp prison cell? Even worse was the shame he felt for not having spoken in her defense. If he had only told Prost the truth, maybe he would have let her go free and taken Marcus instead.

The darkness in the room pressed in on him until he felt suffocated by it. Finally, Marcus flung off his covers and hurried out of his room into the hall. He would go to Kelvin and tell him the truth. He would do whatever he must to help Kaië.

The corridor was dimly lit by a single torch set in an iron sconce. Marcus's shadow stretched across the floor like a ghost. Standing there in the darkness, he felt his old fears rise up inside him. This time he brought his knife with him, though he longed for the blade concealed in Xerxes' staff. During his quest, he had relied on that blade for protection, but with only this small dagger, he felt vulnerable.

Marcus started down the hall, but he had not gone far when the sound of a door opening behind him made him pause. He turned and saw Zyll, dressed in his night robe and cap, slip from his room and walk as quickly as he was able down the corridor in the opposite direction. He did not have Xerxes with him.

Zyll disappeared around a corner. Curious, Marcus followed. When he reached the spot where Zyll had disappeared from his sight, he found a narrow, stone stairwell spiraling upward into the darkness. Marcus climbed the steps, which led to another corridor with several doors along either side.

Marcus heard voices coming from an open door at the end of the corridor. He approached and glanced in. Two men stood inside the small room. One was Zyll.

"You deceive yourself, Taren," Zyll was saying. "You thought that by killing Fredric you would gain power. But power is an illusion, as elusive as a rainbow."

Chancellor Prost stood at a window, his back to the room. He placed his hands on the windowsill and gazed out over Dokur. Zyll continued.

"Yes, I know who is really to blame. And I know how you manipulated Kelvin into breaking Fredric's treaty with the Agorans. You want them to turn against him so that you can gain his crown."

"Well, the treaty will be honored—in time," said Prost. "That is the best I can do. What more can you ask of me?"

"Spare the girl," said Zyll. "Please. Do not punish her for your crime."

Prost did not move from his place at the window. Instead, he raised one hand and swept it over the scene below him.

"Do you see what's down there?" he said. "An entire city. Beyond the city there is a mine, a mine filled with the world's most precious gem, Celestine. It is found nowhere but on Imaness. Whoever controls the mine controls our world, Zyll. Not just Dokur. Not just Imaness, but the world."

Prost turned from the window, his gaunt face even more pale against his blood red robe.

"Fredric hoarded Celestine, kept Imaness isolated to protect it. I, on the other hand, shall open free trade with Hestoria and other lands that will give us whatever we desire in exchange for Celestine."

"At what cost?" pleaded Zyll. "The girl's life? Kelvin's?"

"My dear Zyll, I have sworn my allegiance to the crown. Why, the boy looks to me like the father he never truly had."

"Kelvin has a father."

"Oh yes. The mongrel. Well, recent events have shown how deeply Kelvin cares about *him*."

Marcus felt the anger rising in him. He had to restrain himself from charging into the room and cutting out Prost's heart. But if Prost had killed Fredric, why didn't Zyll do something about it? Why not tell Kelvin the truth?

More secrets. Marcus was sick of secrets.

Zyll's voice was closer now, just on the other side of the door. "Beware, Taren. Do not think your acts are accomplished in darkness. The truth always finds its way into the light."

"So nothing's changed since we were young," said Prost.

"You are wrong," answered Zyll. "You have changed."

The door opened wider, and Zyll stepped through it. Marcus leaned back into the shadows as Zyll walked past him down the hall. Marcus waited for Zyll to descend the stone steps. If Zyll would not punish the guilty, then he would. Marcus didn't care what pain it might cause him, he would use magic to make Prost pay for what he had done to his other grandfather, Fredric.

Marcus was about to slip into the room, but the sound of a new voice, one he did not recognize, sent him back into hiding. Whoever it was had not been in the room before and must have entered through some other door.

"I can take him now," the voice said.

"Not here, Arnot," replied Prost. "We do not need another "accident" within the Fortress. Kelvin might become suspicious. No, the deed must be done in the open, tomorrow in the marketplace. There must be no doubt he is dead."

There was a pause, and then Prost spoke once more. "And Arnot," he added, "bring me back some fresh willenberries while you're there. I do so love willenberries."

Forty-eight

Prost had killed Fredric, and now he planned to murder Zyll, as well. Marcus's stomach clenched at the horrible discovery. He again thought of his vision of Zyll's death. So he had seen the future after all, which meant there was still time to change it. He had to warn Zyll. But first . . .

Marcus leaned his head back against the wall and tried to calm his breathing. He had better do it now before he lost his courage. Holding up both palms, Marcus concentrated. He felt the heat building inside of him and drew energy from every source he could reach within his mind. His chest started to throb before he even stepped into the room. Ignoring the pain, Marcus pushed open the door and leapt inside. A column of orange flame burst from his

222 Laurisa White Reyes

palms, engulfing the room. A second later, it was over. Except for the streaks of black where the walls had burned, the room was empty. Arnot and Prost had already left.

Marcus ran to the door at the opposite side of the room. He tried to open it, but it was locked. Zyll! He had to find Zyll.

Marcus hurried back down the stairwell and through the corridor toward Zyll's room. As he neared, however, the throbbing in his chest grew to an intense pain. His failed attempt to hurt Prost had triggered another attack.

The pain radiated throughout his entire body, his knees threatening to give way. He tried to call out for help, but the pain gripped Marcus so tightly he could not speak. He collapsed to the floor and let his mind fall into the void.

* * *

By the time Marcus had strength enough to stand again, the earliest rays of sunlight were creeping through a nearby window. The pain had diminished to a dull ache, which he did his best to ignore as he got to his feet. He hurried as fast as he dared to Zyll's room and rapped on the door. When no one answered, Marcus tried the door and found it unlocked. The room was empty. Zyll and Xerxes were gone.

* * *

Dokur was quiet this morning. Only a handful of merchants had arrived early to secure the best locations for peddling their wares. Marcus recognized the woman who had sold him his gryphon amulet. He nodded a greeting as he passed, and she smiled in return.

Marcus started across the town square toward the Seafarer Tavern. Zyll had planned to meet Jayson there again today, so it was the most likely place he'd be. The attack from the night before left Marcus feeling drained. His ribs felt bruised, as if someone had punched him. Between that and the real bruises from Eliha breaking a chair over his back, Marcus would probably need to spend the next week recovering in bed. But he didn't have time for that now. He had to find Zyll and tell him about Prost's plans.

He reached the great fountain. The Seafarer was not far now, just on the other side of the town square. He was about to move on when the door to the tavern opened. A bright column of gold light spilled from the doorway, and the figure of a girl emerged. Marcus raised his hand to wave at Lael but stopped when he saw the fear on her face.

"Marcus!" she shouted. "Look out!"

Marcus spun around and drew his knife. A long, steel blade whistled through the air as it came down on him. Marcus deflected the blow at the last second, though his knife was no match for the heavy sword. The force of it nearly knocked him on his back, but he managed to regain his balance just in time to block a second hit.

Lael's shouts brought others to the tavern door.

Marcus heard Lael calling his name again, but his eyes
were focused on his attacker.

The man wielding the sword was a stranger to Marcus,
with deep brown skin and piercing, black eyes. He came at
Marcus with a rapid succession of blows, each one harder
and faster than the one before. Marcus managed to block
some with his knife, others he avoided by shifting or duck-
ing. Every movement sent spasms of pain through him.

Arnot thrust his sword forward, and Marcus jumped
back, barely avoiding its tip.

Then, using both his hands, Arnot swung his blade in
a wide circle, slamming it straight down. Sparks flew as
metal met metal. Marcus's blade held the final assault in
check, but he strained against the weight of Arnot's body,
which now bore down on him until Arnot's face was mere
inches from his own.

"This was supposed to be easy," Arnot spat. "I've tried
to kill you twice before, but that girl knocked you out of
the way of the falling post. I had you again night before
last in the great hall, but you managed to get tangled up
with that Agoran rebel. I had hoped he'd do you in, but
now it's come to this."

Arnot's lips curled into a predatory smile. He pressed
his blade harder, and Marcus knew he could not resist him
much longer. Instinctively, he stepped back, but felt something cold and hard behind him. He was pinned against
the fountain.

Marcus reached back with his free hand and felt the
water behind him. If he froze it, he might have a solid

retreat, but after what he suffered last night, he doubted he would have the strength to cast any spell at all or even enough to continue this fight.

Before he could finish another thought, he heard the loud *thwang* of a bowstring. Arnot reared back, howling in pain. A single arrow tip stuck out from Arnot's side. Marcus looked toward the tavern and saw Clovis there, lowering his bow.

Arnot's body went limp, and for a moment, Marcus felt relief. The assassin didn't want Zyll, after all. Prost had sent him to kill Marcus, but now the assassin was dying.

Suddenly Marcus felt something sharp and hard pierce deep into his stomach. There wasn't any pain at first, just the shock of surprise. Arnot's eyes rolled back in his head, and his body gave a slight shiver as it rolled off Marcus and crumpled to the ground.

Marcus looked at his own body then and saw the handle of a previously concealed dagger jutting out from his stomach like some strange ornament surrounded by a growing stain of red.

Forty-nine

It wasn't long before the pain took hold. Each breath sent wrenching spasms through Marcus's body. The agony made him long for death.

Clovis raced to the fountain, his bow dropped and forgotten at the tavern door. He caught Marcus by the shoulders just as his knees gave way.

"Help!" Clovis shouted, his voice already choked with tears. "Help! Someone!"

Moments later Bryn was beside him. Together they eased Marcus to the ground.

The whimpering child cradled Marcus's head in his lap and smoothed back his hair with a trembling hand.

Some townspeople who had witnessed the attack from the tavern, as well as several merchants, gathered around.

Lael pushed her way through the thickening crowd. "Get out of the way!" she yelled. "Please move aside! He's my friend!"

She dropped to her knees beside Marcus. He tried to focus on her face, but the image was blurred. Finally, he closed his eyes just to keep from getting dizzy.

"Marcus, I tried to get help, but it happened so fast!"

He heard Lael's voice as though it were miles away. When he first saw the blood, he had been afraid, but now with Lael beside him, he felt strangely calm.

"I'm so sorry," she said. "Don't die, Marcus. Please don't die."

But how could he do anything else?

Marcus . . .

Her voice was like an angel's, sweeter than any voice he had ever heard before. Marcus longed to hear her say it again.

Marcus, she said at last, *you must take the key.*

Marcus saw the angel bathed in gold light. She held out her arms to him. He wanted to be held by those arms, comforted by them. Her lips moved again . . .

Take the key to Voltana, she said. *Take the key, Marcus, and find its maker.*

The angel began to fade. Marcus called after her.

Ivanore!

Marcus reached for her, the anguish inside him greater than the pain, but she was already gone.

Mother!

"Pull out the dagger," said another voice. It was Zyll.

"Make room. Give the boy space to breathe. You just might suffocate him before he's had the chance to die."

His grandfather had raised him from birth, loving him like his own son. What would Zyll do when Marcus died? Who would care for him?

Marcus couldn't abandon his master. Not now. Not like this.

Marcus felt a tugging at his chest, but it did not add to his pain, which was already more than he could bear.

"My boy," said Zyll, his voice firm, "you will live. But you *must* hold on a few moments longer."

Marcus struggled to open his eyes. He wanted to see Zyll's face just once more, but try as he might, his eyes remained stubbornly shut.

He felt something warm and familiar. Zyll's hands were on him, gently caressing his wounded body. He heard Zyll's voice break in one brief sob. He had never seen Zyll cry before, but he knew his grandfather was crying now. He had to try harder, for Zyll.

The warmth from Zyll's hands grew hotter and hotter until the heat seemed to penetrate every cell of Marcus's body. It grew so hot that he soon felt as though he was burning. The peace he had known earlier faded and was replaced with pain—searing, agonizing pain.

Marcus's eyes shot open, and a horrific scream exploded from his mouth. Then it was over. The heat was gone. The pain was gone.

Fifty

Marcus stared straight above him at the cloudless sky overhead. He wondered for a moment where he was and whether what he had felt and heard had been a dream. He blinked, then slowly rolled to his side and sat up. Laying his hand over his chest, he felt the damp, bloody cloth of his tunic and the tear that Arnot's dagger had made in it, but where he expected to find a wound, there was only clean, solid flesh.

And then he knew.

"Grandfather?"

Marcus got to his knees and bent over Zyll's body, lying face up beside him on the ground. Clovis stood nearby, holding Xerxes. Both their faces appeared stricken with grief. The expressions of the onlookers revealed the miraculous nature of what they had just witnessed. Clovis, Bryn, and Lael were all in tears.

Zyll's chest rose and fell in uneven, gasping breaths. The blood oozing from his chest was already pooling on the earth beside him.

"No!" Marcus shouted. It was almost too unreal to believe. Zyll had exchanged his own life force for Marcus's. "Why, Grandfather? Why?"

Marcus clutched at the old man's shoulders. He was angry enough to shake him. How could he? There was no way a man as old as Zyll, no matter how strong, could survive an exchange of energy as powerful as this one had to have been.

"You can't die, Grandfather! Not now!"

It was not too late, Marcus knew. There was still time to save him. He had done it once for Kelvin, he would do it again now. Marcus swiped his hand across his eyes, but the tears kept coming. He pressed his hands to Zyll's chest and tried to focus his thoughts, but his body shook from weakness.

"Live, Grandfather! Please live!"

Though desperation compelled him to try, Marcus lacked the strength to succeed. His arms fell limp across Zyll. "I'm sorry," he sobbed. "I'm so sorry!"

With a trembling hand, Zyll reached into his robe and removed the key Marcus had given him when he left for Dokur, the same key Zyll had given Marcus for his quest. Zyll placed it in the boy's palm. His lips moved, his eyes fixed on Marcus.

"He's trying to say something," said Lael.

Zyll's voice was so faint Marcus could barely make out the word.

"Secrets . . ."

"Grandfather?" Marcus said, his voice choked with tears.

"Your mother . . . Ivanore."

"Yes, I saw her. I had another vision, and she finally spoke to me. She told me to take the key to Voltana. It was a beautiful dream, Grandfather."

Zyll drew a slow breath, the air and blood gurgling in his chest.

"Not . . . a dream."

Marcus knew Zyll had only moments left, and yet his gaze was steady, his eyes piercing into Marcus's very soul. Then with his dying breath, Zyll whispered, "Ivanore lives."

THE LAST ENCHANTER

Fifty-one

Marcus had no idea how long he had slept. It was dark outside when he awoke—that much he knew. He sat up and let his feet rest on the floor. He listened but heard nothing except the gentle rattling of his window shutters in the breeze. He knew he was in the Seafarer. He remembered being brought here, and he knew the tavern was always alive with patrons eating and drinking throughout the night. He expected to hear the clinking of dishes, the voices of rowdy guests, the creaking of wood as people walked up and down the staircase. Yet there was nothing but silence.

Marcus had knelt beside Zyll's body for several minutes, though to him it felt like a lifetime. Every memory he had of his grandfather passed through his mind. The countless hours and minutes and seconds they had spent together were not enough, and Marcus felt the sting of losing the one person he loved and who had loved him most of all. It was agony beyond anything he'd ever known. Not even the sobs that exploded out of him could ease the pain.

No one tried to comfort him, for there could be no peace. They let him cry until he had nothing left in him to cry. Only then did his friends wrap their arms around his trembling shoulders and lead him into the tavern to a warm, soft bed where he had promptly fallen asleep.

As Marcus got out of bed, he expected some trace of pain. There was none. He walked to the bedroom door, which was slightly ajar, and saw a faint light beyond the landing downstairs—the fireplace in the dining hall. Hearing voices speaking in whispers, he went to the landing and peered over the rail.

Below him, the dining hall was empty except for a single table in the center of the room. From above, he could only see the tops of four heads but could not tell who they were. He leaned forward a little, trying to hear or see better, and the floorboards beneath his feet creaked.

The heads looked up at him. The first was his father, Jayson. The second was the tavern keeper, Peagry. Marcus assumed the woman with them was Peagry's wife, but when she looked up, he realized it was the amulet seller from the marketplace. What was she doing here?

The last man was a head taller than the other two, with dark skin. A Hestorian. Half his face was tattooed with strange symbols. He had seen this man once, but only for a moment. He was the man Zyll had been speaking with that day outside the Dragon's Head Inn.

"Hello, lad," said the man with the tattoo. "Finished your beauty sleep, have you?"

On seeing Marcus, Peagry hastily rose from the table. "Arla and I will go see about making preparations," he said. Then Peagry and the amulet seller excused themselves and exited the room. Marcus wondered what preparations they needed to make.

Jayson walked up the stairs but stopped halfway to the top. "You all right?" he asked gently. "I know you've had a terrible shock. Clovis told me everything." Jayson waited for Marcus to respond, but his son remained silent. "I should have been there, I know," Jayson continued. "I was supposed to meet you, but I was looking after some personal business with Brommel here." Jayson nodded toward the man with that tattooed face and then added, "Will you come down and talk with us?" he said.

Marcus followed Jayson down the stairs to the table, but he did not sit down.

"Brommel and I were discussing your situation." Jayson took his seat again. "I asked around about the man who attacked you. His name was Arnot, and he was an assassin. Apparently he's got a bit of a reputation over at the Dragon's Head. He was obviously supposed to kill you, but he failed. I don't know who hired him—"

Marcus willed his mouth to move. "Chancellor Prost," he whispered. "I overheard them last night, but I thought he wanted to kill—"

His voice broke off as fresh tears filled his eyes.

"Of course it was Prost," said Brommel, his voice sharp and low. "He's a treacherous snake, that one."

"When news of Zyll's death gets out," said Jayson, "he will know you are still alive—and will send someone else to properly finish the job."

A log in the fireplace broke in two, sending a shower of sparks into the air. Marcus watched the flames flicker and move as though they were alive. He recalled the first time Zyll had taught him to make fire with magic. His attempt had been an utter failure.

"Don't you see, lad?" Brommel said. "If you stay in Dokur, sooner or later you will die."

Marcus looked from Brommel to Jayson and back again. "What difference would it make if I die?" he asked. "And why would Prost, or anyone, go through the trouble of killing—or *defending*—me?"

Brommel and Jayson exchanged knowing glances. Brommel took a long, hard swig of his ale, and then set the tankard down on the table. "Zyll told me about your abilities, Marcus."

"What abilities?" asked Marcus.

Brommel leaned forward, resting his elbows on the table. "You saw him die, didn't you?" he asked in a hoarse whisper. "You saw exactly how it happened well before it happened."

Marcus nodded slowly. He did not want to think of that image now, though it was etched forever in his mind.

Suddenly Brommel seemed anxious, as if he couldn't

sit still any longer. When he stood, he was even taller than Marcus had thought, towering above him in the firelight. But the man was not fearsome in the least. Instead, his face held a kind of awed expression, as though he were standing in the presence of one greater than himself.

"We've waited years for you, Marcus. Some of us thought you'd never come."

Marcus shook his head. "I don't understand," he said, looking to Jayson for some explanation. "Who is 'we'?"

"The Guilde, son," said Jayson. "It's an ancient society sworn to protect those like yourself. Zyll was a great enchanter, with skills he learned as a young man from his father. But your abilities are not learned. They're inherited."

Marcus's legs went weak. He reached for the table and held onto it.

"Inherited?" he asked. "From Zyll? From you?"

"Not from me," Jayson answered.

"Zyll said you have visions of *her*," said Brommel.

Marcus nodded. "I dream of her sometimes. I used to think she was my angel."

"They're not dreams, lad. You have a gift. You can see things, people and places that are far away in distance and time." Brommel grasped Marcus by his shoulders, grinning proudly down at him. "You're a seer!"

Fifty-two

 seer," Brommel repeated, "the first one we've had since—"

"Since Ivanore." Jayson peered into Marcus's eyes, letting the weight of the words settle into him.

Marcus finally sat down in a chair. This was all so much to take in, and yet somehow it made sense. The pronouncement that he was a seer felt right and yet unreal at the same time.

"Before he died," said Marcus, "Zyll told me that Ivanore lives. I saw a vision of her when I was there on the ground, dying. She said I'm supposed to take the key to Voltana and find its maker."

"Aye, lad," said Brommel, finishing off the last of his

ale, "you can't stay here. You are too important to us to be killed off."

"But is it true? Is my mother really alive?"

"Aye," Brommel said with sadness, "the Guilde believes she is somewhere in Hestoria, a captive of our enemies. There is much to explain, but we don't have time now. We must get you out of Dokur."

Marcus looked to Jayson. "But why did Zyll lie to me before? Why didn't he—or you—tell me the truth?"

Jayson gazed at his son, pain and uncertainty in his eyes. "Because I didn't know the truth," he said, "not until yesterday when Brommel told me what the Guilde has only recently learned."

"Where is she?" asked Marcus. All his life he had believed he was an orphan, and now suddenly his mother was alive? "You said she's on the mainland. Does anyone know where?"

"That's a question we've been trying to answer for months now," said Brommel. "Maybe this key maker has some information. The only way to find out is to find him."

Above them on the balcony, Marcus noticed a door opening and saw Lael slip silently from the room. She stood, quietly watching the proceedings below.

Marcus sat in silence for several moments. So many thoughts raced through his mind that he could hardly sort them all out. What was he supposed to do when he reached Voltana? All he had was a simple key. How would he ever find its maker? And even if he did find him, what questions would he ask? So many things weighed heavily on his mind, but one troubled him far more than the others.

"What will happen to Kaië?" Marcus asked Jayson.

At the mention of Kaië's name, Lael stepped back into the shadows.

"If she's found guilty," said Jayson, casting a concerned look in Brommel's direction, "she'll be executed."

Marcus felt sick. "I can't let that happen. It should be me in that prison, not her!"

"Don't be so eager to trade places with her," said Brommel. "Her trial won't happen for several days. By law, the king must oversee all treason cases, and Kelvin is preoccupied with getting ready to attack Hestoria. So we have time."

"Time for what?"

"To discuss the matter with Kelvin," answered Jayson.

"You'll do that?"

"I'll speak with him personally. I promise you, I'll do everything in my power to keep her safe."

Marcus covered his face with his hands to hide his emotion. When he felt he could speak with a steady voice, he said, "Thank you. I'm willing to go to Voltana. But it's on the far side of the island, isn't it? How will I get there?"

"I know those parts well," said Brommel.

"You'll go with me then?"

"Not I. I have a business to run. But my son, Rylan, will accompany you. And your friends can go with you."

Marcus glanced back toward the fire. Its flame grew dimmer. My friends, he thought. How can I ask them to come on such a dangerous journey?

Jayson rose from the table, disappearing through the kitchen door. He returned moments later, carrying Xerxes in both hands. The wooden eagle's face was still and lifeless, but Marcus saw a deep sadness in his expression. Jayson placed the walking stick in Marcus's hands. "I'm certain Zyll wanted you to have this," he said.

Marcus accepted it gratefully and stroked the top of Xerxes' head with his fingertips as if he were stroking downy feathers. He knew, even if no one else did, what Zyll's death meant to Xerxes and how important it was to Zyll that he would be cared for in his absence. If Marcus was to go without friends, at least he would have Xerxes.

"All right then," Marcus said finally, though all confidence had left him, "I'll go at first light."

Brommel and Jayson traded grim nods. Then they excused themselves and left the room, presumably to get things ready for Marcus's journey. Sitting alone in the now quiet room, Marcus hardly dared to consider what challenges awaited him. In the stillness, he heard an almost imperceptible noise coming from the shadows above, a sniff and muffled sob. The sound cut into him like a dagger and yet also confused him. Lael was weeping, but Marcus couldn't fathom why.

Fifty-three

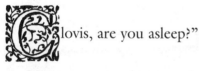lovis, are you asleep?"

Marcus cautiously opened the door to the darkened room and slipped inside.

Clovis stirred on the bed and then sat up, yawning. "Marcus, is that you? Is it morning already?"

"Actually it's the middle of the night, but I had to talk to you."

"All right," said Clovis.

Marcus sat down at the foot of the bed. This was going to be more difficult than he thought. He decided to get on with it.

"It's time for you to go home."

"Home?" asked Clovis, rubbing sleep from his eyes. "What do you mean?"

"I have to leave Dokur. It's not safe for me here."

"Is this about that man who attacked you? You're still in danger," said Clovis, reaching for his bow. "It was my fault. I should have been with you. I could have protected you. I *will* protect you."

"No, Clovis, it's not that," said Marcus. "I mean, you *did* protect me. You're the best friend I've got. But I have to go."

"When?"

"At dawn. I want you to leave with me—"

"Yes, of course. I'll go wherever you need me to, Marcus, you know that."

"—and then you'll go home."

The wounded expression on Clovis's face cut deep. Marcus felt as if he had just betrayed his dearest friend. And in a way, Marcus realized, he had.

Marcus forced a smile, attempting to comfort Clovis a little. "You promised your father you'd return before winter. He'll worry if you don't get home in time."

Clovis tried to hide his disappointment with a weak smile of his own. His hand, which had gripped his bow, relaxed and slid into his lap. "I'll go," he said, though his voice wavered as he said it. He nodded and spoke again with more conviction. "I'll go if that's what you want me to do."

Marcus sensed that Clovis was unhappy with his friend's request, but he was willing to do as Marcus asked even though he didn't agree. At that moment, Marcus knew that Clovis was a greater friend than he had ever imagined.

Leaving Clovis alone, Marcus stepped out into the hall. Below on the first floor, he caught a glimpse of someone slipping through the kitchen door. Marcus followed the figure outside where the sky was full of stars, the moon merely an outline against the night's darkness. The well outside the Seafarer Tavern was nothing more than a silhouette, as was the girl standing beside it. The light from the open door cast a pale wedge of gold on the ground. Marcus paused there and waited for his eyes to adjust. Then he let the door close behind him and stepped forward into the darkness.

"Amazing, isn't it?" he asked, approaching the well. Lael nodded in agreement. They both gazed up into the sky without speaking. After a while Marcus lowered his eyes and watched Lael's face, barely visible in the starlight.

"How did you know I was out here?" she asked.

"I saw you slip out through the kitchen as I left Clovis's room."

Lael turned to look at Marcus. When their eyes met, Marcus's cheeks grew hot. Certain his face was bright red, he was glad it was dark so she wouldn't notice.

"I'm sorry about your grandfather," she said, and by the expression in her eyes, he knew she meant it.

"Thank you," Marcus replied. It was difficult to find words. Words had no place on a night like this, a night in which the stars and the sounds of the sea should be enough. But Marcus needed to speak.

"Lael," he began, "I have to go away for a while. If I stay in Dokur, I have a good chance of getting killed. Anyway, I just wanted to say goodbye."

"Is Clovis going with you?"

"No," said Marcus. "He has to get back to his family. His father's expecting him home soon."

"And where are *you* going?"

"To Voltana."

Lael looked at him again, her jaw clenched in anger. "You're insane. Voltana's the most desolate spot on the island. No one goes there."

"I have to. I think my mother might be alive, and I may find information about her there."

Lael walked around to the opposite side of the well. The darkness there seemed to swallow her up, so Marcus could not see her anymore. Only her voice penetrated the night. "I understand how important it is to find your mother," said Lael. "I've been trying to find mine, too, but so far nothing. I'll go with you to Voltana, Marcus Frye, and who knows, maybe I'll find my mother there, as well."

Lael came the rest of the way around the well until she stood directly in front of Marcus. She was close enough that Marcus could feel the warmth of her breath against his face and smell the sweet scent of apples in her hair. Suddenly he wanted to touch her. He reached out his hand toward her but then stopped.

This was Lael, he reminded himself—Lael who was always trying to make him look and feel stupid. Marcus chastised himself for acting like such an idiot. He had never wanted her to come with him to Dokur. Why would he want her to go with him to Voltana?

"You should go home to Quendel," he said, turning his back to Lael and starting for the tavern. "You can go with Clovis."

"Why would I do that? There's nothing for me in Quendel."

Marcus was irritated now. Lael was being stubborn as usual. Why couldn't she just let him be? "Then stay here in Dokur," he said. "I'll be better off without you tagging along again."

"Excuse me?" exclaimed Lael.

"I don't say that to insult you—"

"I did not '*tag along*'. Our journeys just happened to bring us both to Dokur," said Lael smugly. "So don't bother acting so proud. I would have gone with you to Voltana, but now I have no intention of going, even if you asked me."

"Well, I'm not asking you."

Marcus opened the door to the tavern. The light from the kitchen fell over Lael, who stared daggers at him, though Marcus could swear he saw tears in her eyes. He stepped over the threshold, but then Lael started toward him, her expression suddenly anxious.

"If Clovis and I don't go with you, who will?" she asked.

"There's a man named Brommel who knows that part of Imaness. He said his son will guide me."

"Brommel?" Lael's eyes widened at the mention of his

name, but her expression quickly became stern. "I know who he is. I was told he might be able to find the man who took my mother, but who really knows. Everyone's been so worried about you, he hasn't had a spare moment to talk to me about it."

"You act as if it was my fault I was attacked."

"I didn't say that—"

"Sorry *everyone's* been too busy trying to keep me alive to pay attention to you."

"That's not what I meant. You don't know anything about Brommel or his son. I just don't think you should trust them."

"Who else can I trust?" snapped Marcus. He regretted the words the moment he saw the hurt on Lael's face, but he could not take them back now.

"I see," said Lael, a distinct edge to her voice. "Well, I'm sure you can trust that servant girl. In fact, maybe you should take *her* with you to Voltana."

"Who? You mean Kaië?"

"That's right! Kaië!"

"What does she have to do with this?"

"Everything!" Lael was shouting now. "She's stuck in that prison, and you feel guilty about it. And you should feel guilty, because it's you who should be in jail instead of her."

"Stop it, Lael—"

"But instead of saving her, you're running away! You're running away, Marcus Frye, because you're a coward!"

"I said stop!"

Marcus was shaking with anger now. Lael stood in front of him, breathing hard from shouting. They stood that way, staring at each other, for several moments. What was it about her that made him so angry, Marcus wondered? Could it be because she was right? He didn't want to think about that now. He just wanted to leave Dokur as quickly as possible.

Marcus stepped into the kitchen. "Goodbye, Lael," he said, letting the door slam shut behind him.

Fifty-four

Dawn arrived faster than Marcus would have wanted, but he was ready to go. Jayson and Brommel had left a few hours earlier, taking Zyll's body with them. Marcus had not even gone to the window to watch their cart roll down the cobblestone road toward the Fortress. First they were to give Kelvin the news and then head to the shore to perform the funeral ceremony. In a place and time such as this, there was little opportunity to mourn. The dead must be dealt with as quickly as possible to avoid decay and the spread of disease.

Marcus yearned to go with them. To stay behind felt disloyal to his grandfather's memory, but to go to the Fortress or to remain in Dokur at all would be dangerous. So Marcus spent the few remaining hours of the night gathering what supplies he might need for the journey ahead. Everything he had brought with him from Quendel was still in his room at the Fortress—everything except Zyll's key, which he placed in a leather pouch Jayson had given him for that very purpose. He also had his dagger and Xerxes. Peagry's wife had provided a change of clothing, blanket, food, and a satchel to keep them in.

Bryn and Clovis met Marcus in the dining hall of the inn just before daybreak. Although Mrs. Peagry had cooked hot sausages and biscuits, neither boy had any appetite. Bryn, however, took delight in filling his stomach with as much food as it would hold.

Bryn handed a biscuit to Marcus. "Thank you," Marcus said, slipping it into his pocket.

"You're not hungry?" asked Bryn, his mouth full of food.

"Not today, but I'll save it for later. All right?"

Bryn seemed disinterested in Marcus's answer but was looking around the room impatiently. "Where is Lael?" he asked.

Marcus sighed. He knew how fond Bryn had grown of Lael, though he'd never understood why. Bryn was anything but a real human child, yet he seemed to enjoy playing the role for her, and she liked mothering him. Bryn had promised to follow Marcus to Voltana, but Marcus hadn't had the heart to tell him Lael would not be coming.

"Bryn, there's something you should know," said Marcus. "Lael isn't—"

"—isn't ready yet."

Lael stood at the top of the staircase, grinning. She was dressed in her travel cloak, a bulging knapsack on her shoulder.

"But I will be as soon as I have some breakfast," she added, coming down the stairs two at a time. She snatched a biscuit from the table and took a bite of it, and then cast a guarded glance in Marcus's direction.

"Now I'm ready," she said after swallowing the first bite.

"Fine," said Marcus as he tried his best to hide his surprise and irritation. Though he felt bad about their earlier conversation, he still did not want Lael coming along. But if he were to say so now, Bryn would throw a fit. Marcus would wait until later, when he and Lael were alone, and then try to convince her to go on to Quendel with Clovis.

A few moments later, the door to the tavern opened and in walked a tall, lean young man with straight, dark hair down to his shoulders and eyes that glimmered like jewels against his bronzed Hestorian skin. He looked close to Kaië's age, maybe eighteen or nineteen. The moment Lael saw him, she stopped chewing and held still as a statue.

"Marcus Frye?" asked the young man, scanning the faces of everyone in the room.

Marcus stepped forward and extended his hand. "You must be Brommel's son."

"Yes, I'm Rylan," he said, shaking Marcus's hand. "If you're ready, we should be going. I'd like to be out of Dokur before full daylight."

"Agreed," said Marcus.

Rylan turned to the door and paused. "Are you *all* coming?" he asked.

Clovis and Lael glanced at each other and nodded at Rylan.

"All right then," said Rylan. "Let's go."

Rylan led the small group outside the Seafarer. Once in the marketplace Marcus looked toward the sea. The sky was still dark except for an orange glow just beyond the cliffs. He started walking toward it.

"Where are you going?" Xerxes demanded when they had gone a short distance.

Marcus started at hearing the walking stick's voice, the first words Xerxes had uttered since Zyll's death. "I have to see him," said Marcus.

The orange glow grew larger, and as Marcus approached the cliffs he could hear the crackle of flames mingled with the sound of the waves. Below on the shore he saw Jayson, Brommel, Kelvin, and Prost. Beyond them, floating in the bay, was a wooden raft on which lay Zyll's body, already half consumed by fire.

Fifty-five

should be down there," said Marcus, tears streaming down his face.

"As should I," said Xerxes, making a soft, high whistle that to Marcus seemed as close to crying as he had ever heard from Xerxes.

Marcus held Xerxes at shoulder height so they could watch Zyll's funerary ceremony together. Suddenly Xerxes' staff quivered in his hand.

"Are you all right?" asked Marcus.

"Yes," replied Xerxes, but his staff shook again. "Well, perhaps not. I feel a little strange, actually." Marcus turned Xerxes to face him. The bird's wooden eyes were open wide, and his beak trembled. "Something's happening to me," he said.

Xerxes' eyelids flickered, and his neck twisted in a way Marcus had never seen before. Then Xerxes tipped back his head, and an odd, screeching sound came out of his beak.

"Xerxes!" said Marcus. "Xerxes what's happening?"

Xerxes groaned. His brown, carved feathers rippled. "I think . . . I'm changing," he said.

"Changing? How?"

"Zyll promised me . . ." Xerxes groaned again, and his head twisted unnaturally from side to side. " . . . he promised me that if anything happened to him, I would be transformed!"

"You mean—"

"I'm changing into a real bird!"

Marcus thrust the end of Xerxes' staff into the ground and stepped back. Xerxes' wooden eagle head began to morph. First the beak darkened from brown to black. Then the dull, wooden feathers began to glisten. The staff shortened, part of it spreading into broad, black tail feathers, and another part into two thin legs and feet. The body and head emerged, bulging like a dark fist. Finally two wings unfolded, each individual feather distinct from the next.

"I'm real!" shouted Xerxes, his thick, pointy beak clicking excitedly. He hopped happily about on the ground and cautiously tried his wings.

"I knew it!" he continued. "I knew that old Zyll would keep his word! He made me a real eagle after all!"

Marcus cleared his throat. "I think something's gone wrong," he said.

"Wrong? Of course not! Can't you see? Why look at these wings! These talons, and—wait a moment . . ."

Xerxes turned his head, examining each wing with his small, black eyes.

"No! It can't be true!" he said.

"I'm afraid it is," said Marcus. "You're not an eagle, Xerxes."

"A crow?" Xerxes lamented. "He made me a common crow?"

"Well, just look at it this way," added Marcus, trying not to laugh, "even in death, Zyll had a sense of humor."

"Oh, you think it's funny, do you? I can't believe this! This is so . . . so . . . undignified!"

Marcus burst out laughing. Xerxes cast him a scornful glance before spreading his wings and taking flight. Marcus watched him flap wildly, and just as he disappeared over the rooftops of Dokur, Marcus heard a soft yet angry *caw*.

"Well, goodbye, old friend," said Marcus softly. He turned back toward the bay. The bonfire was far out to sea now, just an orange flicker against the grander gold of the early morning sky. "And goodbye, Grandfather."

Then Marcus turned away and crossed the square to where Clovis, Lael, Bryn, and Rylan waited to begin their journey.

Fifty-six

Marcus and his friends followed Rylan down the familiar road that led from the plateau to the flat plains below. Rylan was a quiet sort, who paced himself well ahead of the others and never looked back to see if they were keeping up. He seemed to be, if not unaware, then uninterested in his companions.

By the time they reached level ground, the sun had risen well above the distant mountains. Bryn held onto Lael's hand much of the time, when he wasn't stopping to pluck pebbles from his shoe or examine some twisted piece of dried vegetation growing on the side of the road. He presented each little treasure to Lael, whose constant flow of gentle praise and encouragement soon wore on

Marcus's nerves. Having a guide who never spoke at all was equally annoying.

About midday they reached the Celestine mine. More soldiers stood guard now than when they had passed before. Each one carried a short sword and shield and wore armor on his chest and head. By the looks on their faces, they were not in the mood to be approached by five young travelers.

"Maybe we should go back and take a different route," suggested Lael. "Rylan, what do you think?"

Rylan said nothing but simply led his party in a wide circle around the mine, avoiding possible confrontation. It was clear he expected the others to follow without question, which they did.

They reached Lake Olsnar by nightfall. When Rylan stopped and began unrolling his blanket, everyone took it as a signal they would be camping here for the night.

"I'm going to the shore to fill my water skin," Marcus said, once he had prepared his own bed.

"Wait for me," Clovis replied.

"We'll come, too," added Lael and Bryn.

As they stood to leave, Rylan, who was arranging a stack of kindling for the fire, held up his empty skin.

"Would you mind?" he asked without looking up.

Marcus hesitated. They had traveled all day without a single word out of Brommel's son, and now Rylan expected to be served? Marcus had half a mind to take that skin and throw it right back at him, but if he offended him, Rylan just might abandon them and return to Dokur. Then how would Marcus find Voltana?

Marcus took Rylan's water skin and headed for the lakeshore, grumbling as he went. He hadn't gotten very far when a loud, high-pitched screech startled him. Suddenly a black ball appeared, rocketing through the air. The mass shot past Marcus, narrowly missing his head, and crash-landed behind a nearby tree. Marcus hurried over to inspect the strange object only to find Xerxes lying on his back, feet stuck up in the air, gasping for breath.

"Oh, praise the gods, it's you!" said Xerxes, moaning in pain. "Oh! My wing! My back!"

"Xerxes! Are you all right?"

"Do I look all right to you?"

"What happened?"

"Well, after I left you this morning, I flew around a bit—exploring, you know—and testing out my wings. It was a lovely experience! The first time I have ever seen anything from higher up than Zyll's elbow! Ah, what splendor! What magnificent beauty!"

"Xerxes? What happened?" Marcus asked more forcefully.

"After a while, I got hungry. I've never been hungry before. I was only wood, as you well know. And I suddenly felt weak and empty. So I thought it would be a good idea to search for food. I foraged a bit and found some berries and a scrap of—"

"Xerxes!" shouted Marcus. "What happened?"

"Excuse me for not noticing you were in such a hurry to fill that water skin!" snapped Xerxes. "If you must know, I was attacked by a falcon! Yes, a vicious, evil falcon determined to have me for dinner—and not as a guest, mind you! I flew here as fast as I could in search of shelter."

Xerxes rolled onto his feet and shook out his feathers. Then he flew up to perch unsteadily on a tree branch.

"You're welcome to stay with me as long as you need," said Marcus.

"Stay with you? Hmmm. I appreciate the offer, but I'm a free agent now. I come and go as I like. But seeing as your company is better than no company at all, I will stay here tonight."

With that, Xerxes nestled his beak beneath his wing and was soon whistling deeply in slumber.

Fifty-seven

By the time Marcus reached the lake, Clovis and Lael were already dipping their skins into the water. Bryn was in the lake up to his waist, splashing happily about.

"Can you believe that guide of ours?" said Marcus.

"You mean Rylan?" replied Lael.

"Does he even know we're following him? He just keeps marching on and on without even acknowledging our presence."

"I think he's arrogant," said Clovis.

"He's just doing his job," said Lael. "He wouldn't be a good guide if he spent all his time chatting, would he?"

Marcus couldn't believe his ears. Lael was always so quick to criticize Marcus when he made even the smallest error. In fact, she *loved* criticizing Marcus, so why not Rylan, who was much more deserving of it than he? Then the answer struck him, making him angrier still.

"Why are you so fond of him all of a sudden, Lael?"

"I'm not *fond* of him," she answered. "I hardly know him."

"Exactly! And yet you're defending him as if he were—"

"Were what?" challenged Lael.

Bryn waddled through the shallow water until he stood beside them on the shore. He shook the water from his body like a wet dog. Cold water sprayed them all.

"Bryn!" shouted Marcus.

"I have to dry myself."

"Well, go do it over there! You've gotten us all wet!"

Bryn apologized and wandered off through the trees, dejected.

"You hurt his feelings," scolded Lael.

Clovis stood up and put the stopper in his water skin. "I'll go after him," he said, following Bryn. "Besides, I think there's only room for two in this argument."

Once Clovis had gone, Lael turned on Marcus. "Why do you have to be so hard on Bryn all the time?"

"Hard on him?" answered Marcus. "Lael, you don't know what you're saying, do you?"

"I do, too. You're too critical, Marcus. You never have anything nice to say to that boy."

"Bryn is not a boy! He's a groc, a monster parading around in human form. Or have you forgotten those creatures that wanted to eat you back in the canyon?"

"He's not like them," said Lael.

"Of course he's like them! He's one of them! But you've been treating him as though you were his mother and he was your child."

Marcus was angry now, but he wasn't so sure it was because of Bryn. No matter how hard he tried to control himself, Lael always found some way to irritate him.

"He wants to be human," said Lael. "He would be a good one if you'd let him." Lael's voice remained calm, and there was a strange pleading look in her eye that, for some reason, only fueled Marcus's temper.

"Bryn will never be human!" he said.

At that moment, Marcus glanced up and saw Bryn and Clovis standing together at the edge of the thicket. Marcus knew immediately he had gone too far this time.

"Bryn, I—"

"It's all right, Marcus," said Bryn, choking back a tear. "Really . . ."

Bryn turned and ran back into the trees. Clovis's mouth hung open in surprise.

"I'm sorry," stammered Marcus. "I didn't mean it that way."

"Of course you didn't," said Lael, getting to her feet and brushing the dust off her trousers. The edge in her voice could have cut Marcus right in half.

Fifty-eight

Jayson stood on the balcony outside Kelvin's private chambers and gazed out over the bay. The sun was setting to the west, casting a deep golden hue across the horizon. The bare masts of Dokur's fleet below in the harbor stood in stark contrast, each one a bold, black gash against the orange-and-violet sky. It would not be long now before they would hoist their sails and set out for the mainland, destruction their only aim.

Jayson spotted the first stars of the night. Marcus had left only that morning, yet already it seemed a lifetime. Too many years had passed with Jayson not even knowing of his son's existence, and he regretted each day they had been separated. Following the Hestorian invasion, he had stayed in Quendel with Marcus and Zyll until the leaves began to turn. Then he left to join his people in Taktani. While he would have preferred to stay with his father and son, the Agorans needed him. But once he led them back to their homelands, Jayson hoped he would never be separated from his family again.

Tonight, however, he could only ask the gods to watch over Marcus on his journey and bring him safely home again. He could also spend his time with his other son, Kelvin.

"This was my grandfather's room," said Kelvin, entering through the door. "Fredric breathed his last breath here."

"A bit morbid, don't you think?" answered Jayson.

"What? That he died here, or that I've made his room my own?"

Kelvin motioned for the guard who had accompanied him to exit. The guard bowed stiffly and then stepped through the door. Though Kelvin closed the door behind him, Jayson was certain the guard would remain posted outside. He could smell the man's scent even through the solid oak door, his Agoran senses far more attuned than those of humans.

"Your guard is nervous," Jayson said.

"I don't see why," replied Kelvin, joining Jayson on the balcony. "The Agoran spy is in chains. There's no more reason to fear."

"Eliha is no spy. He acted on his own. You assume he killed Fredric, and there are those who would prefer you to believe it."

"He killed two of my men. It stands to reason he killed Fredric and also plotted against me. That is why he will be executed."

"And what about the girl? Will you execute her as well?"

Kelvin leaned forward, pressing both palms against the stone rail of the balcony. A cold wind blew from the north, carrying with it the scent of the sea. Jayson sensed the rising tension within his son. It was clear to him that the responsibilities of ruling Dokur were a heavy burden to bear, perhaps too heavy for an inexperienced farm boy like Kelvin. But what was also clear was that Kelvin was determined to fulfill Fredric's wishes to the best of his ability. Kelvin would never cower before an enemy, and he would never accept defeat. For that, Jayson was proud to call him his son.

"You knew her once," said Kelvin after a thoughtful pause.

"Kaië was a small child when I first met her," answered Jayson. "Her mother was Ivanore's lady-in-waiting, but she died, and Kaië was orphaned."

"Marcus told me you and Ivanore took her in."

"We did. She was like a daughter to us. When you were born, she was as doting as a sister could be. She used to cradle you in her arms like a little doll and sing to you."

"Do you think she remembers?"

Jayson turned from the rail and stepped into the room. The woven floor mat cushioned his steps, and he imagined he could sleep quite soundly on it, much like sleeping on a soft pile of leaves in the forest—something he had done countless times. Kelvin followed him into the room and shut the panel to the balcony, turning the lock.

"You know as well as I do that Kaië is innocent," said Jayson. "It is wrong to keep her imprisoned."

"I would love nothing more than to free her, but I've given Chancellor Prost power over this case. I cannot overstep—"

"By the gods, you cannot let that man destroy her!"

"Then what do you suggest I do?" Kelvin's tone was angry, desperate.

Jayson drew close to Kelvin and lowered his voice. The guard still stood outside the door, and Jayson trusted no one. "Listen to me," he said. "Eliha did not murder Fredric. I believe the real killer will be found in your closest circle."

Kelvin stepped back horrified. "Careful," he said. "If you speak of Prost, he is my most trusted counselor—my grandfather's, as well."

"All the more reason to suspect him."

"Impossible."

"Why?"

"Because he's been like a father to me."

Jayson scoffed. "A father—"

"The father I never had before! Now if you don't mind, I've got to get some sleep. You may go."

Jayson nodded stiffly and turned for the door, which opened before he even reached it. The guard had been listening, but how much had he heard?

"I had hoped you and I could spend more time together," Jayson said, pausing at the door. "Zyll was my father, your grandfather. He was killed yesterday, and yet you've said nothing about him. Not a word."

"I hardly knew him."

"You hardly knew Fredric, either. Zyll left much greater shoes to fill than those of a king. It wasn't Eliha or Kaië who killed him. Your throne and your life will not be safe until the true murderer is found."

Jayson glared at the guard as he passed by. Then he paused and sniffed at him. "You need a bath," he said and then strode down the hall and out of the Fortress, glad to leave it all behind him.

Fifty-nine

The night was clear and very, very cold. Marcus and the others huddled beneath their blankets, trying unsuccessfully to stay warm. Marcus imagined they would all be much better off sleeping beside each other to share body heat, but after what happened with Bryn earlier that evening, he dared not suggest it. Lael and Bryn had completely ignored him all through dinner. By the time they were ready to sleep, Marcus felt like an outcast.

As the hours wore on and the temperature continued to drop, Marcus finally got up enough courage to scoot up next to Clovis.

"I'm freezing," he whispered, hoping Clovis would suggest what he couldn't. Clovis did not respond but lay perfectly still.

"Clovis, I know you're still awake, so you might as well answer me."

"How did you know I wasn't asleep?"

"You're not snoring yet."

"I don't snore."

"Yes, you do. Aren't you cold?"

"My fingers and toes are completely numb."

"Mine, too. Well?"

"Well what?"

"Well, don't you think we should do something to get warmer?"

"You could use magic and warm the air around us."

"You know I can't use magic."

"Can't or won't?"

The question pricked Marcus as sure as a briar or a blade. "If I did use magic, it could trigger another attack," he said. "It would take days to recover."

"Right," said Clovis, sounding only partially convinced. "Well, I guess we could share blankets."

"Great idea!"

Marcus shuffled as close to Clovis as he could. They lay back to back beneath both their blankets. Having turned to his other side, Marcus could see Lael and Bryn huddling together nearby.

"I know you're both still angry at me," he said aloud to them, "but if you want to get warm, you're welcome to join us."

Bryn's response was to turn up his nose and curl into an even tighter ball beside Lael. Lael pretended she hadn't heard Marcus at all.

Sixty

When morning finally arrived, Marcus was glad for the sun's first warming rays eroding the thin layer of frost that had dusted them during the night. Marcus had eventually fallen asleep—exactly when, he wasn't quite sure—and waking now, he was surprised at how toasty he felt. Then he realized why. Clovis lay snoring contentedly to one side of him, and on his other side lay Lael and Bryn pressed up tightly against him. He grinned to himself as he lay quietly for a while longer, allowing everyone additional time to enjoy their sleep. Finally, once the sun was fully visible above the trees, Bryn stirred and stretched. Mumbling something about breakfast, he rolled over to face Marcus.

Bryn's face was within inches of Marcus's when he

opened his eyes with a yawn. Suddenly he leapt to his feet, taking the thick pile of blankets with him.

"Bryn," Lael moaned, reaching blindly for a blanket that was no longer there. "Bryn, I'm cold!"

Bryn dropped the crumpled blankets on top of Lael, leaving Marcus and Clovis completely uncovered. Clovis snored on.

"Lael's not the only one who's cold," said Marcus, but the scowl on Bryn's face told Marcus that the oversight had been on purpose. Marcus got up and began gathering wood for a fire. Rylan approached and dropped a heavy bundle of dry twigs at Marcus's feet.

"That should be enough to get started," he said and then brandished a shiny dagger in the morning sunlight. "I'll be back shortly with breakfast." Then Rylan disappeared again through the trees.

Marcus grumbled under his breath as he arranged the twigs into a tidy pile and struck his knife against a stone to light it. After several tries, the sparks finally ignited the thinnest of the tinder, which Marcus carefully nursed to a steady flame. Soon the fire was large enough to add some branches from a nearby dead tree. The heat from the fire warmed the immediate area. Lael came near, and Clovis stirred from sleep to join them. Even Bryn edged close enough to feel the warmth. Using a broken branch, Marcus prepared a spit to roast whatever Rylan would bring back to eat.

Behind the fire, the pile of abandoned blankets stirred. Clovis and Lael froze, as a sharp, angry voice shouted from beneath the moving heap. "Would—someone—get—this—OFF—me!"

Marcus reached over and snatched the blanket away, revealing a fumbling black crow beneath.

"So much for sleeping in!" said Xerxes, stretching out his wings.

"What is that?" asked Clovis, his mouth gaping open in surprise.

"A talking crow?" added Lael.

Bryn, who sat beside her, stared curiously at the bird, but said nothing.

"This is Xerxes," Marcus said.

There was a moment of silence before Clovis responded. "Xerxes. You mean Zyll's walking stick, Xerxes? I wondered where it had gone to."

Xerxes rolled his eyes in annoyance. "Don't sit there gawking—" His voice stopped short. He blinked hard. "You heard me?" he asked. Then he turned to Marcus. "They heard me! Only you and Zyll ever have before."

"We heard you, all right," said Lael, "though how, I have no idea. Then again, after seeing grocs, disappearing cave walls, and miraculous healings, a talking bird shouldn't surprise me."

While Marcus explained Zyll's spell on the walking stick and Xerxes' transformation, Rylan returned with three large quail, which he quietly plucked and skewered while Marcus spoke.

"When Xerxes was a walking stick, only Zyll and I could hear him speak," said Marcus, finishing his story, "but it seems now anyone can hear him."

"Well, I guess having a talking bird around could come in handy," said Clovis.

Lael shook her head. "All this talk about magic spells is more than I can ever hope to understand."

Having grown bored with the conversation, Xerxes flew off in search of his own meal. Rylan attended to the quail, setting them over the flame to cook. He didn't give any of them so much as a glance. Marcus had learned by now that it was pointless to try to start a conversation with their guide. Rylan only spoke when he wanted to speak, and that was rare. Several minutes passed in uncomfortable silence, when Clovis suddenly spoke.

"Marcus, remember the time we sneaked out to the grain mill?" he asked.

"And cut holes in the bottoms of all the sacks?" Marcus laughed at the memory. "I had never heard half the words that came out of Old Man Peeder's mouth that day. We would have gotten away with it, too, if you hadn't burst out laughing."

"He would have found out, anyway. You felt so guilty about it, I had to hold you down behind the woodpile to keep you from confessing!"

"Me confess?" replied Marcus with mock offense. "I'm not the one who borrowed Mrs. Archer's best broom from her back porch to play sword fight with and then broke it!"

"But I had to replace it. Otherwise it would've been stealing."

"Guess you didn't steal that loaf of lemon bread from her windowsill, either."

"I was six years old!"

The two boys laughed and laughed until they nearly forgot about the troubles they'd left behind in Dokur. Marcus could almost forget, for just a few moments, the pain of losing Zyll and of leaving Kaië alone in prison. But a few moments were all he could spare.

"You've been a good friend," Marcus said once their laughter had died down. "I think you've been the best friend I could ever hope to have."

"Well, we weren't always friends," Clovis reminded him. "I mean, we were friends when we were kids, but then we grew apart for a while. You were busy with your apprenticeship, I guess. That day when we left on our quest, I wasn't so sure you wanted me to come with you at all, like I'd hold you back or get in your way. But even if you did think that, you let me come, anyway. I never thanked you for that."

"You don't have to thank me, Clovis."

"But I do. Because of you I fulfilled the quest and gained the respect of my father. I guess that's why it feels so wrong to go back to Quendel now, abandoning you when you need me most."

The quail on the spit sizzled and popped as the skin turned to a deep golden crust. Rylan lifted the spit from the two supports that held it and tested the meat with the tip of his knife. Clear juices bubbled from the punctures and dripped onto the dirt below. The smell of it made Marcus's mouth water.

"Done," said Rylan, slicing his knife down the center of the first bird and separating it into two equal halves.

Clovis was ready with his plate in hand. Marcus dug through his pack for his while Rylan served Lael and Bryn. Marcus thanked Rylan when he received his portion and then carefully peeled a piece away from the bone. He blew on the morsel until it was just cool enough to eat and popped it into his mouth. The meat tasted as good as it smelled. Still, he couldn't help but feel resentful toward Rylan, but why? Was it that Rylan had gathered wood and hunted without being asked? Or was it that Rylan seemed to be so skillful at everything he did, while Marcus still fumbled at even the simplest task?

Marcus glanced across the flames to where Lael nibbled at a wing. Every now and then she dabbed at the corners of her mouth with a knuckle on her left hand, which she somehow managed not to get greasy from the meat. It was the way she held it, Marcus realized, balanced between the thumb and first finger of her right hand and just one finger-tip from her left hand. He tried to think of a word to describe it, how it was different than Rylan or Clovis or himself—all of whom grasped their meat freely with both hands, wiping them clean on their trouser legs. No, Lael was different. She was . . . what was the word? *Feminine.*

Rylan sat beside Lael. He finished off his meal and tossed the remains into the fire. The flames hissed. Then Rylan turned to Lael and spoke. His lips moved, forming words, though his voice was too quiet for Marcus to hear, and Lael was looking at him, listening—and she was smiling.

Marcus stopped chewing. He watched the exchange between Rylan and Lael and felt annoyed at not knowing what was being said. Then for some strange reason, he was angry enough to want to throw his plate at Rylan. But he held tight to it instead, gripping it until his knuckles ached.

Rylan's lips moved again, and Lael laughed. Marcus heard her laughter even over the sound of the fire. It was a light laugh, airy and gentle. The sound of it made Marcus's skin tingle. And then suddenly Lael turned and looked at him—at *him*! And she was still smiling. Marcus's heart sped up as if he had just been caught stealing red-handed. He quickly looked away, hoping she hadn't realized he'd been watching her. But of course she had realized it. Why else would she have looked at him?

Marcus stared at the plate in his hand, his food growing cold. He swallowed hard, and his mouth went dry. She had smiled at him. Yes, she was smiling at Rylan and laughing when he spoke to her, but in that brief moment when she turned to look at Marcus, she was *still* smiling. And somehow Marcus knew *that* smile was meant just for him.

Sixty-one

The trees of the sparse forest north of Lake Olsnar were bare this time of year, offering no shade or protection from the sun overhead. Despite the cool air, Marcus felt the heat of it on his skin, and after a long day of walking in it, he was more than a little uncomfortable from mild sunburn.

The day had also been uncomfortable because of the continued silence from Lael, Bryn, and Rylan. Even Clovis stopped talking after the first hour. Only Xerxes provided some company, perching on Marcus's shoulder from time to time to rest and making disagreeable comments about the dull scenery or the slow pace of the journey. The rest of the time, Xerxes flew overhead or hopped along the ground, scavenging for food.

As they emerged from the trees, a dirt lane lay before them, leading toward the mountains. An hour more along this road would take them to Noam, the village near the mouth of Vrystal Canyon, the only path through the Jeweled Mountains and to Quendel on the other side. The plan was for Clovis to hire a guide there to lead him safely through the canyon and back to Quendel. Marcus had made him swear not to go alone. The grocs that had taken them earlier could still cause trouble, but the Noamish people were known for their skillful hunting of grocs and would provide plenty of protection. Once through the canyon, the journey home to Quendel would take less than two days.

Marcus would not be going to Noam, however, nor would he be following the road. Voltana lay in the northern part of the island, which meant it was time they parted ways. Marcus had originally planned to convince Lael to go with Clovis but had since changed his mind. First, Marcus doubted Lael could be convinced to do anything she didn't want to do. And second, he wasn't so sure anymore that he wanted her to leave.

A pleasant breeze blew. Bits of golden fluff floated weightlessly in the air, changing course at whim. Marcus picked some out of his hair and let it go into a passing air current.

"The last of the willowstalks have shed their seeds," he said. "Winter's coming. It will snow any day now."

Clovis, his bow clasped in his hand, stood with his back to Marcus, studying the landscape. The breeze tousled his hair.

"I can still come with you," he said, turning to face Marcus. "My father would understand."

"Clovis, you know as well as I do that in another week or two the canyon will become blocked with ice and snow. You wouldn't be able to return home until it melts in the spring. Your father is expecting you. He needs you."

"But you need me, too."

Bryn, who had been several yards behind Marcus and Clovis, suddenly sprinted forward through the seed-filled air. Arms raised, he laughed with delight. He ran between Marcus and Clovis into an open field on the opposite side of the road. Lael called to him to be careful. Rylan looked on disapprovingly.

"I do need you," said Marcus, watching the whole scene with amusement. "You're my best friend, and I'll miss you. But you have responsibilities to attend to at home, and I have mine. I will return to Quendel as soon as I can. In the meantime, please take care of Agnes and my cottage for me."

Clovis's head hung low. Marcus couldn't be sure he wasn't crying. But after a few minutes, he lifted his head, dried his eyes with his sleeve, and set his sights toward the mountains.

"You'll come back soon? Before planting season?" Clovis asked.

"I will," promised Marcus.

"And you won't get into any trouble?"

Marcus laughed. "I'm going to a place where humans rarely go to search for what, I have no idea, and someone wants me dead. What more trouble could I get into?"

The two friends looked at each other. Marcus could see the concern in Clovis's face. They had been through a lot together the past few months, and Marcus wondered if he had made the right decision to send Clovis home.

Clovis wrapped his arms around Marcus in a firm but brief embrace. Then he turned back to the road. "Goodbye, Bryn, Lael," he said, waving. Bryn waved back with both arms. Lael ran up to embrace him and kissed his cheek.

"Be safe," she said, "and may the gods watch over you, Clovis Dungham."

Marcus and Lael stood together for a long time and watched Clovis walk down the dirt road. They stood there until he finally disappeared around a bend and over a grassy knoll. Neither of them spoke, but somehow Marcus knew their thoughts were the same. They would miss him, and though Rylan was with them, they did not know him well enough to trust him fully. For the rest of their journey, Bryn, Lael, and Marcus would have only each other to rely on for protection.

Sixty-two

Once they had said their goodbyes to Clovis, Rylan led them off the main road toward Voltana. They traveled across the center of Imaness for two days, saying little to each other. When the first snowflakes began to fall, Marcus was grateful Mrs. Peagry had packed a cloak for each of them. Still, he hoped they'd arrive at their destination soon and be able to rent a room in a warm tavern with a real bed.

On the third day, the ground, forested by barren trees, began to slope upward. As they went over a crest, the landscape changed suddenly. Marcus and company stopped at the top of the hill and gazed down onto the panorama before them. The rocky terrain was gray and bleak, void of life.

Marcus squatted and picked up a jagged rock, rolling it around in his palm. Then he handed it to Rylan.

"It's warm," Rylan said. "We're getting close." He threw the rock as far as he could. The stone landed with a hollow *clack*.

Bryn tugged on Lael's sleeve. "I'm scared," he whispered. Lael wrapped her arm around his shoulders.

"What are you talking about, Bryn?" said Marcus. He was about fed up with Bryn's child act. "What could a groc possibly be afraid of?"

Bryn sulked like a scolded child, his lower lip quivering.

Lael grabbed Marcus's arm and led him out of earshot of the others. "What is the *matter* with you, Marcus?" she said. "Hurting Bryn's feelings at the lake wasn't enough for you, is that it? Or are you determined to make him miserable the entire trip?"

Marcus pulled his arm free and rubbed it with his other hand. Lael had a strong grip. He was sure he'd get a bruise.

"You know I didn't mean anything by it," he said.

"I don't know it, Marcus. Bryn didn't have to come on this journey. He didn't have to rescue us from the grocs. And you yourself have told me more than once how Bryn risked his life to protect you from Fredric's guards. So what is it costing you, really, if Bryn wants to act human?"

Lael turned heel and returned to Bryn, kneeling beside him and drying his tears. Marcus watched the tenderness with which Lael touched Bryn's pink cheeks and the gentle look in her eyes as she spoke to him. It occurred to Marcus that this was a side of Lael he had not known before. In Quendel he had only known Lael as the girl who could fight better and run faster than all the boys—and had resented her for it. But now seeing the compassion she showed to Bryn, his resentment faded.

"Down there," called Rylan, pointing to a dark spot at the base of a distant mountain. Marcus walked over to where the other three stood and saw they were at the top of a steep, rocky slope leading to a wide, barren valley dotted with steaming vents and hot water geysers.

"We should reach Voltana by nightfall," Rylan added. "But be careful. If you stray from the path, you will get burned."

The four of them started down the slope toward the valley below. Their feet sent a waterfall of pebbles and sand down the hill. Marcus slipped twice as he struggled to find solid footing. Behind him Rylan and Lael stepped sideways, slipping and sliding, as well. But it was Bryn who lost his balance completely and slid on his backside past Marcus.

"Bryn!" shouted Marcus. He shot out his hand, attempting to stop Bryn's descent, missing him by mere inches. Bryn rocketed down the hill, screaming all the way. Lael tried to go after him, but Rylan grabbed her by the arm and held her back.

"No point in all of us falling," he said.

Marcus scowled at the comment, but he knew Rylan was right. So he maneuvered down the hill as quickly as he could without endangering himself. Bryn had gone from sight, but of more concern was that they could no longer hear him screaming.

"Bryn!" Marcus and Lael kept calling his name as they neared the bottom of the hill. Every inch they traveled sent more gravel raining down. When they finally reached level ground, they searched frantically for the boy. Xerxes circled high overhead. After a few eternal minutes, he swooped down past Marcus.

"There!" he called, "beside that larger stone!"

Marcus followed Xerxes to the spot. At first he could not see anything, but then he spotted Bryn's thin hand and arm jutting out from a pile of rubble.

Sixty-three

He's here!" Marcus shouted. Lael was beside him in an instant, scooping away the hot debris with her hands. She was in tears as she dug. Marcus dropped to his knees and used his arms to push the rubble away. Soon Bryn lay before them, his eyes closed, his face and arms covered with bloody scratches.

Xerxes perched on the large sandstone boulder nearby. He wagged his beak from side to side, repeating "Poor, poor thing" over and over.

"Is he breathing?" asked Lael.

Marcus held his ear to Bryn's mouth. "Yes, he's breathing!" He took his water skin from his belt and poured some into his hand, using it to wipe away the layer of dust from Bryn's face.

"You're all right. Just open your eyes," said Marcus. To his relief, Bryn moaned softly.

Lael slipped her arm beneath Bryn's head, cradling him gently. "Bryn, please open your eyes."

Bryn's eyelids twitched, and then one lid lifted. Bryn stared up at Lael with one big, brown eye.

"You're so dirty," he said and then opened his other eye. Lael wiped her tears with the back of her hand, though all she managed to do was smear wet dust across her face.

"You're pretty dirty yourself," she said, laughing. She helped him up, but when he tried to stand, he cried out in pain.

"What is it?" asked Marcus.

"My leg hurts," said Bryn.

Lael felt along his left leg. "It's not broken, but he's twisted his ankle. He can't walk like this, Marcus. What should we do?"

Rylan stepped forward and scooped up Bryn in his arms. Bryn whimpered.

"We continue on," said Rylan and started walking. Then he paused, looking back. "Are you two coming?"

Lael touched Marcus's arm. "Come on, Marcus," she said and then hurried to catch up with Rylan.

For a single moment, Marcus wanted to turn back. He wanted to go back to Quendel, back to his cottage, back to Agnes and the grazing fields. But he realized if he did go back, the one thing that meant the most to him would not be there. Zyll was gone, so what would be the point of returning home?

Marcus gazed out at the seemingly endless sea of rock and knew he must keep going. He must continue on, no matter what. He owed it to Zyll.

*   *   *

Marcus wasn't exactly sure what he expected Voltana to look like, but certainly not this. For one thing, it was flat, at least mostly flat. The ground was unlike anything he'd ever seen before—hard like rock, but porous with millions of sharp pits and holes. And the edges of it were curved with layer upon layer formed from countless lava spills from the volcanic mountains nearby as well as the steaming vents scattered throughout the area. The actual town of Voltana had been constructed on the flattest area farthest from the central vent that loomed like a deep, black sea. Even when they had shed their traveling cloaks, the heat from it was unbearable, and Marcus's clothing was soaked with perspiration within minutes. From the looks on everyone else's damp faces, he was certain they were as miserable as he. The only one who seemed unfazed by the heat was Rylan.

"So this is it?" asked Xerxes, landing clumsily on the ground at Marcus's feet. "I flew all the way across Imaness for this?"

Marcus held out his arm. Xerxes hopped up.

Lael stepped in front of them both. She pulled at her tunic, trying to cool off. "Where is everyone?"

"Looks abandoned," said Marcus.

"Couldn't imagine why," Xerxes added sarcastically.

Rylan shot them an amused look, and Marcus could almost swear he saw the older boy laugh. Rylan now carried Bryn on his back in a makeshift sling he had fashioned earlier from a blanket. He continued walking without speaking. Lael and Marcus still stood, gazing out over the barren terrain.

"Maybe we should keep moving," said Lael. "We're getting hungry, and by the looks of it, we're not going find anything to eat out here."

Lael started forward, hesitantly, following Rylan and Bryn toward the town. Watching them go, Marcus tried to shake the uneasy feeling that had settled on him.

"What do you think, Xerxes?" he asked. "Any advice for an old friend about to get himself into a heap of trouble?"

"You could go back," answered Xerxes.

"If only I could," Marcus replied. "If only I could."

Sixty-four

s they neared Voltana, Marcus was even more concerned at the stillness. A hot wind blew a fine, black dust through the air. The buildings looked like extensions of the rock itself, jutting out from it in strange formations. The only way Marcus could tell they were structures at all was by the doors and windows carved into them. He continued to search for signs of life and thought he saw movement between two buildings. He squinted in that direction.

"There," he said. "I saw something. Xerxes, could you scout out the area?"

Xerxes rolled his head back, a sign he was not pleased to use his newfound freedom to do Marcus's bidding. Still, he did not refuse.

"Very well," he said and then took off, flapping his wings unsteadily into the air. Marcus watched as Xerxes' black figure traveled in a crooked path over the town. After a few minutes, he returned.

"Quick! Hide!" he shouted. "They're coming!" Then in a burst of speed, the crow flew off in the opposite direction. Marcus scanned the lifeless buildings. What could have frightened Xerxes?

Marcus noticed that Bryn, too, seemed more anxious than usual. Slung across Rylan's back, Bryn stiffened as though sensing danger. His eyes had an aggressive look in them that Marcus hadn't seen in many months, not since Bryn first transformed into a monster and attacked Kelvin in Vrystal Canyon during their quest for the Rock of Ivanore. Marcus glanced at Lael to see what her reaction was to Bryn's strange behavior, but her eyes were fixed on Voltana, as well.

"What is it?" Marcus asked Bryn.

Bryn curled his lips back and growled. "I smell something," he said, "something not human."

Then Marcus saw them and understood why he hadn't noticed them before. Small, not much taller than Bryn in his human form, three of them emerged from between the buildings. Even then it was difficult to distinguish them from the rocks; their deep gray color camouflaged them well. They approached slowly, upright on two oddly bent legs with long, bare toes and sharp, curved claws. Their arms, though shorter, were just as menacing. Each had a broad tail that tapered to a point and swayed back and forth through the air as they walked. As they neared, Marcus could make out the rough, gray scales covering their bodies.

They each wore a sash across one shoulder, one red, the other two blue. From the strange designs embroidered on them, Marcus guessed they stood for each one's position, or job, in the town. The two with blue sashes carried loops of rope in their hands.

The one with the red sash came forward, its gray eye-slits widening with curiosity. It spoke in sharp, quick syllables punctuated with a series of whistles and trills. It was a language Marcus had never heard before. When no one responded, the creature repeated its message more forcefully.

"Rylan, do you have any idea what he's saying?" Marcus asked.

Rylan stepped forward and placed both of his hands in the air, level with his chin, palms out. The gesture seemed to put the creature at ease. It set down its tail and leaned back on it, resting.

"You can relax," said Rylan. "These are the Pey Wey, native inhabitants of Voltana, but they do speak our language—when they want to. The one in red is what you might call the administrator. Pey Weys are generally wary of outside visitors, but my father comes here every few months to trade. I've come with him a few times."

He faced the administrator, his hands still in position. "My name is Rylan, son of Brommel, the trader. We've come to discuss—"

"What you trade?" The administrator scowled at the visitors, its lipless mouth pinched, nostrils flared in obvious contempt. Behind him, Marcus saw Xerxes alighting on the roof of one of the nearby buildings. The crow proceeded to preen his feathers, casting an occasional glance at the proceedings below.

"Oh no," said Rylan. "I haven't come to trade today. My father will come soon, though, with fresh . . . uh, *goods.* These are my friends."

Ignoring Rylan's response, the administrator stepped toward Lael and looked her over from head to toe. Marcus noticed that, for the first time since they'd left Dokur, Rylan looked nervous.

"Excuse me . . . er," Rylan started.

"Tark," said the Pey Wey as he continued to examine Lael.

"Rylan, what is he doing?" asked Lael nervously, not taking her eyes off the Pey Wey. Rylan continued addressing Tark instead.

"Yes, Tark. Well, you see, she isn't why we've come. She's with me."

Rylan took Lael's arm and pulled her close to him.

"What you trade?" insisted Tark again.

"No trade," said Rylan. He pointed at Marcus. "That one is here to find someone, to obtain information. Marcus, show him the key."

Tark's eyes were on him now. Marcus pulled Zyll's key from his pouch and held it up for Tark to see. Tark came closer and sniffed at it. He tried to take it from Marcus, but Marcus held it against his chest.

"Trade this?" said Tark, exasperated. "This worth nothing. But *boy* . . . "

Rylan spoke again in a hurried tone. "He seeks the key's maker, a locksmith or metal smith, perhaps."

Tark looked again at Marcus, his eye slits narrowing to thin, black lines. One of the Pey Weys behind him stretched the rope taut between his hands. He started walking slowly around to Marcus's left. Marcus tried to keep him in view, but he couldn't face Tark and watch the other one, as well. He decided to focus on Tark.

"Why you want lockmaker?" said Tark angrily. "You lockmaker's friend?"

"I don't really know, actually," answered Marcus. "I was hoping I could meet him. I want to ask him some questions."

"No questions!" shouted Tark. "Only trade!"

"What is this all about, Rylan?" asked Lael. "What's this about trading?"

Rylan, confidant Rylan, actually hesitated. His eyes shifted nervously from Lael to the Pey Wey administrator and back again. "He wants you," he explained.

"Me?" Lael gave a half laugh, but Rylan's expression was serious. "What for?"

"He thinks I'm here to sell your contract."

A change came over Lael's face as the meaning of his words sank in. In that moment, Marcus saw the true depth of the pain she carried inside of her.

"You're a slave trader?" Lael could hardly get the words out.

Rylan shook his head. "Not slaves," he said, "*dents.* Slavery is against the law. People who can't pay their debts sign contracts to work them off instead. It's voluntary. My father collects the contracts and sells them to the highest bidder."

"Your father, Brommel, is a collector?"

Lael's face went deathly pale, and Marcus was afraid she might faint. He knew that her mother had been taken by a debt collector years before, never to return.

"Lael, are you all right?" he asked her.

She seemed to be in a daze. "The woman in the marketplace told me Brommel could help me, but I didn't realize. . ." Her voice faded as she became lost in thought. Then all of sudden, Lael turned her eyes toward him, fear on her face.

"Marcus! Behind you!"

But it was too late. Before he could react, the rope slipped over his head and tightened against his arms and chest. In the next moment, his ankles were bound. He fell forward face-first on the hot ground. His vision blurred, but he saw the other Pey Weys wrenching the kicking-and-screaming Bryn from Rylan's back. At first, Lael tried to fight off the Pey Wey, but Rylan grabbed her arms and held her back.

At the same time, Xerxes swooped down from the building roof, cawing angrily as he beat his wings at the Pey Wey guards' heads. The guards swung their stubby arms at him in annoyance. One struck the bird, and Xerxes flew off again, his left wing drooping in pain.

"Xerxes!" Marcus shouted. He tried to free himself from his bonds, but the more he struggled, the more the ropes cut into his skin.

As the guards dragged Marcus and Bryn away, Marcus saw Rylan speaking heatedly with the administrator. Lael struggled in his grip, but Rylan held her tight and would not let her go. Had Rylan betrayed them? The thought made Marcus sick. He felt sicker still thinking that, if Clovis had been here with his menacing crossbow, the Pey Weys may not have had the courage to attack them. But Marcus couldn't worry about that now. He had to figure out how to get himself and Bryn free.

Sixty-five

Jayson waited as the jailer unlocked Kaië's prison cell. The squeaky door emitted a loud, grating sound as it opened. Kaië sat on the floor in the far corner, her arms wrapped around her knees. A tin plate sat beside her. The bread on it had gone stale and the fruit brown. A rat scurried across the stone floor to taste the fruit. Snatching it between its teeth, it fled back into the shadows.

Kaië looked up as Jayson entered. A faint smile appeared on her dry lips. "Is it time?" she asked. "Have you come to say goodbye?"

Jayson knelt beside Kaië and wrapped his arms around her. She buried her face in his shoulder as tears sprung from her eyes. She sobbed openly without shame.

"Hush," Jayson whispered, stroking her hair. "I have

not come for goodbyes. We still have time. I will do what I can to see that you are freed. Are you well?"

Kaië's sobs calmed a little. "As well as can be expected, I suppose."

Jayson nodded at the plate on the floor. "You're not eating."

"I haven't got any appetite."

Jayson went back to the door and rapped on it twice. When the guard came, he said, "Bring a fresh plate of food for the prisoner."

The new plate appeared a few minutes later, handed through the door by the guard. When the door was again shut, Jayson returned to Kaië. He held out the fresh slice of bread. "It will do no good if you're too weak to defend yourself in court."

Kaië accepted the bread from Jayson and took a bite. As he watched her, Jayson tried to restrain the anger and frustration that had been building up inside of him the past few days. He wanted to tear down these walls with his bare hands and take Kaië away.

"You shouldn't be here," said Jayson. "Not you, Kaië. Not you." He clenched his fist and pounded it against the wall. "Everyone I've ever loved has been taken from me," he continued softly. "My father, Zyll, abandoned me and my mother because the law said it was wrong for them to be together. He left to protect us, but we suffered, any- way. My people were banished from their lands, and my mother died in a swamp. Then my son was torn from my arms and kept from me for fifteen years. Another son I didn't even know about followed. And Ivanore. Oh, Ivanore." He turned to face Kaië. Her shoulders hunched as if she carried a heavy weight.

"I lost her, too," she said, crying again.

Jayson placed his hands on Kaië's cheeks. "Never again," he told her, brushing a tear away with his thumb. "You will never lose anyone again, Kaië. I swear it."

He kissed the top of her head and then reached for the plate. He picked up another slice of bread and held it out to her. Kaië took it and smiled at him gratefully.

The door to the cell opened abruptly as the head guard stepped in. "Chancellor Prost wants to see you," he told Jayson.

Jayson was suspicious of any reason Prost would have for wanting to speak to him. He also wished to stay close to Kaië, at least as close as the law regarding visitors would allow. He might not be able to stay with her in her cell, but he would not leave the Fortress again until her trial. He would keep his word to her and to Marcus. He would watch over her and see to it that she got a fair and honest trial, but in truth, with Prost in charge, there was no telling how much control he had over Kaië's fate.

"What does he want?" asked Jayson, placing a hand on Kaië's shoulder to assure her that he would not be far away.

"I was told to take you immediately to the great room on the second floor and to hurry," said the guard. "It seems you have a visitor."

Sixty-six

Are you sure you haven't been bribed? All this luxury. If you'd been bribed, I couldn't really blame you."

Nathar turned as Jayson entered the great room flanked by two armed guards. Jayson's Agoran friend had traveled all the way from Taktani, the northern swamplands where the Agorans resided. Jayson approached him with open arms. They embraced and laughed.

"This really is amazing," said Nathar, gesturing with his arms to take in the whole room. "Velvet upholstery, gilded picture frames, silk curtains. So this is what Fredric gained from all that Agoran blood? And I thought we had it good back in our grass huts and mosquito-infested swamps."

It was clear to Jayson that though Nathar was pleased
to see him, he was far from pleased at finding him in the
Fortress surrounded by luxury.

"I've been staying in town," said Jayson. "I'm here
visiting a friend."

"Really? And I thought you came to Dokur to demand
our new king give us our land or we'd start a war. Well,
our people are waiting, Jayson. The Agorans want an
answer."

"Don't the elders trust me?"

"The elders know Kelvin is your son but that you may
not have as much influence over him as that sly chancellor
of his."

"Prost. You've met with him already, have you?"

"I called on him, but you arrived instead. It is clear
that neither he nor Kelvin has any intention of honoring
Fredric's decree. We are left with no choice but to take
what is rightfully ours."

"If you would only give me a little more time—"

"Time is the one thing I cannot give. Come," said
Nathar, stepping to the window. Jayson joined him, and
together they gazed down on the outer court of the
Fortress. Beyond it lay the edge of the plateau and the
road leading down to the flat plains and sparse forests of
Imaness's interior. The scene before them was dark except
for the stars—not the stars in the sky, but the stars in the
land below, hundreds of sparkling lights in the darkness.

"Do you see them?" asked Nathar. "Do you see the
torches? Our people have already come from Taktani,

Jayson. They wait for your command either to settle the lands that are rightfully ours or to attack this city."

Jayson looked out over the sea of lights in horror. The Agorans, who had fought so valiantly just months earlier to defend this very city from invasion, were now the invaders. He thought of the people of Dokur settling into their beds, completely unprepared for a surprise attack. He had seen the Agorans in battle and knew there would be no mercy for their enemy. The thought of it made Jayson shudder.

"Your problem is not with the people of Dokur. They are innocent. The decision was Kelvin's. Surely you wouldn't punish the people for their king's wrongdoing?"

"What is a king without his people?" replied Nathar. "Take away the people, the king is no longer a king! We will take everything from him, just as everything was once taken from us."

Had he not tried hard enough to convince Kelvin? wondered Jayson. Had he again failed the Agorans? What was it Nathar said—that the Agorans waited for his command? For *Jayson's* command. They expected Jayson to lead them, and he would never lead them to battle again. Not against an innocent people. He had to find some way to delay what would surely become a massacre.

"I am to meet with Kelvin soon to discuss the decree," Jayson began, hoping his lie was convincing. "He plans to present an offer to the Agorans."

Nathar glared at Jayson suspiciously. "We want what Fredric promised. No less."

"He understands that, but he is preparing for war and has had to consider his options. He will present a fair offer, I am certain."

"When? The Agorans have waited long enough!"

"Just a few days more," said Jayson. "I will hear from him by week's end. In the meantime, tell our people to be patient. As soon as I speak to Kelvin, I will deliver the message to them myself. Are we agreed?"

Nathar studied Jayson's face for a moment, as though searching for any hint of a lie. Jayson prayed he found none. Finally Nathar extended his hand to Jayson.

"Agreed," he said. "But if Kelvin has not answered us by week's end, then war it will be."

Sixty-seven

Marcus guessed it was late at night by how sleepy he felt, but he could not find a position comfortable enough to fall asleep. He and Bryn had been thrown into a holding cell with three irregular stone walls and a panel of metal grating. It reeked of mildew and urine. Marcus covered his nose with his sleeve to keep out the smell but with little success. A pool of stagnant water occupied one corner, with an empty wooden bucket in the other. From the deep brown stains on it, Marcus guessed the bucket was for their personal use, and the thought of it made him want to retch.

Bryn lay curled up on the floor. He had been asleep for hours. Marcus had tried to sleep sitting with his back against the wall and his head resting on his knees, but still he was awake. The jingle of keys signaled the approach of the prison guard. The guard stopped in front of Marcus's cell and grunted some unintelligible sounds. When Marcus did not respond, the guard unlocked the gate and motioned for him to step out. Marcus shook Bryn awake.

"What is it?" asked a bleary-eyed Bryn. Then seeing the guard and the open cell door, he asked, "Has Lael come for us?"

"I don't know," replied Marcus. "How is your leg?"

Holding onto Marcus's arm, Bryn stood up. "A little sore," he said, "but better."

"Can you walk?"

"I think so, why?"

Marcus pointed to the angry guard waiting by the door and the sharp lance in his hand. "I think he wants us to come with him."

They followed the guard out of the cell and down a passageway. Once outside, they were met by two more guards, who bound their hands in front of them with cords. It was late at night, and a line of torches lit a path leading away from town. Marcus glanced around, hoping to see Lael or even Rylan nearby, but there were only the three guards. When one of them shoved Marcus roughly forward, he knew he was in trouble.

"Where are they taking us?" asked Bryn, stumbling along behind Marcus.

"I have no idea."

"What will they do to us?"

"I don't know, Bryn."

They followed the torches across uneven, barren rock until they reached a large structure made of roughly hewn stone. Marcus scanned the darkness for signs of Xerxes, hoping whatever injury he had sustained was not serious, but the crow was nowhere to be found. The guards led Marcus and Bryn through a narrow gap in the structure's side, and they soon found themselves in a circular arena surrounded by a high, sloping wall. More torches lined the edge of the arena, and a hundred or more Pey Weys all sat along the slope. When Marcus and Bryn appeared, the audience cheered.

"Great," said Marcus, "looks like we're tonight's entertainment."

The guards led them to two wooden poles that stood upright from the arena floor. On each one were several metal hooks placed at various heights. The guards grabbed Bryn's hands, still bound, and slipped them over a hook placed high enough above his head that he could not pull himself free. They did the same to Marcus on the second pole. Then the guards exited the way they came, leaving Bryn and Marcus alone to face the jeering crowd.

"Bryn," said Marcus after a few failed attempts to pull his hands free, "now might be a good time to show these people what you really are."

To Marcus's surprise, Bryn cast him a spiteful look. "And what am I *really?*"

"Please, Bryn. This isn't time to hold a grudge. You know I didn't mean anything by what I said the other day. It's just that Lael keeps treating you like—"

"Like a little boy?"

"Exactly! But we both know you could change right now and get us out of here. That would really give these lizards a show, wouldn't it?"

"I'd rather die a human than kill as a groc," Bryn answered, shouting above the roar of the crowd, which had gotten louder. "What about you? Why don't you use your magic to free us?"

Marcus felt his face grow red. "You know why."

"You made a wall of solid rock disappear! Why don't you break these cords or use an earthquake to scare the guards?"

"Because I'm afraid."

"What?" asked Bryn.

"Because I'm afraid!" Marcus shouted. "I'm afraid of what magic does to me! It takes something from me. The pain is unbearable! I can't—*I won't*—go through that again!"

Bryn looked at Marcus, and Marcus thought he saw something different in his eyes, something like understanding.

"Then I guess we'll just have to escape the way any ordinary human would," said Bryn, "with patience, cunning, and luck."

"There's one thing you're forgetting," said Marcus.

"What's that?"

"For ordinary humans, sometimes luck runs out."

Sixty-eight

In the center of the arena was a large pit. At first, the cheering of the crowd drowned out the sound that came from it, the slow *thump! thump! thump!* of something climbing its way up from the depths. As the thumping grew louder, the Pey Weys went silent. The silence was suddenly broken by several earsplitting screeches. The Pey Weys on the slopes held on to each other in what looked to Marcus like fear and anticipation.

The screeching resonated against the stone walls of the arena. Suddenly, the crowd of Pey Weys broke into raucous applause and began to chant, "Rok! Rok! Rok! Rok!"

Marcus's breath froze in his lungs as he waited for whatever was in the pit to emerge. Slowly, a set of three huge claws slipped over the rim of the pit, followed by a

matching set on the opposite side. The creature used them
to pull its massive body up into the arena. As large as
Zyll's cottage in Quendel, its broad, muscular body was
covered with thick, golden fur. It whipped its heavy tail
back and forth and flapped two gigantic birds' wings,
causing a steady, surging flow of hot wind. On its feath-
ered head was a sharp, curved beak large enough to bite a
full-grown man in two.

Marcus gazed in fear and awe at the creature. He had
never seen a real gryphon before. So few people had that
many believed they weren't real at all. Yet here was proof
they did indeed exist. Despite the immediate danger he
was in, Marcus couldn't help but think the creature magnificent to behold.

Beside him, Bryn burst into tears as he jerked desperately at his bonds. "Marcus!" he cried. "Please free us!"

The gryphon's fathomless, black eyes focused on the
squirming boy.

"Bryn, hold still!" said Marcus. "You're drawing its
attention."

But Bryn only cried louder and twisted violently,
attempting to pull himself free.

As the creature lunged forward, its beak and fore claws
extended for the kill, Marcus realized that Bryn would
stay true to his word: he would die as a human.

"Stop!" shouted Marcus, a mass of fear and fury
exploding inside of him. At that moment, an odd sensation
rippled up his arms and burst out of his hands. The Rok
reared back on its hind legs, its head twisting awkwardly

and its wings flapping as if some invisible force had struck it. Whatever went through Marcus had felt solid enough, yet the magic could not be seen with his eyes.

The audience of Pey Weys went silent. The creature dropped its forelegs back to the ground and shook its head, dazed.

Bryn looked at Marcus with an awed expression. "What did you do?" he asked. But Marcus couldn't answer him. He had no idea what had happened.

The Pey Weys began to shout again, trying to incite the Rok to attack. It bolted forward a second time but then came to an abrupt stop as if colliding with some invisible barrier. The creature eyed Marcus hesitantly.

"What is it doing?" asked Bryn. "Do you think you scared it?"

"I don't know," answered Marcus.

The Rok took several cautious steps forward until Marcus found himself eye to eye with it. The creature's breath felt hot and moist on his skin. Being so close, Marcus could make out every detail of its body—the elegant curve of each feather, the downy tufts of fur, the pointed tips of its claws.

"Look," said Marcus, examining the creature more closely, "its leg is chained. It's a prisoner, just like us."

The Rok did not strain against its bonds, nor did it attempt another attack. Instead it blinked at Marcus while turning its head from side to side as if it were curious about him. Then Marcus realized its gaze was focused entirely on his chest. It was the amulet that held its attention, the amulet he had purchased from the woman his first day in Dokur.

"It's a gryphon," said Marcus excitedly.

"What?" shouted Bryn above the increasingly loud displeasure of the crowd.

"Gryphons are guardians of the Seer! Maybe it recognizes me somehow—or at least it recognizes the amulet."

The crowd was heckling the poor creature now, and several Pey Weys threw garbage and stones at it. The gryphon screeched angrily. Turning its back to Marcus, it spread its massive wings, creating a barrier between the crowd and Marcus.

It's trying to protect me, Marcus realized. It's been a prisoner here for who knows how long, yet it's defending me.

As the crowd became more unruly, Marcus could not bear the thought of the abuse this noble creature had, and would likely continue, to endure. The strange force Marcus felt a few minutes before returned. He closed his eyes and aimed his hands at the chains around the gryphon's legs. He felt the sudden surge of power leave his hands. The crowd gasped.

Marcus opened his eyes in time to see the gryphon rise from the ground, lifted by the swoop of its mighty wings. The chains lay broken in pieces on the ground. The Pey Weys, now stunned and frightened, began running up and over the tops of the walls, scurrying like insects to escape, but the gryphon showed no interest in pursuing them. Instead it turned and lowered its face, a grateful expression in its eyes.

"You don't have to stay," Marcus said to it. "We'll be fine."

The gryphon turned its head as if to express doubt, but Marcus smiled reassuringly. "It's all right," he said, "you can go. You're free."

The gryphon blinked its eyes and nodded its beak to show that it understood. Then it flapped its wings, took to the sky, and was quickly gone.

Sixty-nine

Marcus waited for the pain and exhaustion to hit. Despite his determination not to, he had used magic to free the gryphon. What good would he be to Bryn now, crippled with pain? And what had stopped the gryphon from attacking? Some unseen force had hit it. Was that Marcus's magic, too?

Marcus didn't have much time to think about it before the Pey Wey guards were ushering him and Bryn back to the jail at lance point. When they arrived, the guards roughly shoved them both into the cell.

The night's events had taken their toll on Bryn. He was asleep again in minutes. On the other hand, Marcus was wide-awake, rolling the details of the past hour over and over again in his mind. He had fully expected to feel the effects of the magic he had used to free the gryphon. Breaking the chain had required very little effort, but he should have at least felt tired. At worst, he would be doubled over in agonizing pain. Yet he felt nothing. In fact, he had never felt stronger.

"Not tasty?" said a raspy voice from the darkest corner of the cell.

The sudden realization that he and Bryn were not alone startled Marcus. Apparently the guards had brought in a new prisoner while Marcus and Bryn were away.

"Excuse me?" replied Marcus nervously.

"Humans not tasty for Rok? It spit you out, eh?"

The comment was followed by a shrill little laugh.

Marcus bristled. "The Rok has been freed."

The Pey Wey prisoner scooted out of the shadows, its crippled legs dragging along the stone floor behind him. He extended a clawed finger that trembled slightly, per-haps from age, but the creature's gaze was steady. "Rok free, you say? How be it so?"

Marcus hesitated. Telling this stranger the truth was out of the question. The Pey Wey, however, persisted. "Tell Krak how Rok go free," he said.

"Is that your name?" asked Marcus.

"Yes. Krak my name. And you?"

"My name is Marcus Frye."

"Tell me, Marcus Frye, how the Rok be free, and I tell you secret worth much gold." Krak laughed his shrill laugh again.

The strange sound made Marcus shiver. "Fine," he said.

Krak rubbed his hands together like a spoiled child waiting for a delicious treat.

Marcus scratched at the back of his neck, wondering what unseen creatures might be lurking in the filthy cell. "I used magic to free the gryphon, all right?"

"Magic?" Krak gave a skeptical huff.

"Yes, magic," said Marcus, offended. "I'm a master enchanter, so it wasn't anything at all to free it."

Krak stared at Marcus for several seconds and then burst into laughter.

"You don't believe me?" said Marcus.

"Yes, yes, Krak believe you use magic, but you are not enchanter. If enchanter, Marcus would be free with Rok."

Marcus didn't like how this conversation was going. He hated to admit it, but Krak was right. If he weren't so fearful of using his magic, he and Bryn *would* be free. But for now, all he wanted to do was get some sleep. He lay down on the floor with his back to the Pey Wey.

"No, Marcus not confident in self," continued Krak. "Not true enchanter. Krak know only one master enchanter on Imaness. Only one, and he not young boy like you."

Marcus sat up and stared at Krak. The Pey Wey was not laughing now. He wore a very solemn expression and gazed at Marcus with intense focus.

"Why you come here?" asked Krak. "Zyll send you?"

"You knew my grandfather?"

"*Knew?* Zyll gone?"

"He was killed several days ago in Dokur. And he did send me."

"Why?"

"I'm supposed to find the maker of this key."

Marcus reached for the key and held it out in his palm to Krak. When he saw it, Krak gave a knowing nod of his head.

"You have Zyll's chest?"

"Not with me," Marcus replied, surprised. How had Krak known about the chest that held so many of Zyll's trinkets? "But I do have it back home."

Krak leaned back on his tail and rocked gently from side to side for a few moments. Beyond the prison door, muffled voices were speaking.

"Krak have little time," said the Pey Wey prisoner. "Marcus listen well. Not forget. This is Krak's secret. Key opens two identical chests made from wood of same tree. One for Zyll. One for her. She said she come back, but never came. You have key, Marcus Frye. Chest now yours."

The prison door opened, and the Pey Wey guard came in. Behind him was the administrator, obviously displeased. "You talk to key maker like you wanted?" he asked.

So Krak was the maker of the key, the one Ivanore had sent Marcus to find. Marcus looked at Krak, who met his glance with a shrug and a sly grin. "Yes," Marcus said, nodding a quiet thanks to the crippled Pey Wey. "I talked to him."

"Good. You and the boy can go," the administrator said, unlocking the gate. The guard cut Marcus's bonds with a stone knife and did the same for Bryn's. Marcus stood and scooped the still-sleeping Bryn into his arms. Then he nodded toward Krak.

"What about him?"

"You talk to him," said the administrator, "what happen to Krak now not your concern." Then he strode briskly out of the jail.

Marcus started to follow the administrator but turned back. "The chest," he said, making certain the administrator was far enough ahead that he could not overhear. "Where do I find it?"

Krak had already dragged his broken body back into the shadows, but his voice was clear. "My shop near trading post. But be discreet. Crime to take condemned man's property. Everything evidence."

"Condemned? For what?"

Krak did not answer.

"And if I get caught?" continued Marcus.

That shrill laugh sounded again through the darkness. "Then tomorrow Marcus hang with Krak!"

Seventy

rak's parting words and strange, nervous laughter remained with Marcus as he stepped out into the early morning light. The brightness hurt his eyes and he squinted, wishing he could shield his face. Bryn blinked awake and, on seeing Lael standing nearby, gasped in surprise. He wriggled free from Marcus's arms and ran to her.

"Whoa, little guy," she said, giggling. "I guess that means you're glad to see me?"

Marcus stepped away from the guard. He approached Rylan, who spoke with the administrator in hushed tones, glancing every so often at the now-free prisoners. As he neared, Rylan extended his hand to him. Marcus shoved it away. "You let these things take me and Bryn prisoner!"

"I didn't *let* them take you," Rylan replied. "What was I supposed to do?"

"Lael tried to help us, but you held her back."

"I had to! If she had fought them, she would have gotten hurt. As it was, it took a lot of effort to convince them she wasn't for sale."

"For sale?"

"Like I said before, my father trades in contracts. *Human* contracts. He often delivers indentured servants—*dents*—to Voltana to excavate ore. When you asked for the key maker—well, they made arrangements for you to see him."

"Is that what they told you?"

"You spoke with him, didn't you?"

"Yes," replied Marcus, "but only after they tried to feed me and Bryn to the Rok."

Rylan turned a sharp eye on the administrator, whose face was pinched with irritation. "You took them to the Rok?"

"No, I—" the administrator stammered.

"My father's contracts expressly state that his goods are to be used solely in the extraction and production of ore. My father will hear about this."

"Now, Master Rylan, Voltana honors all contracts with Brommel," answered the administrator, his voice oozing with charm. "But we have no contract on these two."

"That's no reason to sacrifice them!"

"Is common to execute criminals."

"You know full well they're not criminals."

"So sorry for mistake. But even so, no telling what can happen to humans here. You leave Voltana, no more problems."

The administrator motioned for the guard to come with him, but as he left, he gave Marcus a warning glance, as if Marcus ought to watch his back.

Marcus watched Lael lift Bryn by his arms and swing him in a circle. Bryn laughed happily, begging her to do it again. Marcus couldn't help but smile at the happy pair. It was hard to imagine them now the way he once had. Perhaps Lael had been right about Bryn, after all. Maybe what he had been did not matter as much as what he was now.

But with Lael it was different. Marcus had known her for too many years to so easily forget all the pranks she'd pulled on him. She had been nothing but a nuisance, like a speck of dust in his eye. It irritated him even now just thinking about it.

He turned to Rylan. "Can you show me where the trading post is?"

Lael set down Bryn and took Marcus by the shoulder. "What are you doing?" she demanded. "You heard the administrator. The Pey Weys want us out of Voltana."

"The key unlocks a wooden chest that belonged to Ivanore," said Marcus. "I have to get it."

"But you'll get arrested again, and getting you out a second time won't be an option."

A light breeze lifted a fine spray of dust into the air. It whirled for a few seconds before settling back down. The jail was situated several yards from the outskirts of the town, where a few dozen Pey Weys lingered lazily in the scant shady spots between the buildings.

"Rylan?" said Marcus.

Rylan glanced cautiously at Lael, then at Marcus. Lael cast Rylan a look that could kill, but both boys ignored it.

"It's not far from here," Rylan said. "But Lael's right. If you get caught—"

"I have to get to Krak's shop," Marcus said. "What's the best way to get there?"

Rylan grinned. "Well, if I were you," he said, "I'd wait until dark."

Seventy-one

Marcus and the others spent the day hiding behind some rocky dunes outside of town. Xerxes kept watch overhead, while everyone else took turns sleeping. Bryn, as it turned out, was the only one of them who had gotten any sleep the night before.

Voltana grew eerily silent once the sun had set. Rylan explained that with the exception of the sort of sacrifices Marcus and Bryn had almost become, Pey Weys did not like being out at night. As cold-blooded animals, they were dependent on the sun and the area's volcanic activity to warm their bodies. As soon as the last Pey Wey was out of sight, they made their move.

Rylan was right about the trading post. It wasn't far from the jail, and the open, barn-like structure was easy to distinguish from the smaller enclosures. Marcus and Rylan crouched behind a flat, stone platform and motioned for Lael and Bryn to hide behind a nearby podium. Xerxes perched on a rock pillar overlooking the entire area, which was illuminated by torches attached to the outsides of the buildings.

"This is a trading post?" asked Marcus, keeping his voice just above a whisper. "It looks more like the auction blocks back home where we sell our livestock."

"The Pey Weys conduct business very much the way the rest of us do," said Rylan.

"But the rest of us auction animals," answered Lael, "not humans."

Above them, Xerxes let out a very soft caw.

"Everything's clear," said Marcus. "That must be Krak's shop across the way, the one with the chains across the door."

Staying low to the ground, Marcus got to his feet and stepped away from the platform. Rylan caught him by his shirt sleeve.

"Careful! The Pey Weys do keep watch. The fact that we can't see them makes me nervous."

Marcus nodded to show he understood. Then he motioned for Lael and Bryn to stay put. He glanced up and down the deserted street and dashed across it to Krak's. Once there, he scanned the front of the building for some way in. A moment later, he heard a noise behind him. He turned and found Lael squatting behind him, a torch in her hand.

"I told you to stay put!" he whispered.

"Oh, is that what you meant by—" Lael pointed her finger, wiggling it in a comical fashion.

Marcus fumed. "You know what I meant. You should have done what you were told."

"When have I ever done what I was told?"

Marcus grunted continued trying to find a way inside that wouldn't draw unwanted attention. He couldn't worry about Lael now. If she wanted to put herself in danger, that was her problem. From the looks of it, though, the front entrance was chained up tight.

"So what's your plan?" asked Lael.

"Magic," he replied, though he did not sound as confident as he had hoped.

"What do you mean, magic? This is not a good time to get hit with one of your episodes, Marcus."

"I won't," he answered. "At least, I don't think so. I used magic last night and nothing happened—to me, I mean. No pain. No fatigue."

"Why not?"

"I'm not sure exactly, but I think things changed when Zyll healed me in Dokur. Maybe he healed not only the knife wound but also the effects from when I healed Kelvin months ago. In any case, I want to try it again, just to be sure."

Glancing around to make certain no one was watching, Marcus focused on a single link of iron. A ripple of power flowed out of him. A moment later, the link glowed white with heat and began to melt.

"Marcus," Lael whispered, tapping on his shoulder.

He ignored her, intensifying his focus on the heavy chain.

"Marcus, don't you think—"

"Shhh!" he responded harshly.

Suddenly the chain link melted through and fell to the ground in a loud, long clatter of metal. The sound echoed against the stone buildings all the way down the deserted street. Marcus cringed and waited for Lael's inevitable snide remark. But none came. Instead, she quickly slipped inside the door. When he didn't follow, she reached through, grabbed his arm, and yanked him inside.

Seventy-two

Once inside Krak's shop, Marcus let his eyes adjust to the dim light. He took in his surroundings. They stood at the front of a small shop with floor-to-ceiling shelves full of items a metalsmith would make: plates, eating utensils, tools, locks and fasteners, jewelry, and an array of decorative items.

Lael set the torch into an iron sconce on the wall.

"Look for a wooden chest," Marcus instructed her. He ran his hands over the surface of the nearest wall. "It's very special so I doubt we'll find it out in the open. He probably has it hidden somewhere, behind a wall panel or in a secret compartment."

"Do you mean a chest like this one?" asked Lael, pointing to a wooden box displayed prominently on a table, a green silk cloth and several silver necklaces draped over its top.

Marcus grunted with irritation. It seemed the humiliation would never end. He strode to the chest and brushed the silk and silver to the floor with an angry sweep of his hand. The chest itself was made of a pale, yellow wood, simply constructed without any decoration at all. The only thing special about it was the brass lock, though it, too, was nothing remarkable. It did, however, bear a striking resemblance to the lock on Zyll's chest back in Quendel.

Marcus retrieved Zyll's key from his pouch. "Here we go," he said and then turned the key. The lock clicked and popped open. Marcus and Lael glanced at each other. Marcus noticed the firelight dancing in Lael's eyes. He looked back at the chest. The hinges creaked a little as he lifted the lid, as a fair amount of rust had accumulated on them. Zyll's chest was full of an assortment of trinkets ranging from broken teacups and locks of Marcus's hair saved from his childhood to pages torn from old books; there were so many other knickknacks, Marcus was not even familiar with them all. He had never been allowed to rummage through the chest but had looked over Zyll's shoulder many times while he dug around for whatever item he needed. But this chest, lined in black velvet, held one item and nothing more: a book, though not a bound book, but a small stack of pages tied together with a red ribbon. Marcus reached in and carefully lifted it out. He guessed there were a little more than a dozen pages, marked with someone's graceful writing.

"What is it?" asked Lael.

Marcus brushed his fingers over the top page. He silently read the first few lines.

"It's a letter to my father," he said, "from my mother."

"Ivanore? What's a letter from her doing here in Voltana?"

Lael's question echoed Marcus's thoughts. At one time, Krak and Zyll must have known each other well enough for their chests to share the same key. Had Zyll given Krak the letter for safekeeping? Or had Ivanore given it to Krak herself? Marcus untied the ribbon and leafed through the sheets that had grown brittle with age.

"What are you doing?" Lael asked.

"Looking for answers," replied Marcus. He tried to read the rest of the top page, but the light was too dim. "Bring the torch here."

Lael did as he asked, holding it just over Marcus's shoulder. They read the first page together:

My Dearest Jayson,

More than a year has passed since you left me standing alone on the cliffs of Dokur. I still can see your face, taste the salt of your tears on my lips as the soldiers tore you from my arms. My heart was torn from me that day as well, carried with you on a ship to a faraway land.

I have waited for your return these many months, but as each day passes with no word from you, I fear that you are injured or dead, for I know that nothing save death would keep you away from me. In my mind, I see you in shackles, your skin bruised and bleeding, and somehow I know it is because of me that you suffer.

If this vision be true, then you cannot come to me. Therefore, I must come to you. Our sons will be safe with your father. He has promised to look after them and has sworn to keep their identities hidden to protect them from those who wish to do them harm.

I had almost forgotten that you know of only one child. I never had the chance to tell you of the second, but no matter. We will all soon be reunited. I leave only this letter behind in the event that you return before I have found you. Should that happen, please wait for me. I also leave with this letter documents I have gathered as evidence against my father's enemies. It is enough to finally loosen the hold they have on the throne of Dokur. With this evidence, Dokur and our children will finally live in peace.

Take care, my love, and protect these pages with your life if necessary. There are those who will go to great measures to see them destroyed. Now I go. I pray to the gods that I will be successful in my quest and that soon I will be in your arms once again.

Your beloved,
Ivanore

Marcus turned to the second page and looked it over as Lael read along with him. They did the same with the next page and the next.

"Those first pages look like legal documents of some kind," said Lael. "A treaty? Contracts, maybe."

"These others are different," noted Marcus, glancing through several other pages. "Look at this one. It goes on and on for six pages."

"What is *Vatéz*? It's in the document's title and appears several times on every page."

"I think it's pronounced 'va-teez,' though I'm not sure what it means. Maybe it has something to do with this list of names."

Lael took the documents from Marcus and read over them while he looked at the final page, which was not a document at all, but a map. From the shape of the land and its markings, it was clearly not of Imaness but seemed to be of the mainland. Of Hestoria. But the locations and other writings on it were in a language unfamiliar to Marcus. He recalled the time magic had helped him translate some text outside the library in Noam during his quest. He might be able to translate this, as well, but it would have to wait until he had time to examine it more closely.

He turned his attention back to the chest and wondered if it would be worthwhile to take it with him. It wasn't too large to carry, after all, and with nothing inside, it wouldn't be heavy. He glanced inside, imagining how much of Krak's jewelry might fit in it, when he noticed the bottom seemed loose.

He pulled back the velvet lining and found that the wooden bottom had cracked with age. He lifted off the broken section and discovered that this wasn't the bottom of the chest at all. Rather, it had been laid over a shallow space, creating a false bottom. Marcus removed the remaining sheet of wood. There, atop several leaves of blank parchment, was a polished medallion crafted solely of Celestine.

Seventy-three

arcus stared at the medallion for several moments. He had seen only one like this before, and the two were nearly identical. The other had once belonged to Ivanore and now belonged to Kelvin. Marcus remembered how Hyer, the leader of the grocs, had spoken of such a stone. He had dismissed the possibility of it being Ivanore's seal since hers had been broken into pieces. But here was a second seal intact! It must have been the very same stone Ivanore had shown to Hyer.

Marcus glanced at Lael. She was focused on the pages. He wasn't quite sure why, but he felt that this seal was meant for his eyes only. He quickly slipped the medallion into his pouch. Just then, Lael called to him.

"Marcus, you need to read this part of the 'Vatéz' document," she said, handing him the pages. Marcus took them and read the passage Lael had pointed out. Then he read it again.

"Is it possible?" asked Lael in alarm. "Could these documents be real?"

"Why wouldn't they be?"

"Because if what these papers claim is true, then Kelvin and Jayson are in real danger."

Marcus nodded. "We have to get back to Dokur right away."

The candles flickered with a sudden whoosh of air. Xerxes flew into Krak's shop, landing clumsily on the table beside the chest.

"They're coming! They're coming!"

Marcus did not need an explanation. He understood immediately that the Pey Weys had likely heard the racket he had made with the chains and were on their way to inspect the cause. Marcus tucked Ivanore's pages into his satchel. Then, using magic, he extinguished the torch.

"Xerxes, tell Rylan and Bryn to meet us outside the village!" he said hastily.

Xerxes hopped onto his shoulder. "They've already gone," he said. "They're out of danger. But you two have got to get out of here now!"

Xerxes leapt from Marcus's shoulder and swooped out the door into the night. Marcus hurried to the door and glanced out. Six Pey Wey guards marched toward them, torches and lances held at ready.

"We can't go that way," Marcus said, slipping back into the room. "Is there another door?"

Lael was already frantically searching the back wall for an exit. She turned to Marcus, shaking her head.

"If they catch us in here, we're finished," said Marcus.

"Then we'll have to fight them."

"All six of them? I'd really like to survive long enough to get home. Look for another way out."

"I did look. That door is the only way in or out of here."

Marcus had only a moment to decide what to do. He hurried to the back wall. "Well, it worked in the groc's cave," he said, pressing his hands against it.

The wall shuddered just as the first guard stepped through the doorway. "Intruders!" he shouted and darted toward Marcus.

Acting on instinct, Lael reached for Marcus's dagger. She swung it forward, its blade clashing with the tip of the guard's lance. The guard lost his balance and stumbled forward.

As the other guards filed in, the walls vibrated again, more violently this time. A sharp, popping sound rang through the shop, and a deep crack appeared in the wall just above Marcus's hands, snaking up toward the ceiling.

"It's coming down!" shouted one of the guards, and they all turned, scrambling to get back outside. The crack widened, and the ceiling opened. Marcus let go of the wall and grabbed Lael by the arm. He pulled her close to him and shoved the broken wall. Marcus and Lael pushed through, falling in a heap on the ground as the building collapsed in a pile of rubble behind them.

"Not again!" Lael pushed Marcus off her.

"Sorry," said Marcus, standing to brush the dust from his clothes.

"Uh, Marcus?" said Lael.

"What?"

"We've got company!"

Seventy-four

he five guards not caught in the shop's collapse stood on the other side of the pile of rubble, shouting angry threats. Marcus went for his dagger but found it missing. He turned to Lael, who held up her empty hands.

"I dropped it coming through the wall," she said apologetically. "It must be buried under all this."

Marcus didn't have time to lament the loss of his knife. He glanced around, trying to decide what to do next. Gather the rubble into a barrier of some kind? Send a gush of wind to throw the guards back? Before he could do anything, however, one of the guards let out a loud *humph!* and then fell to the ground unconscious. Marcus looked behind him. Lael stood with her sling spinning above her head. She let loose a second stone. The next guard grabbed his shoulder and screamed out in pain but kept coming.

Lael snatched another stone from the ground to load her sling as three guards charged forward. Marcus swept his palms forward. A wave of gravel and rocks rose from the ground, pummeling the guard in front. But it was only enough to keep them back for a few seconds.

The last two guards were too close now for the sling. Lael ran back, trying to lengthen the distance between them. Marcus flung another shower of stones, harder this time, and managed to bring one guard to his knees. But before he could repeat his attack, the last guard was on him. The guard kicked Marcus in the chest. Marcus fell backward onto the ground. The guard then lifted his lance with both hands and prepared to plunge it into Marcus.

"Lael! Shoot him!"

"He's too close!"

"Just do it!"

Lael obeyed. As the stone shot forward, Marcus followed its brief trajectory with an intense gaze. Just as it reached the soldier's face, it exploded with such force that the sound of it sent shockwaves through the air. The guard screamed in pain and, grabbing his face with both hands, dropped his weapon to the ground.

Lael's sling spun again. But then suddenly, it was snatched from her hand. One of the injured guards had somehow sneaked up behind her and taken her by surprise. In the next moment, he held her tight against him, a stone blade pressed to her throat. Several of the other guards slowly got to their feet, staggering from pain but still ready to fight.

Marcus froze. What could he do to the guard that would not hurt Lael, too? He had to think fast.

Then, in the sky just beyond the mountains, a dark form appeared. It grew steadily as it soared toward them. Marcus stared, momentarily distracted from the immediate threat of the guard, who also gaped in amazement. The shape approached with such tremendous speed that Marcus had barely taken his third breath before it reached them.

The guard holding Lael dropped his lance and screamed, "Rok!" He turned and ran but not fast enough. The gryphon swooped down, snatched the guard in its mighty talon, and soared straight up as the guard screeched in terror. When the gryphon had reached enough height, it released its prisoner. The guard plummeted to the earth, only to be snatched up again just before hitting the ground. The gryphon took the guard in its beak and flung him. The guard flew more than thirty feet before colliding with an outcropping of porous stone.

The gryphon alighted on the ground between Lael and Marcus and let out a deafening shriek. The remaining guards turned tail and ran. Marcus laughed as he watched them go. "I don't think they'll be coming back," he said.

Lael stood, gaping in awe at the creature that had saved them. "Where did you come from all of a sudden?" she asked.

Marcus approached the gryphon and stroked its neck. "The Pey Weys had it chained up. I let it go, so I guess it thought it owed me one."

"It's a *she*," Lael said, correcting him. "And how did she know you were in trouble?"

"I don't know," said Marcus. He reached up and touched the pendant and thought once more of the words the seller had told him. The gryphon is the guardian of the Seer. Could it be that this gryphon was to be *his* protector?

Xerxes, who had been circling overhead, swooped down and crash-landed on the rocky soil. "Bryn and Rylan are waiting for you," he said breathlessly.

"Good," said Marcus. "Please tell them we're safe and on our way to meet them."

Xerxes immediately flew off to deliver the message.

"We need to get back to Dokur," Marcus told Lael. "We've been gone too long. We don't have much time before Kaië's trial."

The gryphon blinked her eyes, large circles of black. Marcus rubbed her beak. "I think she likes me," he said. The gryphon bowed her head and nudged Marcus from behind.

"What is she doing?" asked Lael.

The gryphon nudged him again, keeping her head lowered.

"I think she wants me to climb on." Marcus tested this by carefully pulling himself up to sit on her neck. He helped Lael to climb on behind him.

"This is incredible!" said Marcus. "It's as if she's always

known me. Do you think she'd take us back to Dokur?"

Lael slid her hands over the creature's downy feathers. "Well, she's certainly large enough to hold all of us."

Marcus drew a deep breath. "All right then. We'll pick up Bryn and Rylan and then head home. Hold on!"

And with that, the gryphon's mighty wings unfurled, lifting them high above the ground. In moments, the entire landscape for miles around became visible, and Marcus thought he could almost see the silhouette of Dokur in the distance.

Seventy-five

"The hour is late," said Chancellor Prost. "There is no need to prolong this trial further."

The throne room was located in the uppermost section of the Fortress, overlooking the southern courtyard below where a gallows was being constructed. The relentless pounding of mallet against spike broke through the silence in the room.

There were only nine people present: the two prisoners accused of treason bound in chains on their knees, Jayson, Brommel the human trader, four armed guards, and Chancellor Prost. Prost stood before the prisoners, his hands clasped loosely behind him. His fingers wriggled like little, white worms as he prepared to pass judgment. He glared down at Eliha the Agoran murderer, whose skin

355

was streaked with blood and dirt. Dark purple bruises decorated his back and arms, evidence of the beatings he had endured. His sleek, feline-like frame was shrunken from hunger. He was so weak that the guards had to pull his chains taut to keep him from falling.

"You, Agoran, have been found guilty of treason and murder!" said Prost. "Having conducted a careful investigation, I have concluded that you are guilty of the following crimes: burning His Majesty's naval vessel *The North Star* and injuring three of her crew; trespassing on His Majesty's property, namely within these walls, and vandalizing said property; and murdering the king and two of his royal guards in cold blood. We have born witness against you. You will be put to death for your crimes. Have you anything to say before I proceed?"

A loud thud sounded from the window, followed by a series of creaks as the wooden gallows was tested. Eliha lifted his face, which bore a defiant and proud expression. "I do not fear death," he said, the words raspy and dry. "Unlike some who run from it, I welcome it! But unless my people are given their lands and the government's noose is forever loosed from their necks, there will be others after me! And we will break your necks with our bare hands for our freedom, if we must!"

Prost looked amused. "I see," he said, smirking. He glanced up at Jayson. "Do you hear that, Jayson? He speaks of others. Is he referring to you, by any chance? I think not. No, I believe his reference to you was in mentioning those who run from death. Hmm? All right then," he continued, motioning to the guard beside Eliha. "Take him away to the gallows. His sentence will be carried out immediately."

Eliha said nothing as one of the guards pulled him roughly to his feet. It was Kaië who cried out, "No!"

"No?" repeated Prost. "Did the prisoner dare speak without permission?"

"You can't accuse him," Kaië said, "until you consider what led him to do it."

"You have no right to speak—"

"But speak I must! This man was taken from his wife—"

"Guard, silence her!"

"—his children left fatherless. He was enslaved in Fredric's mine and imprisoned wrongfully! He demands only that his people be given what was promised them."

"Guard!"

The guard that held Kaië's chains hit her on the side of her head with the grip of his sword. Kaië crumpled to the ground, a fresh trail of blood trickling from her wound. Jayson and Brommel angrily shoved the guards aside and rushed to Kaië.

"Why do you torture an innocent woman?" Jayson shouted, tears burning his eyes. "You know she tells the truth! If anyone is guilty here, it is you!"

"How dare you!" shouted Prost. "Do you know I have the authority and the power to hang you all? In fact, hanging you, Jayson, is something I should have done years ago. I was swayed by Fredric to spare your life and exile you instead. What a weak man he was. You defiled his only daughter, and yet he could not see you die. Well, Fredric is no longer alive to protect you—to protect any of you! I am the supreme authority here!"

"Prost!"

All eyes turned to the front of the room where Kelvin, having entered through his private entrance, stood scowling.

"Sire," said Prost, suddenly polite, "to what do we owe this unexpected visit?"

"I am here to put a stop to this so-called trial."

"You needn't trouble yourself with such matters. You have more important things to attend to."

"More important than protecting the liberty of my own people?" asked Kelvin.

"If you are referring to the prisoners, I assure you, their punishment fits their crimes."

"Is that so? I think Kaië is right. Has the Agoran's history been considered? And what evidence do you have against the girl except for Eliha's testimony?"

"But Sire," said Prost, "they killed your grandfather. You said so yourself."

"I did. But that was before I knew the truth."

"Sire, I—"

"Guards, release the prisoners!"

The two prison guards unlocked the shackles that bound Eliha and Kaië, and their chains clattered loudly to the floor. Eliha, trembling from weakness but still proud, rose to his feet. Kelvin walked past Prost and placed his hand on the Agoran's shoulder.

"Your people are free to return to their lands. I give

my word." Then, holding out his hand to Kaië, he added, "I am sorry I did not come sooner. I promise I will make it up to you in every way possible."

Prost turned ashen. "This is an outrage! I served under your grandfather for twenty years! I have the authority to conduct this trial as I see fit."

"Not anymore," answered Kelvin. "Prost, you are hereby charged with treason against the crown and are to give yourself up to these guards."

"Treason? But you have no evidence against me!"

"Actually, I have more than I need."

From the door to Kelvin's private chambers came Rylan, Bryn, Lael, and Marcus. In Marcus's outstretched hand were the documents from Voltana.

Seventy-six

arcus held up the papers for all to see. "These documents prove that Chancellor Prost's goal since the beginning was to control Dokur's throne and take possession of the Celestine mines."

"Preposterous!" shouted Prost.

"And he is in league with Dokur's enemies in Hestoria—the Vatéz."

Prost gasped and shook with rage. "By whose hand was this claim written?"

"Lady Ivanore," Marcus said, handing the pages to Kelvin.

Prost tried to snatch the papers from Kelvin's hand, but a guard blocked him with his sword.

"Ivanore is dead," said Prost. "Her testimony is invalid!"

Kelvin motioned to his guards. They stepped forward to take Prost's arms.

"I also charge you with both my grandfathers' deaths," continued Kelvin. "You will be bound and tried. You were supposed to be an advocate of justice, Chancellor. Let justice now have its claim on you."

As the guards drew near, however, Prost raised his hands toward them. The air crackled as a thin blue bolt of light arced from his fingertips and struck the guards. They lurched backward, their bodies slamming against the floor. Another guard ran forward and was also thrown aside. Prost raised a single finger, pointing it at a huge marble urn in the corner of the room. The blue light zigzagged through the air. It lifted the enormous urn from its base and hurled it at the guards. It smashed into them, pinning them to the floor.

Prost turned, a smirk on his lips. "Anyone else wish to arrest me?"

Jayson took Kaië up in his arms and ran for the door, but Prost spotted their retreat and, with a slight flick of his wrist, shut and barred the door.

"Running as usual, Jayson. Typical. Do your sons know how you abandoned them, spending fifteen years hiding in your ale while your wife and your people waited for your return? Well, no more! It is time you face your worst demons, Agoran half-breed! There will be no more hiding!"

Prost shot out his arms. The blue light pierced Jayson's body, sending a horrible tremor through him. Jayson tried to keep his grip on Kaië, but he could not. He let her slide to the floor. He struggled against the force that shook him, the strain showing in his face, the veins bulging in his neck.

"Let him go!" shouted Marcus.

Jayson's quaking stopped, and he crumpled to the floor, too weak to move. Kelvin hurried to his side. Finding him exhausted but alive, he then moved to Kaië and tried to wake her. In the meantime, Prost turned his attention to Marcus.

"Oh, yes, I nearly forgot about you—the spare child. I, for one, have had enough of your meddling."

Blue lightning surged from Prost's fingers. The impact of it sent Marcus hurtling across the room, where he crashed against a wall. He felt like he'd been struck by a boulder. Though it left him winded, he managed to stay on his feet.

"This isn't about the mines or power, is it?" said Marcus between gasps of breath. "You want something bigger—more important. According to Ivanore's documents, you've been a pawn of the Vatéz since the beginning—and the Vatéz want the Celestine seals."

Prost's lips quivered in silent fury. His eyes narrowed.

"But she wouldn't give them to you, would she?" Marcus continued, the pieces of the puzzle coming together in his mind. "So you sent her husband away and tried to convince Fredric to kill her baby, but she ran away and took the seals with her. But why? What about them is so special that you're willing to kill for them?"

Kelvin spoke up now. "I don't understand. Prost had plenty of chances to take mother's seal from me. Why didn't he kill *me* for it?"

"Because one is useless without the other," said Marcus. "He needs them both. He hoped you would eventually reveal the location of the second seal. The only problem was that you didn't even know the other seal existed, let alone where it was. But I do."

Prost was so enraged by now that his face was nearly purple. His lips, tight and thin, trembled as he spoke. "Give—them—to—me!"

Nothing in Prost's face or body prepared Marcus for the blow. In half a second, Prost's magic had snaked around the royal throne itself and shot it forward, slamming into Marcus from behind.

Marcus fell forward, miraculously landing on his hands and knees and not his face. A searing pain tore through his back and shoulders as the immense weight of the throne rolled off him and clunked solidly onto the floor.

"Marcus!" Bryn screamed, struggling to break free of Lael's protective grasp. "Stop! Don't hurt him!"

Before Marcus could gather his senses, he saw the glint of one of the guards' swords flying toward him through the air. Prost controlled it with merely a wave of his hand. Marcus dove forward, narrowly missing the blade, which embedded itself in the far wall. He was not to have a moment of rest before Prost sent the marble urn rocketing through the air again, but Kelvin lunged forward, throwing his body against it and setting it off its course to roll and crash against another wall.

Nearby, Jayson moaned as his strength began to return. Prost bent his knees and touched his fingertips to the floor.

The massive stone tiles warped in succession, traveling like a wave toward Jayson. When the wave hit, Jayson flew into the air. Marcus knew at once that when Jayson landed on the hard surface again, he would be seriously injured. Marcus threw up his hands, instantly gathering the air beneath Jayson in an upward gust of gentle wind that cushioned his landing. With Jayson safe on the floor, fear and anger flooded through Marcus's body. He felt a power burst from him, just as it had with the gryphon. He flung out his hands and sent a powerful gust toward Prost, who was thrown back, sliding across the floor.

Prost had not come to a complete stop before he used his magic to uproot several stone tiles, each one as wide as Marcus was tall, hurling them spinning through the air. Marcus avoided the first two with quick maneuvering, but the third struck him in the leg. He cried out in pain, dropping to his knees. The leg was not broken but would be badly bruised.

The fourth came flying, but Marcus sent a current of air that changed its course, sending the stone tile back toward Prost. Prost threw up his arms to shield himself, but the stone landed edge-first across his chest, shattering as it struck him. Prost grasped his wounded chest. He coughed and sputtered, a thin line of blood trailing from the corner of his mouth.

Marcus struggled to his feet. He felt lightheaded and fought off the dizziness that seized him. He watched as Prost grew pale, his body trembling.

"You might as well kill me," said Prost, gasping for

breath. "If you do not, I will kill you!"

Before Marcus could respond, Prost shot out his hand, his bony fingers reaching out like withered branches on a vine. The blue snakes flew across the room, twisting around Lael. She screamed as Prost bent his wrist and pulled her close. She struggled against his power but to no avail. She let go of Bryn, pushing him away from her to safety. And within seconds, she was in Prost's grasp.

Seventy-seven

Bryn, who had been obediently watching from the far doorway, screamed Lael's name. The boy arched his back, preparing to attack. Marcus was again awed at the transformation from boy to beast. Bryn's childish frame mutated in mere seconds, then exploded forth in a terrible rage. Prost lifted not a finger, merely raising an eyebrow as if amused. His magic lifted the groc high into the air. Bryn writhed and twisted, helpless as a fragile sparrow, then slammed onto the floor. By the force of the impact, Marcus knew Bryn had not merely fallen, but that Prost had thrown him down. The monster's figure returned to that of a child who lay whimpering and fearful on the floor.

Marcus could no longer bear to see his friends suffer. He would end this somehow, no matter what it took. He started toward Prost, but the old man held up his hand, fingers spread wide apart, blue light sparking between them. Behind him the giant, stained-glass window shook violently. It suddenly burst into thousands of dagger-like shards that shot forward, filling the throne room with a hailstorm of glass. Kelvin threw his body over Kaië, while Jayson held up his thick cloak to protect them from the assault. Bryn, however, lay in the open.

Marcus leapt forward, positioning himself between Bryn and the flying glass. Placing his palms out in front of him, he focused all his attention massive gusts of air to divert the shards toward the sides of the room. He was successful, and he and Bryn were unharmed. The guards and Eliha the Agoran, however, were not so fortunate. When the assault was over, they lay dead in pools of their own blood.

By this time, more guards—dozens of them—began filing into the room with weapons raised. Kelvin stood and brushed the fragments of glass from his clothes.

"It's over, Prost!" he shouted. "I'm still king, and I command you to give yourself to these guards."

"Never!" Prost shouted.

In his arms, Lael writhed. Prost's eyes rolled back grotesquely as he placed his fingertips on the skin of her neck. The current of magic coursed through her body, making her shake violently. Marcus knew what Prost was doing. It was the same thing Marcus had done for Kelvin and Zyll had done for him—only Prost was using Lael's life force to heal himself. Suddenly, Marcus felt more rage than he had ever known, and he screamed so that every cell in his body threatened to explode.

"Stop!" he shouted. Then, gathering more energy than he had ever dreamed possible, Marcus sent it all in a single, powerful burst across the room. The mass of energy was so dense that it warped the very colors and light of the area around it. It struck Prost with such force that it ripped Lael from his arms and flung her across the room. She came to rest unconscious, but alive, near Jayson.

Prost was thrown backward through the gaping, jagged void where the stained-glass window had been. He managed to grasp the sharp edge of the pane, and though it cut into his hands, he hung there, three stories above the ground.

Marcus began to cross the room to the window. If he had to pound Prost's fists with his own bare hands, he would do it to rid Dokur of the chancellor once and for all. But before he reached Prost, a loud, cracking sound echoed from the hall outside, followed by a tremendous roar.

A guard came running in. "The prison door has exploded off its hinges! Something's down there!"

The floor beneath their feet rumbled with the steps of something massive and heavy. A moment later, the wall separating the throne room from the rest of the Fortress collapsed in a cloud of dust and rubble. The guards shouted and scattered in every direction. In the settling cloud of dust, Marcus saw an enormous dragon. Its black scales glistened in the sunlight as it threw its head back and roared. It lumbered across the marble floor as though obeying a silent command and lowered its head through the window. Prost released the pane and grasped the beast's neck with his bloody hands. With great difficulty, he hoisted his battered body onto the back of the dragon. A moment later, the dragon spread its wings and took flight through the broken window.

Kelvin helped Jayson to his feet, and the two of them joined Marcus near the window. Together they watched the dragon turn toward the sea. Minutes later, it and Prost were gone from sight.

Seventy-eight

Marcus stayed by Lael's bedside for two days, waiting for her to regain consciousness. The Fortress healers who looked after her assured him she would recover soon, but he still worried. Kaië, whose injuries had been minor, stayed nearby, as well, helping where she could. Jayson, of course, refused to be waited on and insisted on keeping his room in the tavern. He and Brommel spent many hours there studying Ivanore's documents late into the night. They provided some clues as to where Ivanore might be, though nothing was certain.

The second night, hours before the sun would rise, Jayson joined Marcus in his vigil. Marcus noted the dark circles under his father's eyes and guessed he had not slept well, if at all.

Jayson pulled up a stool to sit beside his son. "How is she?" he asked.

"Better," said Marcus.

"Good. Brommel is waiting in the hall. When she awakes, you'll let him know, won't you?"

"Of course I will. So have Ivanore's papers yielded anymore secrets?"

"They have." Jayson rested his hands on the edge of Lael's bed, his fingers woven in a relaxed grip. "Marcus, there are many things your grandfather and I should have told you." His fingers tightened, knuckles going white. "You asked why I didn't tell you about your mother, and what I said was the truth. I wish I had known—I *should* have known she was alive."

"It's not your fault," said Marcus.

Jayson pressed his lips together and closed his eyes. A look of remorse crossed his face. "After Fredric sent me into exile, Ivanore came after me. You read that much in her letter. If I had known, I could have protected her. But instead, the Vatéz took her captive."

"Vatéz," said Marcus. "They're mentioned in Ivanore's documents. I don't know anything about them except that they are our enemy."

"The Vatéz are a secret association whose sole objective is to control every other civilized society. They are very powerful, but they lack the one thing that could give them what they most desire."

"Ivanore's crystal seals?"

"If the Vatéz find them, they will force Ivanore to use

the seals to locate and destroy the Guilde."

"Do you have any idea where they are holding her?"

"Only that she is likely in Hestoria. The map may have some clues, but we don't understand the language."

Jayson grew silent. Marcus thought of his mother's letter. She had left him and Kelvin to search for Jayson. Though he understood why she had done it, the feeling that he had been forsaken was like a stone in his stomach.

As if reading Marcus's thoughts, Jayson suddenly continued. "You must understand," he said firmly, "she fully expected to return to Imaness. She did not abandon you. She loves you, Marcus. That's why we are going after her."

Jayson explained the plans he and Brommel had made. Kelvin had agreed to give them a ship and supplies, and they would sail for Hestoria that afternoon. The mission would be dangerous. Prost had escaped and could be counted on to tell their enemies every scrap of information he knew—including the existence of the second Celestine seal. Therefore, Marcus had to protect the seals at all costs.

Seventy-nine

When Lael finally awoke later that morning, Marcus the first thing she saw was Marcus's face. He smiled at her and reached for her hand, still bruised and weak. She tried to return his smile, but a fit of coughing stopped her.

"Shhh," said Marcus. "Lie still and rest."

Lael nodded, but the look in her eyes spoke what her heart wanted to say aloud.

"Everyone's all right," continued Marcus.

"Bryn?"

"Even Bryn."

Lael looked relieved, though she winced in pain when she tried to move.

Marcus adjusted the pillow beneath her head so that she would be more comfortable. "The doctor says you'll be strong enough to go home in a few days. In the meantime, you're to take it easy."

"But I don't want to go home," said Lael, her voice weak but determined.

Marcus shook his head. "I know, Lael. You don't have to go back to Quendel. You have a new home here in Dokur."

Lael looked confused.

"There's someone here to see you," he told her, "someone who can explain it better than I can."

Marcus stood and opened the door, inviting whoever waited outside to come in. A moment later, Brommel and Rylan entered. Rylan held a bunch of orange blossoms in his hand. Lael accepted them gratefully, allowing Rylan to set them beside her on the bed stand.

Brommel nodded approvingly at the girl lying in the bed. "My son tells me you were quite the hero in Voltana, young lady. He says you have the heart of a warrior. Tell me, Lael, have you had any success in finding your mother? That is why you went to Voltana, isn't it? To continue your quest?"

"No, I haven't found her," whispered Lael. "I'm afraid I never will."

"Never?" repeated Brommel. "I'm surprised someone with such spirit as you have would give up so easily. And what if you were to find her? What then? Are you ready to meet her?"

Lael anxiously tugged at the edge of her blanket. Marcus noticed tears coming down her cheeks.

Brommel stepped closer and spoke with the tenderness of a father. "Rylan told me of your sacrifice."

Sacrifice, wondered Marcus. What sacrifice is he talking about?

Two drops fell from Lael's eyes, dampening the blanket in her hands. "It was the right thing to do," she said softly, forcing a smile. "It doesn't matter now, anyway. It was a child's dream, finding my mother after so many years."

"Now, I wouldn't say that," answered Brommel. "You know, I nearly forgot. I brought you something. If you wait a moment, I'll go fetch it for you."

Brommel momentarily stepped out of the room. Marcus wanted to ask Lael what Brommel had meant, what sacrifice had she made. She had, of course, helped him many times along the journey to Voltana and back, but somehow he sensed Brommel referred to something more important. But before he could ask her about it, Brommel returned. With him was the pendant seller from town, the one who had sold Marcus the gryphon amulet and who had been with Brommel and Jayson in the Seafarer Tavern after Marcus was attacked.

"Do you know this woman, Lael?"

Lael looked at the woman and then back at Brommel. "We've spoken on a few occasions," Lael said, "but otherwise we're strangers."

"Are you really so certain, child? Her name is Arla."

Lael turned her eyes to the woman again, with more interest this time. "My mother's name was Arla. . . ."

Marcus watched the recognition dawn slowly in Lael's eyes. Brommel had explained the woman's identity to him earlier, of course, and he had wondered how Lael would react to the news.

Lael tentatively reached out to touch Arla's face. Bursting into tears, Arla grasped Lael's hand in hers and held it against her cheek. As she enfolded Lael in her arms, Lael smiled. "I smell lilacs," she said. Then she held her mother close and cried.

Eighty

Why didn't you tell me who you were before?" asked Lael.

"I would have if I had known," answered Arla, "but I hadn't seen you since you were a small girl. And I never expected to see you again. I didn't recognize you."

"But you knew Marcus."

Arla glanced at Marcus who, until now, had remained a silent witness to this reunion between mother and daughter.

"I felt his power," said Arla, "and when I saw Zyll, it only confirmed what I had suspected. He's Ivanore's son and the new seer."

Brommel interrupted. "There's a very important reason why your mother's been gone so long."

"She sold herself into slavery to pay our debts," said Lael.

"That's partly true," said Brommel. "I went to Quendel that day to collect your father. But he refused to honor his contract and sent your mother in his place."

"Couldn't you have stopped him?" asked Lael. "Why didn't you force him to go instead?"

Arla stroked Lael's cheek. "I went willingly. I thought I'd pay the debt and return to you in a year or two. But when I did return, I learned that your father had told the village elders I had abandoned you, and they believed him. They wouldn't even let me see you."

Marcus saw the pain in Arla's face and knew she told the truth. He imagined Lael must hate her father for everything he had done, and he couldn't blame her. But something else nagged at him at this moment. Though he hated to interrupt, Marcus could no longer keep back the question burning in his mind.

"Arla," he said, "did you know my mother well?"

Arla nodded. "During Ivanore's short time in Quendel, several years before I left, we became friends. She often confided in me about her visions and her desire to find her husband, but she went missing shortly after that. Years later, Brommel and I both became Guardians in the hopes that we could help locate her. But when the Guilde came under attack, the few Guardians who survived went into hiding."

Arla held up the jade pendant she wore around her neck. It was the same one she had shown Lael and Marcus when they first met in Dokur's marketplace, the one with the gryphon carved into it.

"We have all waited a long time for the new Seer to come of age," she said. "And now it's time for the Guilde to unite once again."

"All right, now you know," said Brommel. Despite his brusque tone, Marcus sensed he was moved by what Arla had said. "We have pressing matters to attend to, namely finding Ivanore and destroying the Vatéz once and for all."

"I'm ready to go," said Arla, kissing her daughter's cheek.

"Not this time, Arla," said Brommel. "It will take weeks for Lael to fully recuperate, and she'll be needing assistance. No, for this journey you'll be staying here."

"Then who will go with you?"

Marcus looked at Lael. The happiness in her face at having been reunited with her mother made his heart swell. Things were as they should be. Kelvin would rule Dokur with a just hand. The Agorans would soon inhabit the lands they had been forced to abandon long ago. Clovis was safely home in Quendel preparing for winter. But for him? There was nothing for him here. No reason to stay.

"I'll go," he said.

Marcus stood and squared his shoulders. Touching the shape of Ivanore's second seal still in his pocket, he felt he could do anything. He knew that somehow he had been chosen as its protector—and that only he could save his mother.

Eighty-one

ay I come in?"

Marcus peered through the already open door to Kelvin's council chambers. Kelvin sat at his desk, reading through a stack of papers. He greeted his brother with a smile and invited him in.

"You look busy," said Marcus, sitting in a chair opposite the desk.

"Not at all. Just some reports on the ships' progress. Seems everything will be ready by spring. Unfortunately, that provides our enemy time to prepare for war, too. But no matter. Tell me, how is Lael?"

"Recovering. Thank you for providing for her care."

"It's the least I can do. Father tells me you are going to Hestoria to search for our mother," Kelvin added, pointing to the knapsack slung on Marcus's shoulder. "I wish I could go with you."

"You have other responsibilities," said Marcus. "And you've given us everything we need to make our journey a successful one."

"Not everything," said Kelvin, rising from his chair. He came around the desk, removing Ivanore's seal from his neck. He held it out to Marcus. "Please, take this."

Marcus looked at the medallion in Kelvin's out-stretched palm. "No, Kelvin. It belongs to you."

"Somehow it never felt right that I keep it," replied Kelvin. "I know now that it was meant for you."

Marcus reached into his pocket and removed the second medallion. "I found it in Voltana with her letter."

"So there *are* two of them," said Kelvin.

Marcus looked at both medallions. As he had thought, they were identical in every way. He moved his closer to his brother's to compare them. As he did, they both began to glow.

Marcus drew it back, and the discs returned to normal. The two boys looked at each other, searching for some explanation. Marcus again moved his medallion near to Kelvin's, and again the discs glowed, the light becoming brighter the closer they got.

Marcus turned his over in his palm. "Look at that," he said, pointing to the center of his disc where the shape of a triangle had appeared. Kelvin turned his over and found a triangle there, as well.

"I never noticed that before," said Kelvin.

"The light makes the shapes visible," answered Marcus. "It's as if they sense each other's presence."

"Take it," Kelvin insisted. "Maybe when you find Ivanore, you can return them to her. And you can tell her for me—"

Marcus hesitantly took Kelvin's stone, but the very moment he touched it, a powerful burst of light exploded from both discs, filling the room with such brilliance that everything in it was swallowed up in light.

Marcus shaded his eyes with his arm. He blinked as his eyes adjusted to the brightness. Kelvin was gone. The desk and chairs and the room itself were gone. Marcus alone stood in a perfect whiteness. Sound, too, had vanished, except for the sound of his own breathing. He realized he should be afraid, but what he felt instead was peace.

"Hello, Marcus."

He turned and saw her standing beside him as if she had always been there. She smiled at him, and her smile warmed him to his very soul.

"Hello, Mother," he replied softly.

"I have been calling for you."

"Yes, I know. I'm sorry I couldn't answer you—until now."

Ivanore glanced down at the discs of Celestine in Marcus's hands. She looked up again and gazed into his eyes.

"Things are finally as they should be," she said. *"I am no longer needed. You are the Seer now, Marcus."*

Ivanore turned as if to go, but Marcus called after her.

"*Mother, for all these years, Kelvin and I believed you were dead. Why weren't we told the truth?*"

"*You found my chest?*" asked Ivanore in reply. "*My letter and the other documents inside?*"

"*Yes. You wrote that Zyll kept our identities secret to protect us, but protect us from whom? Your father? Chancellor Prost?*"

"*If you've read those documents, you know of the Vatéz and their hunger for power. If they had found you, they would have used you to blackmail me into giving them the stones.*"

"*Why are the stones so important?*" asked Marcus.

"*They are the tools of the Seer. They focus, even enhance, my gifts.*"

"*And in the hands of an enchanter?*"

"*No honorable enchanter would dare use them. But the Vatéz are not honorable. They use their magic for selfish purposes. They have already killed too many innocent people. If they were to possess the stones, they would destroy us all.*"

"*Zyll told me that you're alive. Others believe the Vatéz are holding you captive somewhere in Hestoria.*"

"*I came to Hestoria to find Jayson,*" said Ivanore. "*Instead, the Vatéz found me.*"

"*And you never told my father about me?*"

The sorrow that crossed Ivanore's face tore at Marcus's heart, bringing him to tears.

"*There are many things I regret, my son, things I cannot explain to you now. Perhaps someday, should we ever find each other.*"

"But we will find each other," said Marcus. *"I'm coming for you!"*

The vision began to fade, Ivanore's figure evaporating like a quickly forgotten dream. Ivanore managed a melancholy smile. *"Yes, my son. Come for me. I am waiting for you where stone meets sea and shadow."*

Just before her image completely vanished from sight, Ivanore reached her hand out toward Marcus, stretching, grasping, her face filled with a horrible longing.

"Marcus," she whispered. The last parts of her to disappear were the tears on her cheeks.

"I'll find you, Mother!" Marcus yelled through his own wrenching cries. *"I swear I'll find you!"*

The light contracted, leaving a dark void in its place. But then, as suddenly as everything had disappeared, it returned—the room, the windows, tapestries, desk, and chairs all where they were before, and Kelvin was speaking as if nothing out of the ordinary had happened.

"Tell her that I want to meet her," Kelvin was saying, "and that I love her."

Marcus held a medallion in each hand, the etched triangles still visible in their glow. Feeling a bit confused by the entire experience, he slipped both discs into his knapsack. As soon as he was able, he would wrap them separately in cloth and find some place safe to keep them.

Kelvin was speaking again, asking if he was all right.

"What? Yes, I'm fine," answered Marcus, standing to leave. "I should be going. Our ship sails at sunrise."

Kelvin accompanied Marcus to the door and held it

open for him. Marcus reached out his hand, but instead of taking it, Kelvin wrapped his arms around his younger sibling and held him tight. "Be safe, my brother," he said. Then Kelvin released him and went back to his desk, drying his eyes with his hands.

Marcus stood at the door for a moment. "I love you, too," he whispered, then turned and walked away.

Eighty-two

The ship stood in port, its ropes taut, pulling at the pier like an anxious child. It was fully stocked for their journey across the sea, and the crew busily prepared the sails for departure. Marcus gazed at it, awed by its massive size. It made him feel powerful, as though with this mighty ship he could conquer the enemy single-handedly.

Xerxes shuffled up to him along the wooden pier. He hopped up to Marcus's arm and climbed to his shoulder. His glossy black feathers were damp with sea mist, and he took a brief moment to preen them.

"It's a good day to sail," said Marcus, breathing deeply.

Xerxes ruffled his feathers. "I suppose it is as good a day as any, though frankly I'd much prefer to stay on land."

"What difference does it make, Xerxes, when you can just fly over water?"

"What difference does it make?" Xerxes crowed. "Land doesn't *move* when you stand on it! I prefer something solid beneath my talons."

"You don't have talons, Xerxes. You have feet, bird feet."

Xerxes made a disgusted sound before flying off toward the ship and alighting on the topmost mast. At the same time, the gryphon soared in and landed on the deck below. She folded her wings and opened her beak in a mighty yawn. Above her, Xerxes rolled his eyes in annoyance.

Marcus laughed at his animal companions and then lifted his pack to his shoulder. Jayson and Rylan each carried a crate of fresh fruit up the gangway and set them on the bow. The crew would store them below deck. As Rylan returned for another, Marcus stopped him.

"Rylan, I have to ask you a question that has been bothering me. Your father said something to Lael about a sacrifice. What did he mean?"

"I promised not to say anything," Rylan began, "but I think you should be told the truth. Didn't you ever wonder why the Pey Weys let you go?"

"You made arrangements with the administrator?"

"Actually, I bribed the administrator."

"Bribed him? With what?" Marcus paused as the truth dawned on him. "Lael traded her gold for my freedom?"

"And Bryn's."

"But she'd been saving that money for years to find her mother. Why would she do that?"

"If you have to ask, then you are a fool. Anyone with eyes can see how she cares for you. Now grab that crate over there and let's get going."

Rylan carried the crate up the gangplank. Jayson leaned over the rail and called to Marcus. "It's time we set sail, son! Come aboard!"

Marcus gazed at the Fortress looming above them on the hillside. Coming toward him were three figures, one leaning on the other two for support. It was Lael, Kaië, and Arla. When Bryn saw them, he called out and ran to them. Marcus followed close behind.

"Lael! Oh, Lael!" Bryn cried, throwing his arms around her waist. "That nasty doctor wouldn't let me see you. He said children weren't allowed!"

"Well, I'm doing a little better now, Bryn, and I'll be getting stronger each day."

"I'm so glad! Marcus, do you think maybe Lael might need someone to look after her while you're gone? Someone to make sure she gets enough rest and such?"

"She does have her mother," said Marcus.

Bryn glanced down, dejected.

"But then again," Marcus continued, "there is really too much work for one person to manage. Wouldn't you agree, Arla?"

"Yes, I do, Master Marcus," Arla replied.

"And the journey we're taking is really much too dangerous for *children*." Marcus playfully ruffled the little boy's hair. Bryn glanced up, a definite look of pleasure and pride in his face.

As Bryn talked excitedly about his plans with Lael and Arla, Kaië stepped forward. "Marcus, I want to thank you for coming back for me. I am deeply grateful."

Kaië leaned forward and kissed Marcus on the cheek. She held her lips there a little longer than Marcus expected, and he wondered if maybe there wasn't a little regret about his leaving.

Kaië took Bryn by the hand then and offered to get him some cookies at the tavern. After waving Marcus a cheerful goodbye, Bryn followed her down the hill into town.

Lael left her mother's steadying embrace and with some effort came to Marcus. He held out his hands to her, and she took them to support her weak legs.

"You've been a lot of trouble, Marcus Frye," she said, laughing a little, "but I can't say I regret coming to Dokur with you. I do owe you an apology, though."

"An apology? For what?"

"I said some mean things about Kaië. She's been very kind to me these past few days, and, well, it would be wrong of me to wish anything but good for both of you."

Marcus peered curiously at Lael. "I don't understand."

"I know how you feel about her," Lael added. "I hope that when you return from your journey, the two of you will have a very happy life."

"You want me and Kaië to be happy—together."

"Yes," said Lael, bristling. "Do you doubt me, Marcus? It wouldn't surprise me one bit, though. You've always been such a selfish, stubborn—"

"Lael, stop," said Marcus. He shook his head, trying not to laugh. "I do care about someone that way, but it isn't Kaië."

Marcus took Lael's hand in his and turned it so that her fingers lay open. He then removed his gryphon pendant from around his neck and laid it in her palm.

"We've had our differences," he continued, "but I hope we can put them behind us. I'll be gone a long time. I don't know what challenges I may face or what might happen to me, but if I know you're here, waiting—"

Lael did not wait for him to finish. She wrapped her arms around Marcus's neck and pressed her lips against his. They stood that way for at least as long as Kaië had kissed him, maybe longer. When they parted, he felt the heat rising in his cheeks, and he saw the glimmer of tears on Lael's.

From the bow of the ship, Jayson and Rylan called to Marcus. The crew had already drawn up the anchor and were ready to set sail. Marcus hurried up the gangplank. Joining his father at the bow, he waved goodbye to those he cared for most. He hoped they would be safe in his absence. He hoped, too, that not much time would pass before he would see them again. In the meantime, he had to trust in the gods to watch over them and to guide him in this new and most important quest: to find Lady Ivanore and, should it be the will of the gods, to bring her safely home.

Coming soon

THE SEER OF
THE GUILDE

Book III of The Celestine Chronicles

Prologue

The girl tried to keep up, but her bare feet burned from the cold, and the air bit into her lungs like icy daggers. She might have stopped running had her mother not held onto her hand so tightly.

The tree root wasn't large, but it seemed to reach up from the ground to trip her. The girl's foot caught on it, and she stumbled forward into a mess of soppy leaves. Her mother did not let go when she fell but tried to pull her back to her feet.

"Please, Orissa. We must keep going," the woman said, gasping for breath. The girl tried to stand, only to collapse again.

"My ankle hurts, Mamae," she whimpered.

Her mother shot sharp glances over both her shoulders, her eyes wide and alert. Her normally golden hair was gray with earth and studded with bits of dried grass. Her arms and face were crisscrossed with red scratches from the shrubs through which they had crawled. Both their dresses had torn. Surrounding them on all sides were thin, white-barked trees, their leaves cast off weeks ago. Even in the moonlight, the girl could see through the naked branches nearly all the way back to the castle.

"They'll have found us missing by now," said her mother. She scanned the spaces between the trees, her eyes darting from one to the next.

"Mamae," said Orissa, rubbing her swelling ankle, "why are we leaving? It is cold out here. I want my bed."

"I told you before," her mother said with endless patience, "I've waited a long time for a chance like this. With Arik gone—"

"Uncle Arik? But he promised he'd come home, Mamae. He promised."

All of a sudden, the sky above them lit up like a bonfire. A brilliant ball of blue flame arched above the trees like a cannonball. Orissa's mother instantly curled her body over the girl, shielding her. Orissa, wanting to see this strange light, peeked beneath her mother's arm. The blue flame came down several yards away from them, crashing through the tree branches. The terrible sound of breaking wood tore through the air, followed by a loud explosion. Orissa clasped her hands over her ears, but just when she thought the noise was over, another fireball landed even closer. Bits of splintered wood and dirt pelted them, and Orissa smelled the pungent odor of smoke.

Her mother pulled Orissa up by her elbows. "Run, Orissa!" she shouted over a third explosion. "We've got to run!"

But Orissa couldn't run. She couldn't even stand. So her mother swung her up into her arms with a grunt. Orissa could see now that some of the trees were burning. She smelled the damp wood as the blue flames consumed them. Not ordinary flames, she realized. Magical ones.

Orissa clung to her mother as she ran on. She could hear her mother's rasping breath as her lungs sucked in air and pushed it out again through her lips in intermittent, white puffs. She could feel, too, her mother's heart thumping in her chest. Orissa was eight years old, and Mamae hadn't carried her in years.

Then, in the distance, Orissa heard the horses. Their hooves struck the ground even faster than the beat of her mother's heart. There were shouts, too, of soldiers calling to each other through the trees, and the voices were getting louder.

Orissa glanced over her mother's shoulder and thought she saw movement not far away. Yes, there it was! A flash of steel near the burning trees.

Another burst of fire exploded right in front of them. Orissa's mother twisted away from the flames, her back taking the brunt of the assault. She clenched her teeth, and Orissa saw the pain in her face, though she did not cry out. Arms shaking, her mother set Orissa down. She frantically scanned the area. As she turned away, Orissa saw that the ends of her mother's hair were singed and the fabric along her shoulders had burned away, exposing raw, oozing flesh.

"Mamae," Orissa said, but her mother quickly held a finger to her lips. A second later, they were on their knees, scooping away loose soil from beneath a large, moss covered boulder. Orissa followed her mother into the narrow crevice. There was just enough room for both of them.

"Shhh," whispered her mother. "We mustn't speak until the soldiers have gone. All right?"

Orissa nodded.

As the horses neared, she felt her mother's arms tighten around her. Her mother breathed heavily into her hair. Orissa's nose wrinkled at the smell of her mother's sweat and blood. From her vantage point beneath the stone, she saw the legs of a horse approach. A soldier slid off its back and walked around the stone, pausing to listen. Orissa held her breath. So did her mother. Finally, the soldier climbed back onto his horse and galloped away.

Orissa let the air out of her lungs. Behind her, her mother did the same. She felt a light pressure on the back of her skull, her mother's kiss.

Suddenly, from the top of the stone, a man's face swung into view. Orissa screamed. The man reached into their hiding place and, grabbing one of her flailing arms, yanked at her roughly. Her mother wrapped her arms around her body, holding her back, but the man pulled so hard, Orissa wished her mother would let her go before they tore her in two. Finally, the man grabbed Orissa's other arm and pulled her into the open. Her mother scrambled out after her.

The soldier gripped Orissa's arms so tightly they hurt. No one held onto her mother, but tears left streaks down her dirty cheeks. Another man dismounted his horse and strode up to them. He was old, with pale, wrinkled skin. He wore a red robe with a wide, yellow sash, and on his face was a satisfied sneer. He traced Orissa's face with one bony finger.

"Yes," he said. "I definitely see the resemblance."

"Don't you touch her!" shouted Orissa's mother.

The man in the red robe flicked his finger, and a rope of blue fire lashed out, striking her on the chest.

"Mamae!" Orissa shouted. She tried to run to her mother, but the soldiers held her back. Her mother fell to her knees, her body trembling from pain. She would have collapsed completely, but two more soldiers grasped her arms, holding her upright.

The red-robed man clucked his tongue like a disapproving parent. "When will you ever learn?" he said, shaking his head. "There is nowhere you can hide from me, Ivanore. Nowhere at all."

Acknowledgements

It is hard to know where to begin, so many people had a hand in getting *The Last Enchanter* on its feet. First, I need to thank those who read various drafts and provided valuable input: my daughter Carissa, my son Marc, my sister-in-law Dorine White, Teak and Tina Bolina, and Jane Zimmerman. Thanks also to the team at Tanglewood— Peggy Tierney, Rebecca Grose, Erin Blacketer, Lisa Rojany Buccieri, and Lauren Wohl—and to Tristan Elwell for his unbelievably gorgeous cover art.

Second, I need to thank my husband, Gonzalo, for his inexhaustible support and encouragement. I honestly could not have done everything I've done the past couple of years without him. Thank you to my parents, Ray and Cyndi White, and my in-laws, Chalo and Gina Reyes, who, in my frequent absences, entertain my kids, drive them wherever they need to go, and prepare meals. And an extra big thanks to Stuart, Brennah, and Jarett—the best fans any mom could ever hope to have.

Next, thank you to everyone who read *The Rock of Ivanore* and asked for the sequel, including friends, family, kids, parents, teachers, librarians, fellow authors, and booksellers. Without you, Book Two would never have happened.

Thanks to The Society of Children's Books Writers and Illustrators for providing such amazing support to me and to thousands of authors worldwide. To the Apocalypsies (you know who you are!)—2012 was the best year ever! And to Joelle Biegel at Barnes & Noble: you are amazing!

Finally, I would be ungrateful if I didn't give thanks to God for the opportunity he's given me to live my dream and to encourage kids everywhere to live theirs, too.

Author Bio

Laurisa White Reyes spent many years writing for newspapers and magazines before mustering enough courage to pursue her dream of writing novels. Aside from her obsession with books, she also loves musical theater and fantasizes about singing on Broadway (one dream she does not intend to pursue). She lives in Southern California with her husband, five children, four birds, three lizards, two fish and one dog.

Please visit her website www.laurisawhitereyes.com and her blog www.1000wrongs.blogspot.com.